A DOG'S
COURAGE

W. Bruce Cameron is the number one *New York Times* and *USA Today* bestselling author of *A Dog's Purpose*, *A Dog's Way Home* and *A Dog's Journey* (all now major motion pictures), *The Dog Master*, *A Dog's Promise*, the Puppy Tales for young readers (starting with *Ellie's Story* and *Bailey's Story*), *A Dog for Christmas*, *The Midnight Plan of the Repo Man*, and others. He lives in California.

By W. Bruce Cameron

A Dog's Purpose
A Dog's Journey
A Dog's Promise
Emory's Gift
A Dog for Christmas
(published in the US as *The Dogs of Christmas*)
The Dog Master
A Dog's Perfect Christmas
A Dog's Way Home
A Dog's Courage

THE RUDDY McCANN SERIES

The Midnight Plan of the Repo Man
Repo Madness

HUMOUR

8 Simple Rules for Dating My Teenage Daughter
How to Remodel a Man
8 Simple Rules for Marrying My Daughter
A Dad's Purpose

FOR YOUNGER READERS

Ellie's Story
Bailey's Story
Molly's Story
Max's Story
Toby's Story
Cooper's Story (forthcoming)
Shelby's Story
Bella's Story
Lily's Story
Lily to the Rescue
Lily to the Rescue: Two Little Piggies
Lily to the Rescue: The Not-So-Stinky-Skunk
Lily to the Rescue: Dog Dog Goose
Lily to the Rescue: Lost Little Leopard
Lily to the Rescue: The Misfit Donkey

A DOG'S COURAGE

. . . .

A DOG'S WAY HOME NOVEL

. . . .

W. Bruce Cameron

PAN BOOKS

First published 2021 by Forge Books, Tom Doherty Associates, New York

First published in the UK 2021 by Pan Books
an imprint of Pan Macmillan
The Smithson, 6 Briset Street, London EC1M 5NR
EU representative: Macmillan Publishers Ireland Ltd, Mallard Lodge,
Lansdowne Village, Dublin 4
Associated companies throughout the world
www.panmacmillan.com

ISBN 978-1-5290-7585-4

1 3 5 7 9 8 6 4 2

A CIP catalogue record for this book is available from the British Library.

Printed and bound by CPI Group (UK) Ltd, Croydon, CR0 4YY

Visit **www.panmacmillan.com** to read more about all our books
and to buy them. You will also find features, author interviews and
news of any author events, and you can sign up for e-newsletters
so that you're always first to hear about our new releases.

Dedicated with love to the memory of my parents,
William J. Cameron MD and Monsie Cameron.
I miss you both so much.

Prologue

Michael "Bud" Butters turned up the stereo because it was playing one of his favorite country western songs—Zac Nelson singing "Life is Wonderful." Bud indulged himself in a high warbling singalong that would have offended the musical tastes of just about anybody. *Life is wonderful.* That, Bud thought, summed everything up pretty well.

Life *was* wonderful. Sixty-two years old with a somewhat—okay, *very*—checkered past, he was closing in on a full year of driving a Freightliner tanker truck, 231-inch wheelbase, 350 HP Cummins engine, 4,500-gallon capacity. Bud Butters, *driving a truck*! For a long time he hadn't even possessed a driver's license, and now look at him. A professional, that's what he was.

With a regular job, he was making steady progress on his credit card bills, though giving up working a ranch to sit behind a steering wheel had supplied him with an uncomfortable tightness to his fifty-four-inch waistband. That's how he registered it: his stomach was the same, it was his pants that were changing.

His route today took him north along Wyoming Highway 26, up to Moran, where he would turn on 191 toward Jackson, eventually continuing south to his home in Rock Springs—some of the most beautiful mountain scenery in the world. People running gas stations were always glad to see him because he was their lifeblood. Once a man of little value to society and himself, he was now an important part of the local economy.

Even better: his son Nate had recently met a gal named Angie, and she was the polar opposite of that poisonous Marna, who
had told Nate he was to have nothing to do with Bud ever again.
Marna refused to believe Bud had turned it around, that he was
sober going on two years, that a man could change. Marna ate at
Nate's soul like acid, turning him against his own father. Which
meant Bud was cut off from his grandson, little Ian—*Not even
Marna's kid!*—and that fact alone almost drove Bud back to the
bottle—at least, that's how it felt, a perfect excuse, *What more
do you need? Any man would need a drink!* But that was just
the seductive weakness whispering to him—he was working the
program, and it works if you work it. The whisper would always
be there, you just had to not engage with it. He went to meetings.
He could sit and watch his friends drink until they fell off their
barstools and not touch a drop himself, though one by one his
buddies had drifted out of his life, ironically made uncomfortable
by Bud's choices.

That was all in the rearview mirror. Life was wonderful. The
random drug and alcohol tests at work further helped keep him
clean. Nate finally came to his senses and vicious Marna was gone,
kicked to the curb, good riddance, and Angie, sweetest thing on
the planet, met Nate at church and stole the boy's heart with pure
goodness. Angie herself had personally called Bud to meet at a
truck stop down in Lander, saying Nate was too ashamed to pick
up the phone. Ian, such a big boy at age ten, ran to his grandpa
and that was it, Bud had his family back.

All you had to do was forgive. It was the magic formula. Good
people forgave Bud, and Bud forgave everybody.

Well, maybe not Marna.

After completing his stops in Dubois, Bud was taking a little
side trip, headed up toward Fish Lake Mountain to visit Ian, Nate,
and Angie.

He navigated the half-full tanker up the mountainous curves
with care. A fuel tanker can both jackknife and roll over more

easily than a traditional trailer. In bad weather, Bud drove almost rigidly with caution, but today was a glorious, windless summer day. The weather was so dry it easily explained why Dubois had once gone by the name of Never Sweat, Wyoming.

Bud had heard all about it one time. Never Sweat. The postal service refused to allow it, insisting on Dubois instead. Faced with a choice between a designation most apt or something forced on it by a government agency, the folks of Never Sweat, with typical cowboy rebellion, accepted the name but not the pronunciation—which was French, for God's sake. *Doo-boyce,* locals called it. Doo-Boyce, Wyoming.

The road twisted and rose steeply, but there was little traffic on this life-is-wonderful day.

Bud appreciated having the pavement all to himself. Some yahoo in a pickup, swerving into the wrong lane, had recently put a coworker of his in the hospital. Worse, Bud's friend's tank had broken loose and wheeled like a gigantic rolling pin down into some oncoming vehicles. The resulting gasoline spill had shut down all lanes of I-80. Nobody died, thank God.

At the crest the song ended, and Bud stopped singing—if that's what you could call what he was doing—and punched the player into silence, pulling over. The descent from here into the valley was breathtaking: soaring stone-faced cliffs, a river below, green aspen trees.

Bud's job was to drive a truck through heaven.

He inhaled and let the clean air whistle out in satisfaction. Little Ian was going to love taking a ride in the big truck with his grandpa. The thought made Bud smile.

From here he could see several fire trucks along a side road below. A stand of dead lodgepole pines climbed steeply up from the river, and the firefighters were conducting a controlled burn to reduce the chance of a disastrous wildfire. Bud didn't really understand the idea behind the whole operation—burning trees to keep them from burning?—but he could see that the firefighters were being careful, arrayed along the fire line, hoses ready to prevent the flames from jumping the break they had cut with their chain-saws.

From his perspective, there had to be a thousand, two thousand acres of dead pines, and he didn't see how the firemen could possibly get to them all.

As Bud eased his big truck forward, his mind was on little Ian, and he committed a rare mistake, letting himself automatically shift up. It would be far safer to keep in low gear, speed checked by the engine.

Bud did not notice as his speed increased, because his heart, so full of love, suddenly seized up inside him. The blockage was complete and the attack immediate and fatal. Bud slumped sideways, his vision dark in an instant, his engine whining as the truck traveled faster and faster.

Down below, the firefighters lifted their heads in unison as Bud's tanker smashed head-on into one of the parked pumper trucks. Then they were running, desperately running, as the tank itself bounded down the steep slope and directly into the controlled burn.

Bud would never know the extent of the disaster his death had unleashed, but almost no one else in the Rocky Mountains would be untouched by it.

One

I was enjoying the sort of nap that, as a dog, I had long ago mastered: sprawled out on sparse grasses, my nose filled with the fresh smell of trees, ears barely registering the small noises of birds and other rustlings. Sleeping outside near my boy, Lucas, his scent giving me an overall sense of his presence, is one of the most wonderful things to do on a lazy afternoon after a walk in the mountains. I was drifting on well-being, happy to be alive.

Lucas shared my contentment; I could tell by his relaxed breathing. He was sitting drowsily in the sun with his dog and his Olivia.

So I was startled when all of a sudden, tension jolted him. I instantly popped open my eyes and lifted my head, blinking away the sleep.

"Nobody move," he urged. I glanced over at him, but then turned my full attention to what I could suddenly smell: a cat, female, a big one, somewhere close, lurking in the bushes. The feral odor was unmistakable.

For a moment I thought it might be a very particular mountain cat, one I knew as well as any animal I had ever met or smelled, but I quickly realized that no, this was a stranger, a new intruder.

She wasn't moving, so I didn't spy her at first. Then she shifted slightly, and I saw her. She was stocky and powerful and larger than the cats who lived in the house down the street, almost bigger than any cat I had ever seen. Her head would easily reach my back. She was spotted, with alert ears held high and a rabbit dangling from her mouth. I could smell the rabbit as strongly as the wild cat.

So, no, this wasn't any animal I knew, though she did bring to mind a mountain cat that was much larger than this one.

The cat and I locked eyes, frozen. Lucas and Olivia were both motionless and tense, but not afraid. "Do you see it?" Lucas asked in the barest of whispers.

Olivia stirred. "I've only seen one other bobcat in my whole life. This is so cool!"

Lucas nodded ever so slightly. "It's beautiful."

I was still staring at the cat and the cat was still staring at me. It was the type of moment I often share with squirrels, when we're both immobile, right before one of us bolts and the chase is on.

I wasn't sure I wanted to chase this particular animal, though.

"I'm going to reach for my phone," Lucas murmured. "Get some video of this. Bella, no barks."

I did not understand why my boy would tell me No Barks when I wasn't barking, or making any noise at all. I noticed his hand creeping ever so slowly, but it was movement enough to remind the big cat that she had other things to do than just stare at two people and their wonderful dog. With motion as quiet as Lucas's whisper, she turned and was quickly in the bushes and gone, though her powerful smell lingered long after she vanished.

If I were going to give chase, now would be my moment. But I did not want the cat, or her rabbit. I had not yet been fed dinner, and did not want to be off in the woods pursuing wild creatures when it was presented.

"Amazing, that was *amazing*," Olivia enthused.

"I've never seen one before. Wow," Lucas agreed. "You know, I used to camp all the time and I never came across anything but elk. But with you we've seen bears, that eagle, a mountain lion, and now we can add a bobcat to the list."

"You're saying I'm good luck."

Lucas grinned at her. "I'm saying that now that I'm with you, maybe I notice more of what's good about life."

"That's sweet."

I wagged.

"Why do you suppose it came so close to our campsite?" Olivia asked. "What does it mean?"

"Mean? What, like a sign, or an omen? A message from the cat gods? I don't think it needs to mean anything. It was just a wild animal checking us out."

Olivia shrugged. "It's just pretty unusual behavior for a felid. Humans are really their only natural enemy."

"Felid!" Lucas howled. He crawled across the grass to Olivia and pulled her onto her back, laughing at her. "What the heck is a *felid*?"

Olivia was smiling up at him. "It's just a name for a wild cat. I was showing off that I know some words that my brainy doctor husband doesn't know. And it *is* almost an omen to see a bobcat sneaking up on people instead of the other way around, don't you think?"

"Maybe it wasn't stalking us at all; maybe it wanted to get a look at Bella. Our *canid*."

I wagged at my name.

"Canid! My husband is so smart."

"My *wife* is so smart. So, okay, what else about bobcats?"

"I know they're territorial, like mountain lions. If a female is in her territory, she's queen and nobody messes with her. But if she accidentally wanders into another female's range, it's open season. She goes from predator to prey. Sort of what would happen if some nurse tried to flirt with handsome Dr. Lucas Ray."

Lucas laughed. "I still don't think Felid the Cat was an omen."

I had the sense that they were talking about the cat and the rabbit, but I didn't feel motivated to pursue it into the trees. My place now was with my people, my Lucas and Olivia. We lived together in a house with a room to sleep in, a room to eat in, and a room where all the food was kept, called "kitchen." Sometimes I would lie on the floor of the food room, just to drink in the wonderful smells.

I never know why, but on occasion Lucas packs things into a car he calls "the Jeep" and drives us up into the mountains. On those nights we sleep in a single, soft-sided room Lucas and Olivia would temporarily erect near the vehicle. That's what we were doing now.

Not long after the wild cat ran off with her kill, Lucas opened some packets and made dinner, an action I found to be a very positive development.

They sat in chairs Olivia unfolded. While I watched attentively for dropped food items, my thoughts returned first to the cat with the rabbit, and then to how her appearance had instantly brought to mind a much larger cat, one with whom I had spent many, many days and nights in these same mountains. Though she grew to be a huge creature, I always thought of her as Big Kitten, because she was a kitten when I met her.

Lucas tossed me a piece of dinner. As I deftly snagged pieces of food out of the air, I realized how the feral odors of the wild cat were more imagined than actually sensed, now that she had faded into the woods with her rabbit. That's what happens in the mountains—it isn't that a dog can't find a particular odor out there, it's that there are so many other smells competing for the primary position in the nose. I gave up trying to track her—she was long gone. In fact, after a time, I was back to reflecting on Big Kitten, calling up the memory of how she smelled when we curled up for sleep together, the snow coming down on both of us in a soft blanket.

Often when I am sprawled at my boy's feet at night I will ponder how different my life is now that I am back with people. For a time, I was a dog who hunted and roamed the trails with a giant cat, and didn't sleep on beds, or get fed dinner twice a day. I was often hungry and afraid, but my companion and I survived. Big

Kitten and I were a pack through two winters, relying on each other.

I usually thought about Big Kitten whenever Lucas and Olivia took me up into the mountains, because it was in the mountains where I first encountered her.

When I found Big Kitten she was smaller than the she-cat I had just seen with the rabbit, and she was alone. Her mother had recently died because of something two men had done to her. That's what I concluded as I sniffed the mother cat's lifeless body sprawled in the dirt, because there had been a loud banging noise and the two men were running toward me, shouting excitedly to each other. The powerful odor of fresh blood clung to the mother feline's motionless corpse, and the air still carried the sharp tang of an acrid smoke that was growing stronger as the men thrashed through the woods, headed in my direction. I was tensed and ready to flee when I spotted the baby cat watching me from the bushes.

I decided in that moment that the big kitten hiding in the bushes, though larger than any adult cat I had ever seen before, was the baby of the gigantic cat who lay dead and bloody in the sand.

I needed to protect her from the bad men. I had the sense that whatever they had done to the huge cat to kill it, they would do to the big kitten, and probably to me as well.

Over time, I became Big Kitten's mother cat. In a way it was a natural role for me, because when I was just a puppy, long before I met Lucas, my mother dog was taken from me by a different set of bad men, and I wound up living under a house with a family of cats. My littermates were kittens, and their mother was my mother.

This lasted a short time, until Lucas took me home, and then I lived with people instead of cats.

I taught Big Kitten how to hunt. She and I went for long, long walks together because I was a lost dog. I had been separated from Lucas, my person, and was making my way home to him. Big Kitten came with me. Along the way, we fed together, and Big Kitten grew until she was much larger than me.

I loved Big Kitten, but I loved being a dog to Lucas even more. So as I did Go Home, Big Kitten remained behind in the wilds, watching me walk away from her, out of the mountains and toward the smells and sounds of a big, open city with cars and many, many people.

As I left Big Kitten and descended toward the streets and buildings and traffic, I couldn't separate my boy's smell from the countless human scents on the air, but I could sense him, feel him, and I knew I would be able to find my way home to him.

I never saw Big Kitten again, but it was not hard to imagine, as I drifted off to sleep many nights, that she was right there next to me, keeping me warm, keeping me company: the best animal friend I ever had.

Often when we took car rides in the Jeep, ranging along bouncy mountain roads, I would thrust my nose out into the wind and concentrate on trying to find her, searching for a single whiff of cat to let me know she was still alive. Thus far I had been unsuccessful, but Lucas always found new places for us to stay, and I thought it likely I would one day see my dear friend again.

I looked forward to that.

Lucas and Olivia were eating chunks of meat, but they did not neglect a good dog like me. I was dazzling them with my Sit. That one always works.

After dinner, Lucas and Olivia and I crawled into the small room where we slept when we were on Jeep car rides. This was our second night and, if past behavior was any guide, we would soon be driving back home to sleep on our bed inside our house.

I didn't mind where I slept, as long as I was with my boy. I fussed to get the soft blankets just right, but eventually settled in between Lucas and Olivia. As I did so, a warmth rose up from within me, because I was with the people who loved me and I loved them. Since the moment I first met Lucas, I knew the two of us belonged together. The reason I never gave up on my long trek back home was because I was his dog. On my travels I met several people who were nice to me and wanted to take care of me, but there was only one Lucas.

As often as I dreamed of Big Kitten, I dreamed of my boy, running with me, or feeding me treats.

Not long after Lucas zipped the door closed, I heard something rustling in the plants outside in the night and raised my head and gave a low warning growl.

"Bella, no barks, okay?" Lucas murmured sleepily.

"Lucas, no snores, okay?" Olivia replied.

Lucas chuckled in the dark. "I've read that wives often pretend that their husbands snore, just so the poor guys will feel guilty."

"I've read that when men snore, their wives will dump water on them just to make the poor guys feel wet," Olivia countered.

Lucas propped himself up on an elbow. "You snore sometimes and I've never complained."

"That's because your snoring drowns mine completely out."

"Well, see how lucky you are?"

Olivia laughed. "This thing you do where you pretend to be really dumb is pretty funny."

"Glad I amuse you."

"Maybe sometime in the future you could pretend to be smart. Like for my birthday, maybe," Olivia teased. "Just one day. The rest of the year you can go back to playing dumb."

They were grinning at each other. Lucas reached over me and touched Olivia's shoulder, and I wagged because his arm was resting on my back. "Hey."

"Hey what."

"I love you, Olivia Ray."

"I love you, Lucas Ray."

I heard a rustling sound and growled again.

"Bella, no snores," Lucas intoned.

"No snores, Bella," Olivia agreed.

I wondered what they were telling me.

"I have a surprise for you tomorrow," Lucas remarked after a long moment of silence.

Olivia stirred. I opened my eyes but didn't otherwise react. "Surprise? What is it?" she demanded.

"Well, clearly, I can't say—that's the nature of a surprise. Surely someone has told you that before."

"Does it rhyme with 'whirl wecklass'?"

"Go to sleep, Olivia."

"How about 'wuby wing'?"

Lucas laughed. "Go to sleep. You'll find out tomorrow."

Two

The next morning, we left the small room with the soft sides still standing and took a car ride in the Jeep. This meant bumpy roads, the vehicle swaying, and wonderful, wild odors streaming in through the open windows. To me a car ride is a car ride and they are all wonderful, but I did understand that when we were in the Jeep it was for a different, more adventurous experience.

I sat in the back seat while Lucas drove and Olivia was buckled in next to him in the front. They were talking, but I heard no words I recognized. Trying to understand what people are saying is not generally rewarding for a dog. I've found it's much better to stick a head out the open window and watch for animals to bark at. Any dog I see out walking requires that I challenge them. They don't usually respond, but they will stare at me in amazement as I pass.

Cats don't pay any attention, but I bark at them as well. I love cats and often try to bark them into a good mood, which never really works. I sometimes bark at squirrels, but I'd rather chase them. Birds I ignore, because who cares about birds during a car ride?

Olivia reached her hand out to touch Lucas on the neck. They smiled at each other. I felt love flowing between the two of them, and I wagged.

Olivia was not living with Lucas when he and I first met. Her scent only gradually came to mingle with his, as if she were an outside cat getting used to living with people a little at a time. My mother cat was like that—she cowered from humans when we all lived under that house, but now there was a woman she trusted and lived with.

I had not seen my mother cat in a long time, but the last time we met, she was happy.

"You know, I would have been fine to cook you a breakfast," Olivia told Lucas.

He smiled at her, "I know you would. But this restaurant in Frisco has the most amazing cinnamon rolls."

Olivia laughed at him. "How are cinnamon rolls part of your diet plan?"

He shrugged. "So maybe it's a cheat day."

"Maybe?" Olivia snorted. Then she drew back. "Wait a minute. Is *that* my surprise? Cinnamon rolls?"

"Um . . . 'minnamon molls'?"

Olivia swatted him playfully on the shoulder.

Lucas grinned at Olivia. "What, are you saying you aren't surprised? It isn't better than a 'wuby wing'?"

"I think maybe I need to explain the nature of a surprise *for your wife*," she informed him loftily. "Cinnamon rolls are a surprise for *you*."

Lucas shook his head. "No, I already knew about them."

I did not spot any dogs until we bumped our way down a steep road and entered what I could smell was a town. Then I saw many dogs, a lot of them off their leashes, running and playing. Lucas kept saying, "No barks," which I took to mean that he didn't understand the rule about dogs seen from the car. I *had* to bark.

There are a lot of things people could learn from dogs, but they are usually too busy to pay much attention.

When we stopped and jumped out, I was only slightly disappointed when Lucas snapped the leash onto my collar with an audible *click*. This town was a place where some dogs could run free and some dogs had to be tethered. Come to think of it, most places are like that.

I was delighted to lead Olivia and Lucas down the sidewalk as the summer sun coaxed wonderful odors from the cement surface. I sat with them at an outside table with a big cloth providing shade overhead.

I patiently waited for bacon to fall to the sidewalk under my feet, knowing that if I stared intently enough at Lucas, he would not be able to resist.

"No begging, Bella," Lucas warned me.

I wagged because if he was talking to me, bacon must not be far behind.

Moments before it was upon us, I heard a gathering roar coming hard out of the hills. Across the street I saw a dog on a leash jerk its head upright, and knew he sensed it, too. Something big was approaching: a huge, unsettling change. When the howling wind slapped us, Lucas and Olivia both jumped in surprise and a piece of paper Lucas held in his lap went flying. I watched with interest as it danced down the sidewalk, almost worth chasing, except I knew from experience that most paper was tasteless.

"Whoa!" Lucas exclaimed as things rattled and cloth snapped. "Out of nowhere!"

A glass fell over and a sweet liquid ran off the table and onto the cement. I licked at it. Lucas and Olivia jumped to their feet.

"Grab everything!" Olivia urged.

A small piece of bread bounced down and I was on it instantly, crunching in gratitude while my people gathered things from the table. As I chewed, the cloth over our heads jolted and banged and then lifted straight up into the air.

This interested me. I had never seen anything like it, and wondered why Lucas had done it.

"The umbrella!" Olivia cried.

I watched as the big cloth thing, now upside down, smashed into the sidewalk and started to skitter down the street. Lucas turned as if to pursue it, but then stopped. Within moments, it tumbled and bounced and then vanished around the corner, chased by grit and sand and small bits of paper.

The wind was whistling and shrieking with such intensity that I couldn't sort out all the smells that were gusting at me. I wagged, though, when a nice woman stepped through a door and out to talk to me. She was the one who had brought Lucas his bacon earlier, so I thought of her as a friend. The door slammed with a forceful *bang* behind her.

"Do y'all want to come inside?" she asked, raising her voice to be heard.

I heard the question, but not the word "bacon," so I wasn't sure if she was addressing me.

Olivia blinked in the swirling dust. "Is it okay? We have Bella."

I looked up at the sound of my name. The woman smiled, reaching for the plates on the small table. "This is Frisco. Everyone loves dogs and nobody complains," the woman assured Olivia. "Last November, one of the locals entered his dog in the contest for mayor, and we had to do the election over because the dog won."

Whatever she was doing sent another small piece of toast skittering across the sidewalk. I strained at my leash, but it remained out of reach.

"Do you want me to go get the umbrella?" Lucas offered.

"It flew down the street and made a right turn on red," Olivia added.

The woman shook her head. "I have two daughters. Every snowboarder in town has a crush on 'em. They see my umbrella blowing by, they'll grab it. Probably there's a fistfight going on right now to see which one gets to bring it back."

Another woman came out to help take plates, but I was too preoccupied with staring at the fallen toast to greet her properly. Bacon-bringing-woman wrestled with the other cloth covers that were still standing on poles in the centers of empty tables nearby. Lucas stepped forward to help, lifting them and collapsing them.

"Thanks—just set them there against the building, I'll send someone to get them," she advised.

Lucas placed the cloth things, now folded skinny, up against the wall. Then he, Olivia, and I followed the woman into the building.

I was astonished. Were we *really* going to leave the toast lying on the sidewalk?

Once inside, it was instantly less noisy than out in the wind. The sweet smells all around me were quite intriguing—perhaps something in here would help me get past the tragedy of the lost toast. People were sitting, and talking, and chewing, and much of what they were eating was food a dog would be interested in. I wondered if any of them knew that.

Lucas smiled his thanks as Bacon-bringing-woman led us to a table and the woman carrying plates set them down. "Wow," Lucas marveled, "huge wind."

Bacon-bringing-woman nodded. "That's the Rocky Mountains," she agreed cheerfully. "One minute, absolutely still. The next, it's like you have a hurricane. We call it 'windshield season' because you have to call the auto glass people every year around this time."

She left, trailing the faint odor of bacon behind her. Some food remained on my boy's plate, though, and in response I did Sit with such dedicated rigidity that Lucas eventually took notice. "Hey, are you going to finish your omelet?" he asked Olivia.

"You mean after that surprise 'minnamon moll' you're still hungry?"

"I think Bella might be interested in some of the cheese."

I cocked my head. Aside from my name, there was a word in there that I both recognized and treasured. Lucas leaned forward and reached his hand out to Olivia's plate. "Hey, Bella," he crooned softly. "Would you like a t-i-i-iny piece of cheese?"

T-i-i-iny piece of cheese! I focused on his fingers, nearly trembling, as they descended slowly, the delicious bouquet of cheese pouring from his hand. My nose was twitching and I was licking my lips. Finally, the morsel of deliciousness came all the way down within reach. As gently as I had ever done anything in my life, I took the t-i-i-iny piece of cheese from between his fingers, my mouth exploding with the flavor.

T-i-i-iny piece of cheese was one way that I knew Lucas loved me.

There was no more bacon, though.

It was a very friendly place, with people stopping to coo over me as they passed our table. Most of them offered a hand to sniff and I easily detected sweets and meats. I knew from experience, though, that they wouldn't be giving me any treats. They weren't *that* friendly.

Humans possess the power to conjure up food items of remarkable delicacy, yet they actually spend little time eating. It's one of the most baffling things about people—they can produce treats at will, yet they seldom think to do so.

After a time, Bacon-bringing-woman came and took away all the plates.

"Hey, let's go check out that museum," Lucas suggested.

"Don't you want to get back to our campsite?"

"We'll hike," he agreed, "but I've never been in there and neither has Bella."

"You think dogs are allowed?"

"In a town where dogs run for mayor?"

When we left the restaurant, I immediately swerved to the table beneath which I had last seen my toast, *but it was gone*.

I loved my boy, but he had taken me inside without regard for the food on the ground, and now some other undeserving creature had snatched up my treat.

I was sure Olivia and Lucas were as devastated over the loss as I was, but we had someplace to go, so I tugged at my leash as we crossed the street. I did not know where we were headed, but I would strongly lead Lucas there nonetheless.

He pushed open a door and we entered an old, musty-smelling, creaky building. Odors wafted toward me, strange and never before encountered. I wagged, not understanding what we were doing, but happy we were doing it.

It turned out to be one of those places where Lucas and Olivia wanted to walk slowly and stop often and talk to each other. So I did a lot of Sit, and I scratched behind my ear, and I yawned, and I wondered if it would be good dog behavior if I flopped down on the floor for a nap.

There were tall boxes made of wood and glass, and Lucas and Olivia kept stopping and staring at them. "That's so beautiful," Olivia admired, touching a finger to the glass.

There was something inside the box, but from where I sat, I couldn't tell what it was.

"Though grey wolves are not officially reestablished in Colorado, there have been a number of sightings that suggest they've made their own way into the state from Wyoming and other places where they've been reintroduced," Lucas said. "This specimen was shot and killed outside Monarch in 1939."

"I love it when you use your NPR voice," Olivia mocked gently.

Lucas grinned at her. "I just thought it would be easier for you to understand if I read it to you than if you read it to yourself."

"Well, most of it was completely over my head, of course, but maybe you could mansplain things to me in simpler words," she teased. "For example, do you know what stuffed animals are stuffed with?"

"Of course," Lucas replied smugly.

"What?"

"They're mostly stuffed with . . . stuff."

Olivia laughed.

We would move forward a little bit, then stop, and then start again, like a male dog marking territory. This is the type of behavior a good dog puts up with.

Finally, Lucas pulled me around the corner of one of the boxes and I stopped absolutely still. The fur on my neck rose as a sensation like a shiver moved along my spine. I stared in disbelief.

There, standing in front of me, eyes glittering and teeth visible in a partial snarl, was my old friend.

Big Kitten.

Three

Lucas chuckled. "Bella thinks that cougar is real."

"If I saw it out of the corner of my eye, I'd probably have a heart attack. I mean, it's kind of freaky how alive it looks," Olivia admitted.

I heard my name but did even not glance at Lucas. My attention was focused on the creature in front of me. In every way it looked like Big Kitten, and even smelled a little like Big Kitten. She was posed in a familiar stance, so cat-like and powerful. What often seemed to me a cautious posture in housecats was always, for Big Kitten, a languid, serene confidence. As her hunting companion I never felt threatened by her athletic limbs or great, deadly claws. But now I saw a terrible menace in her posture, aggressively making a stand in a human dwelling.

It was Big Kitten. And yet, as I stared, I realized it wasn't her at all. This creature stood motionless and did not track my movements with her eyes. An involuntary growl found its way out of my throat as I faced this unnatural apparition. What was this Big Kitten–like thing that was at once her and not her? I did not understand and I felt vulnerable and afraid. Big Kitten seemed unnaturally different, and I wondered if Olivia and Lucas could be in jeopardy.

"It's okay, Bella," he whispered to me. "It's just taxidermy. It's not real. It can't hurt us." Lucas stepped forward and put his hand on the Big Kitten thing, stroking its forehead as if it were a dog.

The thing did not react, didn't lift its head and purr as I knew Big Kitten would if Lucas touched her.

What had happened to her? She was as still as death, but she didn't smell dead. She didn't smell alive, either. Mostly, she smelled like this dusty, dry room. My eyes told me this was my friend, but my nose told me nothing at all.

Lucas beckoned to me. "It's okay, Bella. Come see."

I knew the word "come." I took several cautious steps forward, still feeling the tension in my every limb. I was ready to flee or fight, bite or bark.

Neither Lucas nor Olivia seemed at all frightened, though, so I finally approached the frozen cat close enough to thoroughly sniff it up and down its length. Was this really Big Kitten?

Olivia petted the cat-thing on the head as well. "You don't think about how huge these creatures are until you see something like this."

"These felids, you mean," Lucas corrected. Olivia smiled.

I picked up odors of human hands and chemicals and, very faintly, something that had once been alive but now was as stiff as a corpse long dead by the side of the road. I looked up at Lucas and wagged, completely confused. This might have been Big Kitten at one point. If so, something had changed her so absolutely she was now a not-cat, a not-animal. My fur still a ridge along my spine, I growled again.

Lucas bent down and ran a reassuring hand along my back. "It's okay, Bella, it can't hurt you. Look; there's a deer."

I followed Lucas across the room to where a tall and motionless deer stared without seeing into the room. It smelled much the same as the Big Kitten thing. Next, Lucas led me to what had once been a fox.

We were in a place where animals looked as if they were alive, standing and staring alertly, but they were not.

I did not like this place.

Lucas and Olivia walked very slowly, talking quietly. I followed them because I was a good dog, but I kept my eye on the not-Big-Kitten thing. I could not shake the sense that at any minute, she would break from her frozen posture and come to me and rub the top of her head against me and purr, as she had done so many times when we were traveling together.

During my time with Big Kitten in the mountains, I had missed Lucas so much that, even now, it was unpleasant to recall those days of anxiety and hunger. But now, in this room, it was Big Kitten I missed. I wondered if she ever missed me too; if she'd searched the mountain wilds for her dog, the way I always sniffed for my Big Kitten.

A man on the other side of the room was setting things on a shelf, and I saw him sit down abruptly, as people sometimes will. He put a hand over his face and slumped forward a bit, as if he were getting ready to sleep. Even from this distance, I picked up some unhappiness in him. Something was wrong with the man.

He looked like he needed a good dog, and I trotted over to him, trailing my dropped leash, to see if my presence might make him happier. This is something I'm very good at—providing cheer to sad people.

As I drew right up to him, his face collapsed into a deep frown that didn't alter as I approached. Everything changed for me in that moment: I recognized the sharp tang of his sweat and the unmistakable odor on his breath.

Alarmed, I sat at his feet and whined, but no one paid attention—not even him. So, I barked.

"Bella," Olivia called from across the room. "No barks!"

No Barks could not apply here. I was doing as I had been trained. I continued to bark. I was letting everyone know that there was something very wrong with this man.

"Bella," Lucas asked me as he and Olivia walked over, "why are you barking?"

I now held my boy's focus, so I took the next step. I put both paws on the man's knees and barked right in his face. The man did not respond normally to that. He only blinked at me in confusion.

"Sit!" Lucas commanded.

I sensed the alarm in his voice and knew I had done the right thing. I did Sit. Lucas bent forward and put a concerned hand on the man's shoulder. "Are you all right, sir?"

The man nodded. "Yeah. Sorry. Just got a little winded."

"Have you ever had a seizure? Do you have any form of epilepsy?"

The man shook his head. "Not that I know of. Seizure?"

Lucas nodded in confirmation. "My mother used to have them on a regular basis. Bella always sensed when one was coming on and would signal, like she did just now. There is a high pitch to her bark that we all learned to recognize. We eventually got her trained and certified as a seizure-detection dog. Her signal's to put her paws up on a person and bark that high bark. Are you sure you're okay?"

The man rubbed his chest. "Tell you the truth, I'm having some pretty bad acid reflux lately. I've been taking antacids, but they haven't been helping."

"Does the heartburn get worse when you exercise?" Lucas asked.

The man nodded. "Sure does. Not that I get much exercise. Been meaning to join a gym."

"Sir, I am a first-year resident at Denver Medical. I have to say you are presenting like a cardiac patient, and Bella's signal might mean something's going on." Lucas turned to Olivia. "I think it would be a good idea if you called 911," he observed calmly.

Olivia nodded and walked away briskly, pulling out her phone.

"Bella," Lucas commanded, "you stay."

I did Stay, not understanding what we were doing. That same sharp tang was still in the air, more intense than ever. Lucas knelt to peer into the man's eyes. "I'm going to get my medical kit out of my Jeep. You rest here, all right? I'll be right back."

The man nodded. I watched in alarm as Lucas left the room and then *left the building*. I was on Stay, but none of this made any sense to me. I did not like it when my boy was out of my sight. Olivia was across the room, still talking to her phone. I whined anxiously, trying to tell her: *We need to follow Lucas!*

Moments later my boy was back. I wagged happily, relieved to see him. I also anticipated a treat because of the perfect Stay I was maintaining. Quickly, though, I picked up on his urgency. His movements were hurried as he set a big bag next to the man's chair. Lucas rummaged around inside as if looking for dog treats, but when he pulled his hand out, he held nothing except a small packet. My boy ripped it open and pulled out a tiny object, and my nose immediately confirmed that, whatever it was, I wouldn't want to taste it. Lucas put his hand on the sitting man's shoulder, and the man glumly raised his head.

"Sir? I want you to chew this aspirin, okay?"

The man was still sad and still emitting the same acute odor. But I knew my training and I wasn't supposed to be barking now.

I wondered if I was still on Stay. I looked to Olivia for guidance, but she continued holding her phone to her face and did not glance my way.

"Aspirin? Won't that make my reflux worse?" the man objected. "I was told not to take any aspirin."

Lucas shook his head. "No, it's all right. I don't think this is reflux, sir. Chew it slowly, please."

The man nodded. "It seems like a lot of bother." He reached out a hand and Lucas handed him the uninteresting treat. The man popped it in his mouth and began chewing, a dour expression on his face.

I had the sense we were all waiting for something. I glanced back at not-Big-Kitten, feeling almost guilty that, due to these human affairs, I had neglected to check on her. But she had not moved and was still staring vacantly at nothing.

"How do you feel now?" Lucas asked. "Any change?"

The man swallowed and shrugged. "Feeling kind of punky now."

"Punky?"

The man's gaze drooped and became as vacant as the not-Big-Kitten's.

"Sir!" Lucas shouted urgently. The man slumped forward and Lucas reached out and grabbed him under his arms and lowered him to the floor. My boy turned, his face taut with tension. "Olivia!"

Olivia ran across the room, holding her phone. "They're coming!"

Lucas was lying with the man now, his head on the man's chest, kind of like how I sleep with Lucas at night.

Olivia stared.

"It's 1:35 PM and I am starting CPR," Lucas announced. Olivia put a hand over her mouth and Lucas began pushing on the man's chest. He was speaking, but not to me. "One, two, three, four . . ."

I decided the command to Stay was no longer operative. I eased over to stand next to Olivia because I was afraid and did not understand. She dropped her hand down and smoothed it over the top of my head and I felt safer.

I glanced in the direction of the door because I heard a loud and familiar noise building in the distance. Sometimes when we are enjoying a car ride, a vehicle will approach us very quickly, making a sound just like this—a high, warbling wail. Moments later, two big trucks pulled up—I could see them out the front windows of the building. The second of the two vehicles was enormous; its wailing cut off abruptly. People jumped down from the truck and opened the door, their footfalls heavy as they charged into the room, carrying boxes. Lucas stood up and backed away from the man on the floor. Two men rapidly snapped open their boxes while a woman knelt and began pressing the sleeping man's chest, mimicking my boy's actions.

"He coded at 1:35. I've been doing compressions since," Lucas reported.

Olivia put her phone into her pocket. "That didn't take them long at all."

Lucas picked up my leash. "Good you called when you did. Let's give them room."

Apparently, we were now going for a walk because we left the place with the man on the floor and the weird not-animals, and stepped out into the sunshine where some men and two women were standing by the big truck and the even bigger truck. I noticed bright lights flashing silently on the roofs.

I started wagging in joy. I pulled on my leash, dragging my boy toward a heavy man with darker skin, a very good friend I had not seen in a long time.

Lucas laughed in surprise. "Mack? What are you doing here?"

Four

Mack turned and I registered, not for the first time, how much bigger he was than Lucas. Not taller, just thicker. His face opened up in a wide grin, and even *that* was bigger.

"Lucas! And my favorite girl, Bella."

Mack was one of my old, dear friends, but I no longer saw him on a regular basis for reasons only humans might know. I still accompany Lucas to Work every so often. I go to a big room where everyone knows my name. Often the other person in our family, Mom, is there too. Mom will lead me to rooms to see people. Work is where I first met Mack. He was a sad man who needed me.

I am a good dog who provides comfort to the men and women who congregate at Work, sensing when they are sad and need special attention. Mom, too, needs my attention sometimes, and I have also learned to let her know when something is wrong, when her skin suddenly flashes hot with a smell similar to the lying-down man in the room of not-animals.

Mack knelt down to see me.

"You live up here now, Mack?" Olivia asked.

Mack stroked my fur. "Sure do."

About the time Lucas and Olivia moved to a new house and took me, but didn't take Mom with us, Mack stopped showing up at Work. His absence was immediately apparent. I noticed the lack of his scent at once, and his odors gradually faded from soft chairs and couches. Humans come and go and dogs have to adjust, but as long as I never had to say goodbye to Lucas, I accepted this as just being part of life.

Mack was still giving me that broad grin. I wagged because he was happy. When I first met him, he had been a sad and quiet man, but over time he seemed to gain strength. I jumped up to lick his face.

"Oh, you pretty girl, Bella," he praised. He was telling me he loved me; I could feel it in the soft stroking of his hands. "I miss our conversations, Miss Bella." He held his face in position so that I could lick both cheeks. "Okay, Bella. Okay," he sputtered as I planted a kiss directly in his mouth, "that's enough." He stood up. "Man, it's good to see you two."

They all hugged. I wagged.

"I had no idea you had moved to Summit County," Lucas said.

Mack was still grinning. "It wasn't long after your wedding. I drove up to Frisco for a weekend and stayed the summer. Got a job cutting down all the trees hit by the pine beetle. Acres and acres of lodgepoles, all of 'em dead and ready to burn. The county realized they needed to be better prepared for forest fires, and some positions opened up with the department."

Lucas gestured to the two trucks, then to Mack. "It makes me feel good to see you like this, Mack—working for Fire and Rescue, I mean."

Mack nodded. "I know what you're saying. Far cry from being inpatient at the VA, isn't it? Part of me thinks that as much help as I was getting at the hospital, with Bella the amazing super support dog and the twelve steps and Doctor Gans, I really needed to break away, get a change of scenery. I came up here and, well, obviously I'm not a soldier anymore, but fighting fires seemed like the closest civilian thing to it. I applied almost a year ago, but they just put me on as a regular in the past thirty days."

"Long time to wait for a call back," Olivia observed.

Mack shrugged. "Well, up to then, I'd been a volunteer in training, so I was working and learning the job. I can't tell you what it means to me to be doing this, to have a regular job, helping people. Speaking of . . . how's your mom?"

Lucas nodded. "Better than ever. She's out of state attending a school for training therapy dogs. She says she wants to do it more than anything."

"Because of Bella," Olivia added.

"You're a good dog, Bella," Mack said softly.

It was nice to have everyone talking about me. I decided a good Sit was in order and waited patiently for Lucas to notice.

"So, catch me up. You still in medical school?" Mack asked.

Lucas shook his head. "Graduated. Now I'm doing my residency at Denver Medical. And Olivia's a full-on vet tech. She works for an animal rescue outfit. I thought *my* schedule was impossible, but as long as there's one more pet to save, she doesn't stop."

"Your schedule *is* impossible," Olivia mock-scolded him.

The door to the place with the not-animals opened and the three people trundled out the lying-down man on a rolling bed. He was wearing a plastic cup on his face and a machine on his chest. For a moment, no one spoke. I kept doing Sit.

Olivia pulled her phone out. "Mack, give me your number. We come up here camping all the time. We'll be in touch."

"That would be great."

I watched curiously as the rolling bed was loaded into the big boxy truck that was parked behind the huge truck near us. This was a day of many events that a dog could only observe without comprehending.

Mack and Olivia stood with their phones pointed toward each other.

"Hey, Mack, let me know what winds up happening. To the guy, I mean," Lucas requested. "It's the first time I've done CPR on anything other than a mannequin."

"You okay?" Olivia asked him.

Lucas shrugged. "Yeah. I mean, I just went with my training and wasn't really thinking. But now I just want him to survive."

He gave them a half-smile. "I know what I'm saying sounds a little strange."

"No problem," said Mack. "I'll follow up. And I don't think it's strange at all. I think that's how it goes. The paramedics talk about that sort of thing, how running code blue on somebody makes you feel responsible or something. Well, my ride's leaving, I'd better go."

He hugged everybody, especially me. I licked him in the face, loving him, glad that we had finally reconnected and hoping we would see him soon. I sensed, though, that he would not be coming back to sleep with us in the soft-sided room. He would be leaving with his friends. This is what people do—get in vehicles and drive away, sometimes with dogs, sometimes without.

When the two trucks rumbled off, they no longer made the hideously loud wail, though I heard one of them start up again once it rounded the corner. Far in the distance, a dog answered the truck with a lone, thin howl.

Olivia put her hand on my Lucas's shoulder. "You sure you're okay?"

My boy lifted his shoulders and let them drop. "I've just never had the experience of having someone's life literally in my hands."

"Let's take a minute, let Bella run around in the park," she suggested.

We walked toward the clean, powerful smell of a river rushing loudly under a bridge, and then we walked along the stream until we came to a grassy, open area. Lucas unclipped my leash. I stared up at him. "Well, go on, silly," Lucas urged with a smile.

I put my nose down, inhaling the dog and people smells from the grass, then froze in utter shock. A squirrel was quietly bounding along, stopping every so often to dig in the dirt, seemingly oblivious that there was a dog right here!

I crept forward, head low, confident I would catch the creature this time. I was so focused I did not notice a small dog, belly close to the ground, racing across the field.

The squirrel raised himself up on its two back legs and stared at this other looming threat. I made my move, my nails digging in the dirt. The squirrel unfroze and launched himself toward the bushes on the riverbanks. He clung to a set of low branches, which bowed under his weight. He sagged closer to me. I could still catch him!

The small dog reached the base of the bush at the same moment, but it was too late. The other dog was male and immediately lifted his leg, even as the squirrel leapt nimbly to a thin tree and scrabbled up to the top.

How lifting a leg was supposed to do any good at all was something only a male dog could understand. I sniffed the area to be polite, but did not engage when the small dog play-bowed.

Big Kitten understood how to hunt. This dog clearly didn't. When I flushed prey, Big Kitten would remain motionless, tracking with her eyes, and not waste energy bounding after something she couldn't catch, even if we were hungry. Whereas this dog had blundered right into the middle of my stalking advance. I obviously would have caught the squirrel if it hadn't been for the little male dog interfering.

Another dog, also male, ran over from where his people released him from his leash, and that made it okay to play with the little dog. The three of us chased one another, stopping only so the males could mark a shrub or a big rock. Then someone threw a ball and we chased that, though once the big male had it in his mouth, there was nothing left to do but return to Lucas and Olivia.

Lucas snapped my leash onto my collar and we walked back to where we had met up with Mack, but he and the loud trucks had not returned, so we climbed into the Jeep for . . . a car ride!

I sat in the back seat, my head out the window, smelling animals on the wind—odors that in no way resembled the smell of the animals not-alive in that odd room with the glass boxes.

I did not believe the big, frozen cat was Big Kitten after all. I had made the mistake of trusting my eyes and not my nose. I felt better now—I liked to think of Big Kitten out in the wild and not standing rigid in a dusty room with a sick man lying on the floor. Though now, as hard as I tried, I couldn't find her scent anywhere in the air currents.

Olivia pointed. "What does that light mean?"

"What?"

"On your dashboard. The red light."

Lucas peered down at something. "Oh, that must have just come on. I've never seen it before."

"It says 'Airbag,'" Olivia noted.

"Yeah," Lucas agreed ruefully. "It means there's some kind of malfunction in the airbag. That'll be expensive."

"So, if we crash, the airbag won't go off?" Olivia demanded. "That seems more important to me than the cost of fixing it."

Lucas gave her a reassuring look. "Don't worry, if we crash, I'll throw my body in front of you."

"Great," she replied. "That's all we need, another excuse for you to throw your body at me."

They both laughed, so I wagged.

"Seriously, though," Olivia pressed. "Is that what it means? We get in a collision, no airbag?"

"Sure, it could mean that. Or it could mean the airbag will go off without warning. Driving along a mountain road, and *bam*! Face full of nylon."

"O-kayyy," Olivia answered slowly. "Would you let me out here, please?"

Lucas grinned.

I caught a quick and intense odor and knew we had just passed something dead in the sun—another sharp contrast to the stiff creatures in the musty room.

"You know what I like about you?" Olivia said. "You have every right to be proud of yourself for graduating from med school and being a resident. But whenever people ask what is going on with you, you always also tell them about me and my job and my life.

You're a good husband, Lucas. I probably could have done better, but you're okay."

"Oh, you could have done far better, Olivia," Lucas promised her.

Olivia reached over and put her hand on the back of my boy's neck. It gave me a warm feeling to see that. They were doing Love to each other.

Lucas eventually stopped back where we had left our smells and the small cloth room. We were going to spend another night out in the mountains! That meant I would be together with Lucas and Olivia the whole time. At home, I was often alone for almost unbearable stretches of the day. But here, outdoors, I would always have my boy within sight.

Lucas pulled a familiar metal box out of the Jeep, sweeping tantalizing fragrances through the air as he set it down. They were food odors, strong ones—especially after he fiddled with it and heat began blossoming from within. The smells were like memories, reminding me of grilled fish and other meals from days spent in the mountains.

I watched Lucas attentively as he placed some meat inside the smoking box. Sometimes when we were doing this, going up into the mountains in the Jeep and spending the night in the tent, Lucas would build a fire in some rocks and cook food on long sticks. Tonight, though, Lucas seemed happy with his metal box. (I know *I* was happy.) As usual, my own dinner came from a crinkly bag, but there were some scraps from Olivia's plate that Lucas placed in my bowl. I ate those first.

A dog knows it's always important to eat the best treats before turning attention to anything else.

When the sun dropped behind the mountains, the air chilled and we were soon inside the soft-sided room. I slept between Lucas and Olivia, my head on Lucas's chest the way his head had been on the chest of the man lying on the floor.

I was drowsily aware of the metal box and it still smelled wonderful.

The night was far from quiet. Small creatures scrabbled around, their odors wafting into the cloth room. An occasional fox screamed, which always startled me. A dog barking at night is a beautiful, peaceful sound, but the call of a fox is disturbing.

I imagined Big Kitten out there hunting creatures and bringing them back to me so that we could share a meal. She preferred to do her stalking in the darkness, while a dog likes to hunt in the day to see prey like the squirrel I was set to catch before that small male blundered into the situation.

I could not smell her, though, and did not know where she was. What I could smell, faint but undeniable, was smoke.

Five

I awoke just as birds were calling to one another about the impending sunrise. I sat up, concerned. What had begun at night as a barely detectable odor of smoke had become much more powerful, though it somehow had managed to not penetrate my sleep. Worried, I gazed down at the shadowy forms that were Lucas and Olivia. I felt afraid and wondered if I should nudge Lucas. I did not know how he would react to that. I imagined him being unhappy and speaking to me sternly, as he sometimes did in the middle of the night when I had a perfectly good reason to bark at something.

In the end, I decided to sit and wait for them to awaken, even as I felt my fear rising. Out there somewhere in the mountains, there was a fire.

A very big fire.

The acrid tang grew stronger, picking at my nostrils, flaring them. The odors were on me like a pressure, and I waited restlessly, yawning and staring at my boy's face, and at Olivia's, willing them to wake up and do something that a dog couldn't—fix the smoke.

Light gradually filtered in the sides of the soft room, and with the dawn came irregular, strong gusts of wind, rippling the walls. After a particularly howling burst seemed to move the entire room, Lucas yawned and looked at his watch. "Good morning, Bella."

I wagged and leaned forward to lick his face. I felt so much better now that he was awake. He would know what to do.

"Okay, thank you for the kisses. That's enough. Okay!"

Olivia groaned as Lucas crawled to the tent door and unzipped it. I followed him out into the morning, squatting, watching him peer up into the sky. Strong blasts of wind blew pebbles and dust at me. I blinked the grit out of my eyes and watched my boy for clues as to how we should react to the smoke.

With a rustling sound, Olivia stepped out, stretching her hands above her head. "I need coffee," she declared sleepily. "Wow, windy day."

"Weirdest cloud over there. See?" Lucas replied. "Strange color. It's not supposed to rain today, just high winds."

Olivia followed his pointing finger and frowned. "That's not a cloud. That's smoke."

"Smoke?"

"It's a fire. A *huge* fire. Don't you smell it?"

Lucas inhaled deeply. "No, not really. Do you?"

"Yes. Somewhere out there, something's really burning. Look at it!"

"Let's hope it doesn't head in this direction." Lucas began opening and shutting boxes, one of which was called a "cooler," where the delightful perfumes of meats and cheeses wafted out on cold air. I wagged while he banged some things together and decided that I liked the cooler even more than the hot metal box.

Olivia wandered away and stood with her back to us, head tilted up. I kept my eye on Lucas, though so far he had not pulled anything edible out of the cooler.

"I'm pressing the coffee," he called to her.

Olivia rejoined us. "Hey, I have a bad feeling about this."

"The fire, you mean?"

"It might be coming this way. Hard to tell. The wind is kind of blowing all over."

Lucas looked around. "Do you think it's coming up from the valley? We could get trapped up here if it does."

"It's for sure coming from the direction of the valley, but when

you look down you can't see any flames. Just black smoke. I wonder if maybe we shouldn't leave, just as a precaution."

"We were going to hike to the summit today."

"I know, but . . ."

Lucas passed her a metal cup and she drank from it. They were
staring at each other but not talking. Dogs stare at each other, too,
but usually it's because we're just astounded to see another dog.

Lucas sighed. "I guess the smart thing to do would be to pack
up, head down to a town where we can get a cell signal, see what's
going on."

"Vail? Frisco? Leadville?"

"Probably back to Frisco."

"Why do I think the deciding factor might be a certain bakery-
slash-restaurant?"

"Rhymes with minnamon molls," Lucas agreed cheerfully.

"How nice, another surprise for your wife."

Car ride!

Lucas put everything back into the Jeep and I sat in the back
seat as we slowly ascended a steep rutted road, swaying and jounc-
ing. Olivia's window was down but I didn't thrust my nose forward
in the space between the seat and the door because the smoke
made it unpleasant. The smell was much stronger than it had been
when the sun was rising. I hoped at the end of this car ride we'd
be in a place where the air wasn't heavy with the sooty scent of
burning wood.

Eventually Lucas cranked a tight turn and then sped up,
headed downhill. "It's getting worse," he told Olivia. "Roll up your
window, would you?"

I registered without disappointment as Olivia's window slipped
up and seated itself with a squeak. On the other side of the glass,
the tree-filled hill rose up sharply on Olivia's side, while on my boy's
side it plummeted nearly straight down. The wind continued to
punish the swaying branches.

I could feel a gnawing anxiety growing in both of them. Olivia reached her hand out and touched Lucas's neck, but I took no comfort from the gesture because she was so tense. "We're going to be okay, though, right?" she asked. "Lucas?"

He gave her a pensive look. "The problem is, we don't know where the fire even *is*. And with this wind, it could be heading right toward us and we wouldn't even know it."

"I'm glad we left when we did."

"Is this where I'm supposed to say, 'My wife was right'?"

"Again," Olivia corrected. "Your wife was right *again*."

"Yeah. I'm glad we left when we did. The smoke is getting thicker by the minute. For all we know we're driving right toward it."

"Do you think we should turn around, then?" Olivia pressed worriedly.

"Maybe. Can you look on your phone and see where the road takes us back in that direction?"

She pulled out her phone and began touching it fondly. "Well, that's not helpful. I can't pull up maps. I don't have a signal, either. No bars."

I glanced at her. I knew what No Barks meant, but did not know why she would be saying it now. I sneezed, which did nothing to clear the tickle from my nose.

Lucas coughed. "I've got it on recirculating, but it's still getting pretty bad in here." He reached forward and touched something and the air began blowing loudly from the dashboard.

Olivia shivered. "I feel like the wind is trying to push us off the road." Her hand reached up and gripped a handle above her.

"There's that scenic turnout not far from here, remember? We'll get out there, see what we can tell about where the danger is. Okay?"

Olivia nodded. "Sounds good. Maybe I'll be able to get a signal from up there, too."

"We're going to be fine, honey."

Olivia reached out and touched a tender hand to my boy's neck again. He slowed for a tight bend in the road.

"Lucas!" Olivia screamed.

Lucas slammed the Jeep into a stop so abruptly that I nearly toppled from the seat.

We had found the fire.

In front of us, all the trees were burning, flames roaring loudly up into the blackened sky. As we watched, a tree crashed across the road, sparks dashing off with the wind as it smashed onto pavement. The smell was overwhelming.

"The trees are burning on both sides of the road!" Olivia's voice cracked with dread.

An awful terror poured from Lucas as he backed up, swung the Jeep around, and raced back up the way we had just come, the engine roaring loudly.

"My God. . . ."

Olivia's eyes were wide and horrified. "The whole world was on fire back there!"

"Did you see how fast it was moving?"

"No—I mean, I just saw flames everywhere. Lucas, what do we do if the fire's in front of us, too?"

Lucas glanced at her, then grimly turned his attention back to the road. We were swaying into the turns, and outside the windows the trees were flying past in a blur, shaking their limbs at us. I was too agitated to lie down, so I just stared out the front, the smoke so strong in my nose that my eyes were tearing up. I panted with agitation. I wanted to do Go Home, to have a t-i-i-iny piece of cheese, to lie in bed with Lucas and Olivia and have everything be normal. To be gone from this scary place.

"Whoa!" Lucas shouted. A car came flashing around the corner, its horn blowing, and Lucas veered to avoid it, his wheels crunching on gravel, the Jeep sliding. I was flung up against the door. My boy wrestled with the wheel and we skidded to a halt, sideways on the road. "He nearly hit us! Are you okay?"

"Yes. Yes. But where's he going? That way's the fire." Olivia reached over the seat and I licked her hand. "You okay, Bella?"

"He'll find out soon enough," Lucas replied grimly.

We started moving again, still headed uphill.

"We just need to find a place out of the smoke, see what's going on."

"I don't understand how we can go from a normal July day to a forest fire so quickly," Olivia fretted. "There was no warning."

"It's the high winds. They can make a tiny fire huge and push it at speeds over twenty miles an hour."

"It's so nice to be married to a man who watches the weather channel," she replied.

Lucas grinned at her. Then I felt the Jeep slow. Olivia gasped.

Up ahead of us, more trees were burning. The fire was a wall and it was coming straight at us. At us *fast*.

Lucas twisted in his seat, staring behind us as he backed up, the engine whining tightly, while all around us the trees seemed to explode, columns of smoke and fire blasting out toward us.

I barked, hating the fire.

Olivia was weeping. "Oh God, Lucas. We're trapped."

"Hang on."

The Jeep yawed to one side as he spun the wheel, and then we were going forward again.

"We just came from here!" Olivia protested wildly. "This way is the fire!"

"I know." Lucas stopped the vehicle and we all sagged forward. He gave Olivia an intense look. "Okay. Get in the back seat. Put Bella in her harness." He leapt out onto the road and ran to the back and started pulling things out of the Jeep. Instantly the choking smoke was much worse.

Olivia twisted in her seat uncertainly to watch Lucas gathering items from the back. "What are we doing?"

"See that lake down there? If we can get to it, we should be safe. There's an island maybe fifty yards out with no trees. Nothing to burn, surrounded by water."

"*What?* We can't drive down *there*. There's no road—there's not even a trail. It's too steep—it's the side of a mountain!"

Lucas came back around, carrying something. I whined. I did not want to be locked in the Jeep with Olivia, I wanted us to all be together. The fire all around us made me want to press up against my boy, to climb in his lap and be held. He opened his door. "Here's her harness. I think this whole area could be engulfed any second, so we don't have much time. I know it's really steep and rocky, but there's no other way to go. We've got to get to the lake, and if we try on foot, we're not going to make it. The fire's coming too fast."

"Okay," Olivia said. "I trust you."

He left his door open and returned to the back of the Jeep. Olivia scooted her seat forward and climbed over it and slid in next to me. I licked her face but was not wagging because she held my harness. I did not like the harness due to the fact that it kept me from roaming freely in the back seat, cinched into place by the belts. She buckled me into it while Lucas took the flattened pad we usually slept on in the soft-sided room and shoved it into the space between me and the back of the front seats. A familiar motor buzz started up.

Within seconds, the flat pad began growing, pushing at us. Olivia pushed back on it. "Air mattress?"

"Air bag's out, remember? This should help cushion the two of you. It's going to be a rough ride."

"Take the doors off," Olivia responded.

Lucas stopped, looking at her questioningly.

"We don't know how deep the lake is. If we sink, we're going to want to be able to get out," she explained.

Lucas nodded and was soon wrenching at the Jeep's soft doors, setting them down at the side of the road.

The sleeping pad kept growing. "I think it's inflated enough!" Olivia called to Lucas over the top.

The sound of the motor ceased. Lucas jumped in the open door and clicked his belt in place and looked over at us.

"I love you, Olivia."

"I love you, too, Lucas."

They stared at each other a moment and the fear was so strong I panted with it.

Then Lucas said, "Hold on to Bella."

Six

Olivia put her arms around me as the Jeep lurched forward. Within moments we were bouncing and jerking, the vehicle rocking with hard slamming crashes that *hurt*. Olivia cried out as a vicious impact sent us hurtling into our harnesses. The engine was screaming and Lucas was clinging to the bucking steering wheel and a tree limb hit the windshield with a huge *bang* and then there were glittery pebbles flying everywhere. We tipped one way and then way over the other way and hit something that stopped us, throwing me forward against my belts.

"Oh God, Lucas!"

"Hang on!" Lucas grabbed at the stick on the floor and the Jeep careened backward, then forward again. He desperately twisted the wheel and teeth-rattling impacts rammed my body in all directions. The harness held me but forces tore me back and forth, so many jarring shocks shaking us I couldn't focus my eyes. "It's a cliff!" Lucas shouted. Then suddenly we pitched forward, no longer shaking, an odd floating sensation, and I heard Lucas yelling something else and then with a tremendous concussion we jolted to a halt and we were upside down and water was pouring in from the sides, rushing all over us.

"Lucas!" Olivia screamed. She unsnapped her harness and fell headfirst into the water. I felt her hands on me and my buckles released and I dropped into the water, too. She reached over and shook my boy by his shoulders.

"Lucas! Are you okay?"

Lucas sputtered, pulling his head out of the water. "Airbags worked after all," he mumbled. With a snap of his belts he fell down and now all three of us were in the water, but I was the only one swimming.

I did not know why we were here but I was relieved the car ride down the steep hill was over. Thrashing, we made our way out of the Jeep, which was lying with its wheels up in the air. Lucas ducked his head in the water and pulled out the sleeping pad. "Flotation," he explained. "Even partially inflated, it'll work. Let's get to that island."

At first Olivia and Lucas waded, but then they were swimming, each holding on to one edge of the sleeping pad, which was sagging but floating. They were gulping air.

The water was *cold*. I felt it as a penetrating ache in my bones. I did not know what we were doing, why we decided to drive into the lake, but I was glad to be with my people.

Before long Lucas and Olivia were wading again, and then my paws struck rocky bottom. I climbed out onto shore and shook myself. A trembling seized my body and my legs were shaking. We were on a small rocky place out in the lake, with water on all sides of us. The inconsistent clouds of heat, arriving on the dancing wind and then blowing quickly away, did nothing to dispel my bone-deep chill.

Olivia and Lucas stood and held each other.

"I thought we were going to die, Lucas," Olivia whispered. "I really did."

He nodded and swallowed. "I've never been more afraid, but we made it."

I climbed up on my rear legs and put my paws on his hips and thrust my head into their hug so they'd know I loved them both. They needed my comfort—I was a good dog who could sense such things.

Lucas smiled down at me, then frowned at Olivia. "You're cut."

Olivia pulled her sleeve back and I smelled the blood as it ran down her arm. "Oh wow, I didn't even feel it. Maybe when the windshield blew out?"

Lucas examined the bleeding gash. "It's going to take a few stitches." He looked around. "Okay, I'll go back to the Jeep and get my kit and a few other things."

"*What?* You can't swim in that water again! It's too cold."

"I won't. Swim, I mean. See? Look to my right, see how much more shallow the water is over there? I'll wade to shore. I won't ever be in over my head."

"*There?* That's where the fire is! You can't be serious."

"Obviously I won't go all the way up on shore where the trees are burning. As soon as the water is shallow enough, I'll turn right and get to the Jeep." He picked up the sleeping pad, coughing into his fist. "I'll take this along. Don't worry. I'll be okay."

"I'll go with you."

"I know you would, but I want you to keep pressure on that arm. I realize it's risky, but it's the only way we're going to survive. We need the cookstove and dry clothes—we could literally die of hypothermia if we don't do something."

"I'm just terrified you're heading straight where the fire looks the worst!"

"You watch, I've got this."

Olivia wiped tears from her face. "Wait. Wait. When we were driving down the mountain, when I thought we were going to be *killed,* all I could think of was how important you are to me. I can't lose you, Lucas. I can't have you die on me."

Lucas put his hands on her shoulders. His teeth were chattering. "That's what I thought, too. How lucky I am that I met you."

After another fierce hug, I was mystified when Lucas turned and, dragging the sleeping pad, marched over to the shore and walked out into the water. What were we *doing*?

I followed, though, because I was his dog.

For the most part I could touch bottom in the icy lake, but

what concerned me far more was that we were heading straight toward smoke and flames. In front of us the steep slopes sent hot, billowing clouds to the sky, the wind thrashing the burning trees in a storm of sparks. I kept looking up at Lucas. I would follow him, but I did not want to go ashore where everything was on fire.

"Okay, Bella, that's close enough." I was relieved when Lucas turned and headed in the direction of the Jeep. His body was quaking violently, and when the lake bottom dropped he stumbled and seemed weak. I swam close, anxious and afraid.

At the Jeep, he heaved me up so I was standing on metal between the wheels. He ducked into the Jeep, returned with his hands full, and piled things onto the sleeping pad, which cratered when he placed the cooler on it. His hands trembled when he patted the pad. "Okay, let's go, Bella."

I leapt into the water and paddled after him. We cut a different path back than on the way out, and I saw that the shrieking fire and smoke were much closer to the Jeep and the shoreline than they had been before. We swam for a distance, and then Lucas was wading again, breathing in short gasps. My feet finally found purchase, but the lake bed was uneven. Lucas tripped and went down.

"Lucas!" Olivia rushed forward, splashing, while I anxiously nosed my boy. He was on his hands and knees and his face was almost touching the water. Olivia reached under his arms, dragged him upright, and half pulled, half carried him to shore, his hand still gripping the sagging sleeping pad and the items he had placed on it.

Once on dry land, Lucas struggled to his feet.

"Your lips are blue!" Olivia told him. I heard the alarm in her voice.

"Cookstove," Lucas croaked. He began pulling off his wet clothes. "I should have grabbed an extra bottle of LP."

Olivia lifted the familiar metal box off the sleeping pad, and when she opened it, I turned my nose toward the delicious odor of meats past. "We're good, there's plenty of gas in the tank." There was a coughing sound and then I felt heat wafting out of the box.

Lucas bent and picked up rocks the size of his fist and placed them in the box and slapped the lid shut. His hands were shaking uncontrollably as he fumbled with his backpack. "We need to heat our cores first," he slurred. "Put on dry clothes, honey."

Olivia reached into her pack as Lucas struggled into a thick shirt and some pants. Soon she was yanking a sweater over her head. "I can't feel my hands or feet," she complained, her teeth clicking. "It's like getting dressed wearing oven mitts."

Lucas pulled out two towels, grabbed a long metal tool, and opened the box. "Okay, we'll roll the heated rocks up in the towels and hold them between our chests and our clothes. We warm the center mass, our torsos, first, then the extremities." He pulled out the rocks and placed them on a towel. He folded this up and handed it to Olivia. "Put this under your shirt."

"You first."

"No, I'm okay."

"Lucas, you look like you're *dying*. Your lips are almost black."

My boy nodded and shoved the rolled-up towel into his shirt and put more rocks in the box and closed it.

"I was watching the fire up in the hills while you were at the Jeep," Olivia said, her trembling forcing a warble into her voice. "You wouldn't believe how fast it's spreading. A whole hill, one minute fine, the next completely on fire. It's more like a bomb going off than anything."

Lucas shook his head grimly and took out the rocks. They smelled different, having been cooked. He put them on a second towel and rolled it and handed it to Olivia, who thrust the bundle up her sweater.

"How does that feel?" he asked.

"It feels fantastic."

This was how we passed much of the day—I watched as the two of them put the warm rocks in towels and placed them in the front and back of their clothing. Eventually they started rubbing me with the towels, and my skin felt alive under the deliciously warm cloth. I spontaneously ran around the shoreline, which took almost no time before I was right back where I started.

Lucas opened the cooler and peered into it. I watched him hopefully. "I'll make coffee, and we should eat these hard-boiled eggs and some cheese, get some fat into us. Shivering takes a lot of energy. How are you doing?"

Olivia smiled. "A lot better."

The whistling wind blew hot, smoky air at us, and sometimes glowing pieces of wood sparked as they landed on the stony shore of our island.

"Okay, I hate to say this, but it's time for me to get to your cut," Lucas told Olivia.

"Why do you look so serious? It's just a little cut, right?"

"Well, sure, but it hasn't stopped bleeding, even with the towel tied around it. I'm going to need to put in stitches."

"Okay," Olivia replied slowly. "But you can do that, right? I mean, you've done it."

"Yes, of course. On, um, grapes."

"What?"

"I haven't actually stitched a person yet. We've been practicing on grapes."

"Oh my God, you went to medical school to become a *fruit doctor*?"

Lucas laughed. "I'm pretty good at it, don't worry about that." Then he stopped laughing.

"Don't worry about that. . . ." Olivia repeated. "About *that*. What *should* I worry about?"

"I, uh, don't have any actual anesthetic in my kit."

"Oh."

"So it's probably going to hurt a little."

"You're going to stick needles in my skin and it's going to hurt *a little*."

"A lot. It's probably going to hurt a lot, honey. I'm really sorry, but I don't think we've got a choice."

Olivia sat on a rock and Lucas pulled out a small bottle of very strong-smelling liquid and a square cloth. "Isopropyl. This will sting," he warned.

Lucas gave Olivia's arm a bath. She sucked in air and winced and I felt a flash of pain from her. "You okay?" he asked.

"Just get it over with."

I did not know what was happening, but it seemed to me that Lucas was hurting Olivia. She looked off in the distance, biting her lip, but when I followed her gaze, I saw only the flaming trees and black smoke whipped into the air by the raging wind.

"All done. That was amazing, Olivia. I would have screamed my head off," Lucas admired.

"That's why men don't have babies," Olivia responded lightly. "If they did, every family would have just one child."

We cuddled together on the oddly floppy sleeping pad for the night, but it wasn't long before I caught the scent of an animal, wild and intense and unfamiliar. I lifted my head and stared into the odd light—the glow from the fires was diffused by the smoke, but I could see something standing in the shallow part of the lake, something very big.

I growled a warning. Olivia sat up. "What is it, Bella?" She put out her hand and stroked me reassuringly. Then she gasped. "Lucas! Wake up!"

Lucas was instantly alert. "What is it?"

I stopped growling because I had done my job and alerted my people.

"It's a bear. See?"

Lucas peered into the dark, and now we were all staring at the huge, hulking creature, whose dank odor wafted to me, strong even with all the smoke. "Is it a grizzly?"

Olivia shook her head. "No. Grizzlies are extinct around here. But it's a huge black bear, which can be pretty dangerous."

They were saying "bear," and I decided that's what this wild, dangerous-looking animal was called. *Bear.*

"Wonderful," Lucas drawled. "What do we do?"

Olivia thought for a moment. "I think for now we just keep an eye on it. He's running from the fire; he's not interested in us."

I smelled another animal, too—several of them, a pack. Soon my eyes confirmed what my nose told me as deer emerged from the gloom and stepped into the shallow water.

"Look at that," Lucas murmured.

"They are standing right next to a bear," Olivia marveled. "But they're so afraid of the fire, they don't even care."

Lucas and Olivia put their heads back down eventually, but I maintained my vigil. I knew that the big bear was a danger to us and would not allow it to come any closer.

When the sun rose, the bear wandered off, and so I finally stretched out to sleep. When Lucas woke me by yawning, the deer were gone, too.

The smoke smell was still heavy upon us, but the flashing flames had receded for the most part. The winds were calmer and I could hear a few birds reassuring each other from deeper in the woods.

Lucas stood and surveyed all directions. "Fire's mostly out."

"It burned everything. There's no more fuel," Olivia agreed.

"How did you sleep?"

"I think I slept. I was completely exhausted from all that shivering. But I kept waking up and watching the fire. It was almost beautiful, you know? But I was afraid it was somehow going to make it to our island."

Lucas nodded. "Same here. I was worried we might be overcome with the smoke, but the wind kept blowing it away."

They cooked eggs on the hot box and gave me some. For a long time, neither of them spoke.

Finally, Olivia set down her coffee cup. "Okay," she said.

Seven

Lucas nodded. "Okay." He stood and carefully looked around. "I don't think it would be safe to leave this island in any direction except straight back behind us, our six o'clock, if the Jeep's at twelve. See how pretty much everywhere there are still jets of smoke coming out of the ground? We might step in a hot spot and burn ourselves. But behind us, that rocky area didn't get hit with fire. There's no foliage for fuel. So, what do you think? Should we try going that way?"

Olivia drained the last of her coffee. "I'm game. I don't want to spend another night here, that's for sure."

Lucas and Olivia put on their packs and went wading. I stayed next to them but the frigid water was deep enough for me that it was mostly a swim. An intense odor of smoke rose from the surface as I paddled.

"The lake is just black," Olivia commented despairingly.

"And *cold*," Lucas agreed.

When we were close enough to the smoking shore that I could walk in the water without it touching my belly, Lucas put down a cautioning hand. "That's far enough, Bella."

I didn't know what he was saying to me but I stopped to look at him and sensed his approval as I heeded him.

"You could burn your paws, Bella," Olivia told me.

I glanced at her when she said my name.

Lucas turned and waded along the shore. "My feet feel like ice blocks, but I think we need to stay in ankle-deep water and see if we can get to that gully."

My boy's pull on my leash kept me from climbing onto shore. I gingerly picked my way over the pebbles and small stones under my feet. I did not see any squirrels or any ducks or any creatures worth chasing, but at least I was no longer swimming.

When we finally stepped out of the water, we were in a rocky area that sloped upward with no trees or bushes. I stayed close to Lucas.

"This is probably the streambed for when the snowmelt fills the lake," Lucas speculated. "Let's head upstream and see where it goes."

The rocks clattered as Lucas and Olivia led me up the slope. Wind gusted hard at us, blowing smoke up my nose and making it difficult to smell anything else, which was why I didn't detect the animals until we were upon them. They were bright white, with bushy coats and horns coming out of their heads. All were bigger than I, and any dog knows a pack is more dangerous than any single creature.

I growled a low warning.

"Mountain goats!" Olivia exclaimed.

Lucas nodded. "I don't think I've ever seen them at such low altitude. It's okay, Bella."

"Do you think this means the fire got all the way to the summit of the mountain?" Olivia asked anxiously.

"I'm guessing these guys didn't wait to find out."

Lucas commanded me to do Heel. Heel is where I am supposed to remain right by his side and not run off despite provocation— even a squirrel. I am not always a good dog when I am asked to do Heel but that is because where we live there are a lot of squirrels who try to take advantage of the situation. I don't consider that to be my fault, but Lucas does.

I could tell the reason my boy wanted me to do Heel was because the big creatures were eyeing us nervously and moving ahead of us as if we were chasing them at a slow speed.

Lucas grinned. "I've never been this close to a mountain goat before."

He kept saying the word "goat." There were no goats around that I could see, just the odd shaggy animals who were not dogs but probably wished they were.

At a place where the path broadened out wider than a street, the strange not-dog, not-goat creatures bunched together and then suddenly reversed course. Lucas yanked my leash as he and Olivia jumped to the side. The horned animals raced past us, their hooved feet making ringing impacts on the rocks. I saw several juveniles running with them. They seemed to have no trouble skipping across the loose, rocky surface.

"Whoa!" Lucas exclaimed. He held my leash taut as the shaggy not-dogs thundered past. He shook his head, marveling at the sight. "What do you suppose spooked them? Us?"

Olivia shrugged. "Honestly, I think the fire has them in panic mode. They're just trying to stay safe."

When the last of the animals was beyond us, Lucas played out the leash and we went back to our walk.

The sun was much higher in the sky when we followed a dark dirt path and came out onto a road that was rutted and filled with stones. "What do you think we should do now?" Lucas asked. "Uphill? Or down?"

Olivia pointed. "Down."

So now we were walking in the middle of a road. It was much easier. There were places where trees were fresh and green and still standing, and places so barren and burnt that my eyes stung and I felt an oppressive, sooty heat pouring out of the ground.

The road twisted and turned, but I had faith that Lucas and Olivia knew where we were going. Humans always know.

I had my nose down and was not really watching my boy when he exclaimed, "Hey, look. It's a car."

Olivia and my boy led me to a car that was sitting with its windows rolled up. Olivia put a hand on Lucas's chest. "Honey, I'm afraid there might be somebody in there. Somebody who's . . ." She trailed off.

"I'll check it out." Lucas stepped forward and put his hands to his eyes and leaned down and pushed his face right up against the window of the car.

I looked up at Olivia for an explanation as to what we were doing now.

"Nobody here." Lucas opened the door and I heard a chiming sound. "Keys are in it. Let's see if it starts."

"But the owner could be around here somewhere," she protested. "I don't think we can just take it."

Lucas walked around to the other side of the car and shook his head. "This thing is all scorched on this side, and the tires are blistered. I think whoever was driving this got out somehow and escaped. I don't think he's coming back anytime soon."

"So we're doing *Grand Theft Auto* now?" Olivia asked.

Lucas wiped his forehead with his sleeve. He grinned at her. "Not at all. We left our Jeep, now we're taking a Toyota. It's sort of like a lending library. Leave one, take one."

Car ride!

Lucas did not roll down the windows, but when he started the car, delicious air began blowing from the front to where I sat in the back seat.

"Almost out of gas. Maybe that's why he stopped."

"Hope he was able to get a ride from somebody."

The tension that had been crackling between the two of them had eased, but I could still detect an undercurrent of worry. They were both sweating, and their sweat smelled of fear. I panted anxiously.

We drove downhill. At one point, I felt the car engine stop vibrating, though we were still rolling.

"Coasting. Conserving gas," Lucas explained.

"But can you stop? Aren't they power brakes?"

Lucas pushed his foot down and I felt the car slow. He nodded at Olivia. "We're okay, and if we run into a problem, I'll turn the engine back on."

As we rolled quietly along, I heard something approaching from down the hill in front of us—a heavy engine sound, familiar. I stared at Lucas, waiting for him to hear it, too. We rounded a bend, our new car still silent, and Lucas sat up straight. "Whoa!"

He reached forward and keys jangled and our motor came to life. He steered us to the side of the road and stopped. I watched out the window, wagging, as the source of the loud noises drove past us—two lumbering trucks of the kind that Mack liked to ride, followed by a steady procession of cars, all headed in the opposite direction. I noticed several people waving their arms at us out the windows.

Lucas turned to Olivia. "They're all going uphill. Fools."

Olivia laughed. "What do they know?"

"I guess maybe we should join them." Lucas sat for a moment while the rest of the cars flowed past. Then I swayed as our new car turned around and headed up the hill, following the line of vehicles.

Olivia twisted in her seat, smiled at me, and then stared out the window behind me. "Hard to say what's going on downhill, but obviously there's a reason the trucks are going this way and not that way."

"I'll see if I can catch up and we can ask them."

We started moving faster, but then after a short while, the car went quiet again. Lucas steered over to the side of the road and we coasted to a stop. "How would you feel if I told you we just ran out of gas?"

"Huh," Olivia replied pensively. "So now what?"

Lucas pressed his lips together and shrugged. "You have any cell reception yet?"

Olivia pulled out her phone and frowned at it. "Nothing."

"We're probably not going to get anything for a while. I imagine the fire can't be good for the cell towers." Lucas shrugged again. "I guess we walk uphill."

Walk! Still on leash, I sniffed along the side of the road, finding animal smells but no dogs. Heavy gusts of wind whistled at us.

"How many cars and trucks would you say passed by?" Lucas asked.

Olivia reflected for a moment. "Maybe . . . twenty? It was a lot."

"My guess is that they're all from a small town from somewhere down the mountain and they just did an organized evacuation. So even though we don't know where we're going, they do."

"What if where they are going is a dozen miles from here?"

"You wanted to hike today, remember?"

We walked steadily. At first I pulled on my leash, eager to get wherever we were going, but after a time I fell into step next to my people and just opened my nose to the experience.

"How's your arm?" Lucas asked.

Olivia glanced down. "Good. No bleeding, and I don't really feel it. All that work on grapes really paid off."

I could still smell smoke. It danced in and out on the air currents, sometimes heavy, sometimes a mere tickle, but always there.

I glanced back the way we'd come because I'd heard it again, that same engine noise. After a moment, both Olivia and Lucas halted, twisting around to look behind us.

In the far distance, another one of those huge trucks ponderously approached us. Lucas handed my leash to Olivia and stepped out into the middle of the road. He waved his arms and the big truck eased to a halt. A man leaned out the window, but it wasn't Mack.

"We ran out of gas," Lucas told the man.

"That your Toyota back there?"

Lucas nodded. "Yeah. Well, no, but it's a long story. Is there fire down the hill? We were passed by a lot of cars."

"Not yet, but it's coming. We just cleared the last people out of the town of Norwalk. You two like a lift?"

Car ride in the big truck!

Lucas and Olivia sat on a metal seat and talked to a man who was dressed like Mack, while I lay at their feet. The heavy vibrations on the floor made me drowsy. I slept, but jumped to my feet, wagging, when I felt the truck come to a halt.

"What's going on? Why are we stopping here?" Olivia asked.

"Hard to say," the man dressed like Mack replied.

We climbed down. Parked in the road up ahead were the two huge trucks, plus a line of other vehicles. People were standing up out of their cars, opening doors, and I saw a small brown dog and a larger white one. The white one strained at his leash to reach me, but his person held him fast. I wagged but stuck to my boy's side as we joined a circle of people.

Suddenly, I smelled Mack! He was here, but there were so many other people that I couldn't tell where.

A man in a white shirt stood in the center of the ring of people. "Okay, I don't know everything, but here's the situation. The fire has jumped the break we dug yesterday, blocking our way going forward. And as you know, the way back downhill takes us to the middle of the evacuation zone. There's no easy way to say this, folks. We're right in the path of the fire."

Whatever the man in the white shirt was saying, it caused people to stiffen and start talking to one another, alarm audible in their rising voices.

"You mean we could die up here?" a woman asked.

White Shirt Man nodded grimly. "I've radioed for help. They're putting county resources to working on a way to get us out of here. But for the moment, we're trapped."

People were talking even more loudly. I looked over at the big white dog, and he looked back at me. We were both doing Sit.

"We need to go back to town," someone said loudly.

"They said the town was going to catch on fire," another person objected.

"There's a trail," someone offered.

"What? Please, quiet down!" White Shirt Man called loudly to the crowd. "Sir, would you repeat what you just said?"

A thin man wearing shorts stepped forward. "It's an old two-track, about a thousand yards back. I ride down it sometimes. It leads to an old mining camp, and there's a road from there to the highway."

"Show me."

The thin man and White Shirt Man pushed through the people and walked away. As everyone returned to their cars or stood around to talk, I saw Mack and dragged Olivia over to him. His back was to me, but he turned when I jumped up and put my paws on him.

"Bella?"

"Well, hey, Mack. This is getting to be a habit." Lucas greeted with a tight grin.

Mack gave me a hug and I licked his proffered hand. "Were you two down in Norwalk?"

Olivia shook her head. "We were camping and ran from the fire. It was . . . We had a challenging night."

"Man, I was thinking about you. I knew you were spending the night in the mountains and was worried. I tried to call you, but my phone's not working. I'm glad you're safe." Mack brightened. "Oh, one of the reasons I wanted to call is that my captain passed me a message. That guy from the museum? He made it. He's breathing on his own, even."

I glanced up at my boy, sensing his relief. He touched my head with his hand when I nosed it. "That's great to hear. Thanks."

"Congratulations, Doc," Mack said. "You saved a life."

Olivia hugged Lucas. "I'm so proud of you."

I turned because the white male dog was lifting his leg upwind of me. We stared at each other for a moment.

"So, what's the latest, Mack? How big is the fire?" Lucas asked.

Mack shook his head. "I don't think we know that yet. It's just moving faster than anyone expected." He gestured up into the air. "This wind."

"Are we going to be rescued? Helicopters?" Olivia asked.

Mack looked worried. "I don't know."

When White Shirt Man returned, people once again surrounded him. I lost track of the white dog but saw the small brown one. She was a female and was panting nervously.

"Here's what we need to do," the man announced loudly. People instantly fell silent. "Any SUV or pickup with a high clearance, you're going to be fine on the two-track. We'll send the fire trucks down ahead of you. Small cars, though, the trail is too rough. So, grab what you need and let's consolidate into the vehicles that can make it."

A man dressed like Mack shook his head. "We're going off-roading. In a *fire truck*."

White Shirt Man nodded firmly. "I'm not going to lie to you, this could get pretty bad. But we better go *now*."

People immediately began talking and leaning into their cars and pulling things out. Then they were leaping into trucks and shutting doors with a *bang*.

Mack turned to us. "Want to ride with me?"

Eight

I was astounded when we climbed up on Mack's truck for a car ride—not in it, *on* it!

I was lifted up onto a flat surface. I saw that many people were crammed into seats in the front, but some of us, including Mack, were on the very top, toward the back wheels. Some of Mack's friends stood on small metal platforms on the sides, clinging to handles. My boy took a firm grip on my collar with one hand and grasped a metal rail with the other. Olivia was next to him, holding the railing with both hands.

Cars were backing up and turning. I watched alertly for the big white male dog and the small nervous female. I wanted to bark at them from the roof of the truck.

We bounced and creaked as we drove back down the mountain a bit, following the other two big trucks. We were the last truck in a line of vehicles. The trees along the side of the road were lush with leaves being thrashed by the ever-present wind. I expected the warm blowing air to whisk away the smoke, yet the bite of burning wood never left my nose. Nobody talked, but everyone coughed occasionally.

I brightened when we rattled to a stop. White Shirt Man stood on an outside platform of the truck, at the front of the halted procession. He leaned forward and pointed. "That's it!"

White Shirt Man and some of Mack's friends jumped down as the driver opened his door and stepped out. They stood with their hands on their hips, staring into the trees as if watching for squirrels. I wagged, thinking we were going to climb off the truck ourselves, but other than loosening his grip a little Lucas made no move to go anywhere.

"You want me to drive down *that*?" the driver demanded.

I looked to Lucas, who was watching the conversation. His hair and face smelled like smoke. He glanced at me but did not issue any commands.

"Well, now," Mack murmured. "*This* will certainly be interesting."

Olivia shook her head. "How can they expect the truck to make it down that? It's not even a real road. The fire trucks are too wide."

"I think you're right," Lucas agreed, "but if this part of the forest starts burning, I want to be on the truck and not on foot. Probably be okay."

"You'd be surprised at what fifty thousand pounds and six hundred horsepower can do," Mack interjected. "We've never gotten stuck in snow, and we can mow down small trees like they're nothing."

"Not going to be fun if the truck tips over, though," Olivia pointed out.

Mack grinned at her. "What part of that wouldn't be fun?"

Olivia shook her head at him and Lucas laughed. I wagged at the familiar sound.

Mack's friends returned to the trucks, which snorted back to life. Lucas's hand tightened on my collar again. With a lurch, we started to drive into the trees. We were moving more slowly, but our truck was swaying from side to side, sometimes to such an extent that Olivia and Lucas exchanged glances, their eyes wide. We kept hitting thin trees, cracking them loudly. With every jolt I slid a little, my claws digging fruitlessly at the slick surface underfoot. Here, in a place where the fire had not touched, the ordinary sound of the leaves being tossed in the stiff wind was comforting to me, but I was starting to understand that we were probably soon going to be smelling burning wood and seeing smoke and flames. Something had changed in our world. But as long as my boy kept me with him, I knew he would make sure I was never in danger.

We twisted and turned and bumped and were so jarred I had to stand with my legs splayed to keep from being flung. Several times Olivia and Lucas were tossed into the air and then landed hard, looking uncomfortable. When we all leaned precariously to the side, my boy's arm went rigid as he held my collar, and he took in a breath and didn't exhale until the truck righted itself.

"That was close!" he exclaimed, then coughed. "What do we do if we think we're tipping over?"

We were all jolted as the front of the truck swiped a tree, and then we started to lean again.

"Jump," Mack replied grimly.

Lucas looked at Olivia. "I'll throw Bella as far as I can. Then we go together, okay?"

We leaned over even farther. Olivia nodded tensely. "Do you think she'll understand to get out of the way of the truck?"

Now we were *really* leaning. I felt Lucas start to lift me up in the air. "She'll have to."

"I'll help you," Mack said. His hands reached out and grabbed me on either side, just in front of my tail.

With a *boom,* the truck straightened back up. I skidded on the metal surface, nearly falling over. I wagged at my boy, seeking reassurance that this was all intentional. People understand things about car rides that dogs don't. They know where they are going, and they know why sometimes the windows are down and sometimes they are not.

In front of us, the line of vehicles rose and fell into the deep ruts in the road. I peered at them but still couldn't spot the other two dogs.

There was another *bang,* a rattle so fierce along the length of the truck that Olivia gasped.

"Hang on!" the driver yelled.

"Good dog," Lucas told me.

I found myself thinking of the last car ride in the Jeep. That too had been a steep and bouncy journey. I hoped we weren't going to drive into a lake again.

A few moments later, the truck stopped weaving and made a really sharp turn. Suddenly we were on a road that was much less bumpy, with gravel crunching underneath the tires. Lucas and Olivia grinned at each other, and I could feel my boy's relief in the way his hand relaxed on my collar. We gained speed, the truck vibrating beneath us.

"I wouldn't want to do that again," Mack observed.

Olivia leaned forward and looked at him. "We're so lucky you showed up. We'd still be walking."

Mack smiled and shrugged. "Some things are just meant to be."

"You seem to be doing really well with this, Mack," Lucas observed carefully.

"Yeah." The two of them exchanged a long look, and then Mack turned to Olivia. "I don't know if I ever told you, but I was at the VA for PTSD. So you'd think this whole situation would be coming at me all kinds of ways, right? But nobody died this time. It's not the same as Zhari. It's . . ." He shrugged. "I can't explain it. But this feels important, and positive, and the other thing just felt tragic and horrible."

The smoother ride lasted for a long while. I was able to lie down, conscious of my boy's hand still resting on my collar. From that position I wasn't able to spot squirrels and other dogs, but some car rides are like that, and dogs simply have to adjust.

Before long I recognized the smells that meant we were approaching a town. After another swaying turn, we saw buildings on each side of the road, and our truck slowed.

A man dressed like Mack was standing in the middle of the street. He waved at us and the trucks all stopped. I climbed to my feet to watch.

The man walked to the lead truck and looked at the driver. "Welcome to hell," he greeted. He climbed up and stood on the outside of the driver door and pointed and we trundled slowly forward.

Cars filled the streets, some of them honking, many with dogs. I responded to them appropriately.

"No barks, Bella."

Though Lucas clearly did not understand the situation—there were dogs *in cars*!—I did as I was told, even though No Barks is one of those commands that rarely results in a treat for a good dog.

Lucas looked from one side to the other. "Where are we?"

"It's Paraiso," Olivia replied. "Maybe thirty thousand people. I've come up here before when their shelter has too many animals and they need me to take some back down to Denver."

"It looks like all thirty thousand people are trying to get out of Dodge," Mack observed.

"Lot of traffic," Lucas agreed.

Mack pointed. "That's going to be the command post up ahead in the city park, all those big tents."

The truck drove a little bit farther and stopped and the engine died. I yawned and wagged as people climbed down to the street. Mack swung himself over the side and then reached up to help Olivia down.

Lucas snapped my leash into my collar. "Okay, Bella."

He lifted me up and I went limp in his arms. It always felt good to be held by my boy. Grunting, he handed me down to Mack, who gathered me to his chest and then set me on the ground. Lucas hopped down and grabbed my leash. "All right, now what?"

Mack clapped Lucas on the shoulder. "We made it. I'm going to get back to it. Glad you guys are safe."

"Thanks for everything, Mack."

Mack reached down and petted me the way people do when they are leaving a dog.

"Let's go see what we're supposed to do," Olivia suggested.

We left Mack and his friends and their trucks and walked a short distance to a grassy area where several male dogs had recently lifted their legs. The steady hum of cars moving slowly in the roads, closely following one another, was a constant presence, as was the much fainter but still detectable odor of burning wood.

I saw many people milling around next to big white structures that reminded me of the soft-sided room where we slept next to the Jeep. These were much larger, though, and they rattled and rippled in the stiff wind.

A woman climbed up some metal steps and stood on a large wooden box. I squatted in the grass near the freshest male dog mark, announcing my arrival to any dog paying attention.

"What's going on?" Lucas asked a tall man.

The man turned and looked at Lucas with a cynical expression. "We've been listening to government employees make announcements. So far, that's about all that's been accomplished," he replied drolly.

"The whole town's evacuating," a woman next to the tall man added. "There's been a line of cars and trucks backed up since dawn. Some people are waiting until the last minute to leave because they don't want to get stuck in traffic."

"So the fire's coming here?" Olivia asked anxiously. "To Paraiso?"

The tall man shrugged. "No one has said anything definite yet."

"Attention! May I have your attention!" the woman on the box called.

Several people yelled right back at her, saying things like, "Hey! Listen up!" Two people whistled, the sound harsh and shrill on my ears. The sound of voices quieted, though I could still hear the cars on the road behind us.

"I'm Whitney Walker, district wildlife manager," the woman on the box announced loudly. Apparently, we were not going to go anywhere soon, so I sat and waited for Lucas to decide what to do next.

"At times like these it's easy to forget about wildlife," the woman continued, "but obviously they are even more impacted by all this than we are—they can't get in cars and drive away. So we all need to understand just how many thousands of animals have been displaced by this fire. That means they are out of their territories. They are lost, confused, and frightened. Some predators are very territorial—like cougars as an example—and they react to being forced to leave their comfort zone in unpredictable ways. Stay away from them, all wildlife, even deer. They should all be considered dangerous. Especially do not approach *hurt* animals. A hurt animal might see you as a threat and try to protect itself."

I picked up a scent rising sharply above the smoke and turned my head to see a car driving by us with goats sticking their heads out the window like they were dogs. They didn't bark the way dogs would, but they stared at me and I stared at them. What was this place, I wondered, where people took car rides with goats?

A new man clumped up the wooden steps and stood next to the woman, who moved to the side. He clapped his hands together. "All right, eyes on me, I need your full attention," he called in a near shout.

"We're standing here not saying anything, how much more attention do you need?" Olivia murmured quietly. Lucas grinned at her.

"I am Deputy Steve Holcomb with the Colorado Division of Homeland Security and Emergency Management," the man began. "I have been in contact with our command center. We have fire to the north, the west, and the east. Our only escape lies due south."

Whatever he was saying upset the people standing around next to Lucas and Olivia. Some of them spoke quietly to each other.

"Okay, everyone, settle down," the man commanded. "I'm not finished."

Olivia rolled her eyes at this.

"We are in control. National Guard trucks are headed this way, accompanied by fire companies from Eagle River, Clear Creek, and Jefferson. They should be here within an hour and a half. This town is under mandatory evacuation orders. If you have a vehicle, you need to get in it and go. *Now.* Otherwise, remain right here at the command post. The National Guard is our only way out, and we're not waiting around for anybody once the trucks get here."

A man in a wide-brimmed hat raised his hand. "I can see the fire from my home," he stated. "It's many miles away. The second peak over. I don't think you need to panic."

The man on the box frowned. "I am not *panicking*," he corrected testily. "We've got gusts up to fifty miles an hour. That means the fire is moving at top speed. Coming at us from three sides. Understand what I'm saying, here?"

"After we leave, then what?" someone else asked. "What's going to happen to Paraiso?"

The man looked around. "This place is going to burn to the ground."

Nine

Whatever words the man had just uttered, people flinched away from them like a dog being told *"Bad!"* Some raised their hands to cover their mouths. Everyone was upset and began talking to each other in louder voices. I stretched, feeling their tension. Lucas was calm, though, which was comforting. He and Olivia exchanged glances.

"Hey! Quiet," the man on the box shouted. "I need your full attention, here! I'm not done."

The man directly in front of Lucas raised his hands to his mouth. The motion caused the distinctive smell of cooking meat to waft toward me, and I lifted my nose to it. "Hold on. This is our home," Meat-man called to the man on the box. "You can't ask us to just abandon everything. There's still time to do something."

"Mandatory means mandatory," the man on the box replied tersely.

Meat-man glanced at the people on either side of him. They were like Lucas: the same age, and all men. They were shaking their heads.

"You want us to leave our town and just let it *burn*?" another man shouted from the crowd.

The man on the box put his hands on his hips. "You're not listening to me. You have to leave. This is not a request. I am in command. If you've got a functional vehicle, you need to be in it."

Meat-man spoke again, his voice rising above everyone else's.

"We're going to fight this fire and save our town. Don't even try to stop us."

I noticed several people nodding at this.

"If you do not follow orders, you will be subject to arrest," the man on the box countered sternly.

"Who is going to arrest us, *you*?" someone jeered.

I felt a mood stirring the crowd the way the wind was blowing smoke, a rising anger passing from person to person. Lucas stirred and I put my nose up to touch his hand.

"You are disobeying a direct order from the government," the man on the box said. "You want, we'll wait for the National Guard to explain things to you."

Olivia turned to Meat-man and his friends. "Do you really think you can save the town?"

Meat-man nodded. "It's just a question of how much time we've got. We know what to do—cut down trees, dig a firebreak."

"We were camping near Vail Pass when this thing hit," Lucas told him. "The whole situation went south pretty quickly."

Olivia nodded in agreement. "The fire whipped up so fast that there was nothing we could do. It was like the mountain just exploded. No one would have been able to save anything. We were lucky to escape with our lives. What happens if you get trapped here?"

This caused the men to glance at one another in a way that suggested they were communicating without speaking.

"That's a risk we will have to take," one of the men said finally.

I shuffled a bit closer to Meat-man's delicious odors.

Olivia looked at Lucas and shrugged. "If it were my home, I guess I'd feel the same way."

Lucas nodded. "Best of luck, guys. We're going to get on one of the troop trucks and evacuate."

People began drifting away from the man on the box, who had turned his back on everyone and was speaking to somebody else. I followed Lucas and Olivia to talk to the man in charge.

"Excuse me," Lucas said.

The man whirled and scowled at Lucas. "You and your buddies are going to burn up here and I don't give a damn," he spat.

I decided I did not like him.

"They aren't my buddies. I don't know them," Lucas replied mildly. "I'm just coming over here to tell you that I'm a first-year medical resident and I'm offering to help."

The man shook his head. "You're a little late. We already evacuated everybody who needed medical attention."

"The way you talk to people makes them not want to do anything you say," Olivia informed him coldly.

"You want trouble, lady?" the man replied threateningly. "If you want trouble, you've come to the right place."

Lucas stepped in front of Olivia. His voice remained soft. "What kind of trouble are you talking about, exactly?"

The man stared at Lucas for a minute, then turned away. "I don't have time to deal with people like you," he muttered.

Olivia stepped forward and opened her mouth and Lucas put a restraining hand on her shoulder. "Hey, I see sandwiches and water in that tent. Let's grab something and wait for the trucks."

Olivia's posture softened and she relaxed, nodding. Lucas took us across the lawn to a soft room from which tantalizing odors came flowing out, pushing past the smoke. He grabbed some succulent-smelling bundles and Olivia found water bottles. She cracked one open—"Here you go, Bella"—and poured the refreshing water into her cupped hand. I drank gratefully, licking her fingers in the process.

Lucas pointed. "I have another Mack sighting." He waved, and I saw Mack, who was standing with his friends, nod and smile. I hoped he would be joining us.

"Let's find someplace less crowded and sit down," Olivia suggested. "Have a meal like normal people."

"Sure," Lucas agreed. "Hey, Mack!"

Mack came over and I wagged, happy to see him. He put a

hand down and I licked it, tasting dirt and smoke in equal measure.

"They've got sandwiches in the tent," Olivia told him.

Mack nodded. "I'll get one in a sec. I guess the evacuation isn't going very well. There's really only one road going south, and it's all jammed up. The trucks that were sent to come get us keep getting stuck in traffic."

"Should we try to catch a ride with somebody, or wait for the National Guard?" Olivia asked.

Mack shrugged. "I don't know, hard to say. The fire trucks will be leaving last, but we've got good communications, so we'll be monitoring the situation in real time. I'll hold a place for you, if you want—just be sure to tell me if you manage to snag transportation from somebody else."

"What is the real-time situation, Mack? How bad is it?" Olivia asked.

Mack looked grim. "Bad. They're calling it the largest fire in United States history. Wyoming, Idaho, Colorado—it's all burning."

"But we're okay here for a while?" she pressed.

Mack gave her a frank look. "I know it pissed people off to hear it, but we're abandoning Paraiso. We expect the town to be hit pretty hard. Soon as the trucks arrive, we're loading up anybody left and getting out of here."

For a moment no one spoke. I stared meaningfully at the delicious-smelling bundles in my boy's hands, but he didn't notice me. "Okay," he acknowledged. "Meantime, we're going to head down the street a little, find some shade, and eat."

"Okay. Don't go far, though."

"We won't."

"Here." Mack reached for his belt and unbuckled something that looked like a big phone. "Keep it on channel nineteen. That's the coordinated-response frequency. You'll hear everything, including the 911 operator. You'll know the second the trucks pull up. Don't delay when that happens, man. Get back here fast."

Lucas accepted the big phone. "Thanks. I mean, roger that. Ten-four, over."

Olivia held out her hand. "Maybe an adult should carry the radio."

They all grinned and we left Mack. Confused, I looked over my shoulder several times to see if he was going to follow us, but he was busy talking to other people.

Lucas faced Olivia. "All we can do is wait."

"I guess. I'm going to duck into that pharmacy for just a second," Olivia said. "Then we can have a picnic."

Lucas frowned at her. "Why? What's wrong?"

Olivia sort of cocked her head at him. "What's wrong? What's wrong is that when a woman says she needs to get something from the pharmacy, her husband isn't supposed to ask her a lot of questions about it."

"I've been trained to ask questions."

"And I'm training you to mind your own business," she responded lightly.

They smiled at each other and then Olivia left us to go into a building. I looked up expectantly at Lucas, uneasy that she was out of our sight. This happened all the time, of course, but in this place, on this day, with the smoke and the wind, I was anxious. I wanted us to all be together and to get back in the Jeep and go home or to a dog park.

Olivia came back and I greeted her happily, putting my paws on her chest so she would bend over and let me lick her face. "Bella, you nut, I was only gone for five minutes. I got some dog food."

"Oh, great idea. There are some picnic tables over there," Lucas said. "Let's go sit and eat and talk about something besides the fire for a while."

We crossed the street and Lucas and Olivia sat down at a wooden table. I climbed underneath it, listening to the delightful sounds of paper being unwrapped to release the bouquet of meat and cheese into the air. I felt confident I would be getting a treat soon, and I was not wrong; Lucas reached down with a pinch of meat, which I gobbled eagerly. I was, I realized, hungrier than usual. Then Olivia put a paper on the ground. I wagged excitedly at this promising development. She leaned over and pulled the lid off a can and all the smoke odors fled before the blossoming bouquet of the meaty meal she emptied onto the paper. I attacked it instantly. It was delicious almost beyond belief.

"Good dog, Bella," she told me. I wagged and she sighed. "I know it sounds crazy, but I feel like I can relax, finally."

"Relax. With fire coming at us from every direction," Lucas repeated skeptically.

"Like you said, all we can do is wait. Trucks will be here soon, and you heard what they told us, the fire is miles away," Olivia responded. "Even the wind seems less forceful than it was. And I'm enjoying a sub sandwich with my husband. A lunch date. So, yes: relaxed."

I frantically licked the paper, chasing the phantom taste of my dinner, then stared up at them alertly, waiting for a hand to drop more treats.

"I don't think I've ever been more frightened than I was driving down the mountain toward the lake, with the fire coming, making all that noise," Lucas whispered after a moment.

Olivia went still. "I was terrified, too. But you said we were going to be okay, and said it with such assurance, that I believed you. It's what gave me the strength to sit there in the back seat and just hold on."

Lucas leaned forward and took Olivia's hand in his. "And you gave me strength. This whole way, I couldn't have made it without you."

Olivia and Lucas talked more while I did Sit at their feet, waiting patiently. Then a movement caught my eye and I lunged to my feet, staring in disbelief. A pack of unknown creatures plodded slowly and solemnly toward us, filling the width of the street.

Huge creatures. They were shaggy, with dark fur and wicked horns. Each had a head the size of my dog bed. Threatened, I bolted to the end of my leash and strained, barking furiously at them.

"No barks, Bella," Lucas admonished. "Those are just some buffalo passing by. They won't hurt us."

I was astonished to be told No Barks. Did he not see these enormous monsters coming straight at us? Sometimes people say or do things that a dog cannot hope to understand. I stopped barking, though, because I was a good dog and I knew to behave when there was still meat on the table.

"Displaced by the fire," Olivia murmured. "That one in front is the size of an SUV."

Lucas nodded. "He's enormous. I've seen herds of buffalo before, but never this close."

The fur was up on my back and I allowed a growl to rumble through me despite No Barks.

"You know," Lucas remarked, "I read somewhere that there are more injuries to people in Yellowstone from bison encounters than all the other animals combined."

Olivia stirred. "Maybe we should take our lunch and go somewhere else."

"They do seem to be bearing right down on us, don't they?"

Olivia and Lucas stood and I looked up at them, wagging. And then the most wonderful thing happened. Lucas leaned down to me, extending his fingers pinched together around a very tiny morsel.

"Bella?" Lucas said to me. "Do you want a t-i-i-iny piece of cheese?"

He and Olivia laughed as I focused all of my concentration on those fingers. The smoke, the wind, and even the monsters on the street were forgotten. I tentatively licked the cheese from between my boy's fingers, wagging happily. *T-i-i-iny piece of cheese* meant that Lucas loved me.

We left the table, my eyes on the savory paper bundle still in Lucas's hand. We rounded a corner and I was conscious of the huge creatures continuing their slow stroll in the direction they had been going and not turning to follow us.

They knew better than to mess with a dog.

"It's raining!" Olivia exclaimed.

I was conscious of the faint tickle of something landing on my fur. I shook it off.

Lucas was staring into his palm. "That's not rain. Look. They're tiny kernels of hard ash, blown here on the wind."

"Maybe we should get back to the camp," Olivia suggested.

They stopped walking when the phone on Lucas's belt squawked. The noise sounded vaguely like a human voice.

"911: What is the address of your emergency?"

"There's a fire up on Tribute Ridge."

I cocked my head because the tone of the almost-voice seemed upset and afraid.

"Yes, ma'am, we're aware of the fire on Sherwood Mountain."

"No, lady, you're not listening to me! This is on the ridge, Tribute Ridge!"

Lucas and Olivia exchanged solemn glances and we started walking again, our pace quickening.

Ten

Something was scaring Lucas and Olivia. I went alert, scanning with my eyes and nose, looking for what it might be. Of all the moods a dog might sense in people, this one, the sense of impending danger, was the easiest to detect, coming to me as clearly as a shout. Yet the cause of human emotions isn't always evident. I wanted to be a good dog and help Lucas and Olivia face the current threat, but I didn't know what it was.

The phone on Lucas's belt was still making scratchy, squawky noises.

"If you feel you are in danger, you should evacuate immediately."

"Do you know where Tribute Ridge is?" Lucas asked Olivia.

"No. I've never heard of it."

"Let's make our way back to tent city."

She nodded. "Good idea. Let's go left at the next corner—I think buffalo rush hour has probably moved on by now."

We turned at the end of the street and Olivia slowed down. "Oh no!"

Lucas followed her gaze and shook his head grimly. "Do you think people just left their dog here to die?"

At the word "dog," I realized that I smelled one. A male was watching us from a yard, not barking or moving. A chain sagged from his collar to a metal rod protruding from the ground. We stared at each other, each of us frozen at the sight of another dog.

Surely *this* wasn't the source of my boy's apprehension. It was a *dog*.

"Hey, boy," Lucas called to him softly. "Are you friendly?"

The dog shook himself, bowed, and wagged.

"Do you want something to eat?" Lucas asked.

Lucas cautiously approached this new dog and I watched in utter shock as my boy opened the paper bundle and pulled out a piece of *my* meat. I started to move forward to address this issue, but Olivia tightened my leash. "No, Bella. Stay."

I almost always hate Stay.

Lucas fed some of my food to the male and then reached down to the chain and unsnapped it from the stake. The dog did Sit, and received some more meat. I was doing Sit, too, right behind my boy, and he wasn't even looking at me! I stared up at Olivia in astonishment, but she ignored me, even though I was doing Sit and Stay and getting no treats!

Lucas led this new dog over to me. The male was big and light colored with his short tail up and stiff, but wagging a little. We politely smelled each other under the tail, and then he dashed over to a bush, pulling Lucas at the end of the chain, and lifted his leg. To show him I was friendly, I sniffed his mark. I was wagging in a way intended to show that I understood he was just happy to be with people and wasn't going to try to take any more of my food.

Lucas gave Olivia a helpless look. "Now what do we do?"

"We need to take him to the shelter so he can be evacuated with the rest of the animals," she said.

"Do you know where it is?"

She nodded.

"Is it far?"

"Nothing's far in this town. I'll show you."

We went for a walk, though I was somewhat suspicious of this new male dog who seemed so at ease with my people. Where were his humans, that he had to share mine? His chain clinked and rattled when it struck the street. I found it annoying.

Like most males, he held us back because he kept stopping to sniff other marks and lift his leg on them. I trotted pointedly next to my boy, displaying better, more treat-worthy behavior. We all halted when the male made another mark, and Olivia took the opportunity to bend down and grab the metal tag on his collar. "Gus," she declared.

I could tell by the way the male brightened that this was his name. He looked to me, and I glanced away. I already knew Lucas and Olivia could do amazing things, and coming up with this treat-stealing dog's name seemed among the least of these.

Olivia released the collar. "Are you a good dog, Gus? Yes, you are, you're such a good dog."

Gus wriggled in pleasure. I looked away from Olivia. I did not like her speaking in such tones to a new dog and hoped we would not be walking with him for long.

The phone on my boy's hip made a familiar noise. *"911: What is the address of your emergency?"*

"Chambers Road! Fire!"

"Which . . . where on Chambers Road?"

"I gotta go, the fire's right here!*"*

"Oh my god," Olivia breathed. "Do you suppose that's close to where we are?" I picked up on her distress, even more heightened now, and glanced up in concern.

Gus, if that was his name, was busily examining an old urine spot and didn't react.

Male dogs aren't usually good for much more than that.

Lucas fiddled with the phone. "I'm going to . . . I think I'll turn down the volume on the walkie for a little bit. We've still got plenty of time before the trucks are supposed to be here. I don't think we need to listen to every 911 call."

Olivia nodded. "Okay," she agreed shakily.

Hearing her speak, Gus looked up at her, so I knew he was one of those dogs who reacts more to women than men. Because he was finally aware something might be wrong, he turned his gaze on me. I ignored him.

We all walked steadily for a while. I hadn't been asked, but I was essentially doing Heel, pointedly sticking to my boy's side while Gus yanked around at the end of his chain without discipline. Then we came across another dog. This one also had light fur, and was smaller than I, but was far shaggier than Gus or me. Unlike Gus, she was running free, untied behind a wire fence that surrounded the front yard, and she was wagging with excitement as we approached. We stopped at the gate, and I had a sinking feeling our pack was about to grow even larger.

"Hello?" Olivia called loudly.

She opened the gate and the male dog and I followed her into the yard. Lucas dropped our leashes so we three dogs could freely examine one another. Though she was female, when Gus lifted his leg, she smelled his mark and then squatted as well. I don't usually do that.

Olivia strode to the house and mounted some steps, knocking on the front door and then opening it, sticking her head in. "Hello?" She turned and shook her head at Lucas. I watched in concern as she passed into the house, but she returned moments later carrying a leash. She came over and clipped it into the new female's collar. She looked up. "This one's named Trixie."

"And the family just left her in the yard?"

Olivia shrugged. "Nobody home."

I watched, perturbed, as Lucas knelt and ran his hands through the female's shaggy fur. "Hello, Trixie. I can't believe your family took off without you. What if the fire comes through here? What's wrong with people?" He stood back up and we all left the yard. I did not know what we were doing; I only knew that we now had two more dogs walking with us. Lucas held us females on leashes, while Olivia clutched Gus's chain in her fist.

"I don't want to think they left their dogs on purpose," Olivia replied cautiously. She was jerked forward when Gus sensed that a particularly interesting male had sprayed the base of a street sign. The female sniffed at me in a friendly way. "I think maybe they were just caught up in the flow of traffic, or maybe they panicked when the evacuation order was issued."

"Sure, that could be. Or maybe they're in another town and couldn't get back to Paraiso. I imagine they're not allowing traffic to come *toward* the fire," Lucas suggested.

The road underfoot turned to gravel, and along its sides, fewer houses and more trees appeared. We turned and followed a narrow, rutted driveway that ventured up a steep hill. At the top we found a long, low building. As we approached, I heard some dogs barking and could tell the two new dogs could hear them, too. The building had a glass door, which Olivia pulled open. As soon as she did, we were blasted with the strong odors of many dogs and cats. The new female was wagging furiously but Gus seemed unsure. I was with my boy, so I followed him and Olivia into the building with confidence.

"Hello?" Olivia called.

A short woman with long, light-colored hair came swiftly through an open doorway and hugged Olivia. "Oh my God, what are you doing here, Olivia?"

"Lucas, this is Diane. Diane, this is my husband, Lucas."

"Oh!" Lucas exclaimed as the woman hugged him. He seemed startled. "Nice to meet you, Diane."

Diane. She wiped her eyes and laughed briefly. "I'm sorry, I'm just so scared."

Gus was sniffing at a couch along a wall as if getting ready to lift his leg on it. Many male dogs mark when they hear barking. I don't do that.

Diane smelled of dogs and cats and tears when I sniffed her hand.

"That's our dog, Bella," Olivia told Diane, "and we found these other dogs, Gus and Trixie, abandoned by their owners in their yards."

Diane nodded. "The evac orders came so fast and they just made everybody go and it was utter chaos and they said no one could take their dogs. It was *horrible*. We've got eight dogs and more than a dozen cats that weren't here yesterday."

"That's ridiculous," Lucas interjected. "How could it possibly matter if they took their dogs with them?"

Diane shrugged. "I think most people felt the same way, but everyone was shouting orders at them. Like, in a total panic. The sheriff came and told me I had to leave immediately but I'm like, "So what about the animals?" and he didn't have any kind of answer. So . . ." She shrugged again.

Olivia reached down and petted Gus, who wagged and glanced at me, and I reflexively wagged back. "Well, these two are sweethearts. They won't give you any trouble."

"We'll find room for them," Diane agreed.

"When will they be evacuated?" Olivia asked.

Diane gazed steadily at Olivia. "They won't be."

Olivia gasped. "*What?*"

"My brother went into town to see if he can find someone to help us. A lot of people are planning to stay and save the town. We are going to try to keep the building from burning down because if that happens, we'll lose all the animals here."

Lucas tapped the phone on his belt. "You may be okay. I hear the fire is still pretty far out. Tribute Ridge? Maybe it won't get up here."

Diane stiffened. "Tribute Ridge? That's only twenty miles from here. I thought it was on Sherwood Mountain."

"I don't really know the area."

"We'll stay and help you," Olivia assured Diane. "Don't worry."

Lucas stared. "Stay and help," he repeated. "Didn't we just decide to get on the National Guard trucks when they come?"

I noticed that the female was gazing in the direction of all the barking, her ears alert, her head cocking from one side to another. So many dogs were giving voice to their fear at the back of the building.

"We can't let these animals *burn alive,* Lucas," Olivia implored.

Gus flopped down on the floor with a sigh, apparently unbothered by the distressed barking from down the hallway.

Lucas was frowning. "Olivia . . ."

"You heard the people in town saying the same thing Diane just told us. A bunch of them are staying. They're going to fight the fire. We should help."

"They're doing it because these are their homes."

"These are innocent animals!"

Lucas gazed at Olivia for a long moment. I could feel strong emotions pouring off of both of them, but I couldn't tell if it was fear or anger. The other two dogs didn't seem to be paying attention to the people.

"Lucas is right," Diane interjected softly. "This is our town, not yours."

Lucas and Olivia were still staring at each other, doing that thing of talking without words. Finally, my boy walked to the window and looked out. "Okay. I think the thing to do, then, is to take down the trees right next to the building. Also, the wooden fence. Maybe." He turned back to Olivia. "I don't actually know. But that's what the guy at the briefing was saying, the one who's going to stay and fight. Make a firebreak."

"Good," Olivia agreed. "And we should radio Mack. Maybe the fire department can help."

"And don't forget my brother," Diane reminded him. "He's got chainsaws and so do his friends."

The three people went to sit at a table. I was unsure what I was supposed to do about the two dogs who had recently joined us. They weren't a *permanent* part of my pack now, were they? They reacted to all the human movement by climbing into a couple of soft dog beds, but I followed my boy and sat loyally beneath the table at his feet.

I heard the same squawking noise as before. Lucas spoke to the phone. "I need to contact Mack Fletcher. This is Lucas Ray."

"*911: What is the address of your emergency?*"

"*There's fire on both sides of the road!*"

"*Where are you, ma'am?*"

"*Katsen Road, by the school!*"

"*You need to evacuate. . . .*"

"*I can't! There's fire everywhere! You've got to help me!*"

"Katsen Road?" Diane gasped. "That's out where I live. That's practically here!"

"*Lieutenant.*"

Lucas looked at Olivia. "That's a firefighter."

"*This is Lieutenant Gibbens. Go.*"

"*Lieutenant, this is Jordi. The hill is on fire, sir, it looks like a lava flow!*"

"*Go to channel five, Jordi.*"

"*There are people driving cars with* flaming tires*!*"

"*Jordi! Channel five, now!*"

Lucas and Olivia and Diane ran out the front door and I followed. The other two dogs remained inside. Everyone was staring at the sky. "Why is it orange?" Diane gasped.

"That's from the fire," Lucas responded grimly. "I thought it was supposed to be far away, still." He held the phone to his face. "Mack Fletcher, Mack Fletcher, come in."

"*I've got eyes on Fletcher, hang on.*"

"*911: What is your emergency?*"

"*I'm trapped in my house! Everything outside is burning. 891 Silver Road!*"

"*Lucas? Change channel to twenty.*"

Lucas played with his phone. "Mack?"

"*Hey, where are you guys? Are you okay?*"

"We're at the animal shelter. Listen, it's packed with abandoned pets."

"We got to get you out of there, Lucas. The fire's coming faster than anyone thought. The National Guard trucks should be here soon. Can you get to the command post, or should we come get you?"

Lucas and Olivia stared at each other. Lucas lifted the phone to his mouth. "Mack, I . . . I'm sorry. We can't leave."

"Repeat that?"

Olivia leaned forward. "We can't just let these animals burn up, Mack."

There was a long silence.

"You said the animal shelter?"

"Yeah," Lucas responded.

"You guys stay there. I'm coming."

Eleven

As we stood in the front yard, two trucks came rattling up the driveway. I pulled at my leash, interested because the first truck's pickup bed was full of dogs, who started barking when they saw me.

Diane waved, smiling. "That's my brother Dave."

There was a loud *screech* as the trucks stopped. A man slid out and opened the tailgate and the dogs jumped to the ground. Two of them immediately began fighting, both large males, snapping and trying to climb up on the other's back. I watched tensely, the fur rising on my back. The other dogs circled the altercation uneasily.

"Hey! Hey!" the man yelled.

People always join dog fights with their voices.

Diane ran forward and the two male dogs backed away from each other. She seized the collar of one of them and the man who had been yelling grabbed the other one. Both dogs were still growling, but I could tell they were relieved to be pulled from battle.

I understood why they had gone after each other; the tension rippling off of the people was almost unbearable. Something was going on, something awful and beyond canine understanding, and it was frightening all of us. I looked up at Lucas, seeking guidance from my boy.

"I don't get it," the man observed as he dragged the big male up to us. "They were fine on the truck."

Diane put a leash on two of the new dogs and guided them through the gate and into the house while the new man followed, still gripping the collar of the big black dog who had been fighting. The dog stared at me as it was dragged past. The rest of the dogs hesitated, sniffing each other, then turned, sticking together as a pack, and followed Diane. The door shut behind them. I remained with my boy.

Men hopped out of the second truck, and I wagged because I recognized the scent of one of them—it was Meat-man, the angry local man from earlier. He held out his deliciously fragrant hand to Lucas. "Hey," he greeted. "I saw you guys earlier down at the staging area. Name is Scott, Scott Lansing."

"Lucas Ray," Lucas replied. I glanced up at his mention of his name. "This is my wife, Olivia."

Everyone wrestled with just their hands for a moment. Meat-man gestured toward his friends. "David said you're going to put a firebreak around the shelter. We're here to help."

"Thank you so much," Olivia replied.

"So, we brought chainsaws, axes, and shovels," Meat-man advised, looking grimly purposeful. "We're going to make a stand. No one can tell us we have to just let this town burn. These are our homes, our lives. We might not be able to save everything, but we're going to try. I got six guys, including me. We all grew up in Paraiso together."

My boy nodded. "We'll take all the help we can get. We can't leave either. If this building goes, all the animals inside the shelter will burn."

Meat-man nodded. "That's what Dave told us. We'll make this one of our top priorities, I promise."

The other men were unloading metal objects from their truck. I picked up the slick smell of oil and dirt. They set their things on the ground with heavy thuds.

I heard something approaching, and waited patiently for Lucas and Olivia to hear it, too. Finally, an enormous truck swung up the

driveway. I wagged because I had been on top of that truck! There
were no people atop it this time, only the man driving and Mack,
who jumped down from the open door when it came to a halt. He
walked over to us and I wagged, licking his hands in greeting. He
watched the men from the two small trucks carrying their obviously heavy items over to the trees in front of the building of dogs
and cats, then turned to us with a grin. "Your chariot has arrived,"
he announced.

Lucas and Olivia glanced at each other. "Mack . . . ," Olivia began cautiously.

Mack held up a hand. "Look, I know you're trying to do the
right thing, here. But I've been trained for this, and *I'm* not staying. Nobody's staying."

"Not nobody. There are dogs and cats and a couple of rabbits in
there," Lucas responded bluntly. "If we leave, and the fire comes
up here, they'll be cooked alive."

Mack fixed Lucas with a serious look. "The fire *will* come up
here, Lucas. And it won't just be the animals who get burned to
death."

One of the men from the trucks stood close to the house of
barking dogs and yanked at the tool in his hand and there was a
sudden loud mechanical roar. He bent down at the base of a tree
and the nature of the roar changed to something deeper-throated.
I didn't like the sound. Beyond the stand of evergreen trees where
the men had gathered with their metal machines was an expanse
of grass that sloped downward to the dirt road. On the other side
of the road were many trees.

Mack and Lucas seemed tense, which made me uneasy. They
stopped speaking and we all watched as more machines joined
their hideous voices in a chorus of loud shrieks.

I heard a *crack* and a moment later, a thin tree one man was
attacking with his machine fell to the ground with a muffled *thud*.
Soon another one followed. The machines in their hands were
somehow bringing down all of the trees, which lay at their feet.

Mack nodded at this and then turned back to Lucas. "These people live here, man, it's their home. And I get that they don't want to leave, won't leave. Maybe if I lived here I would feel the same way. But you two have to come with me. The fire can't be more than an hour away. It's zero percent contained at the moment, and by the time it's through they're saying it's going to burn six million acres of Rocky Mountain forest. That's the size of New Jersey. This isn't just a wildfire, it's an inferno. The flames and the heat can't be stopped."

"Do we know how it started?" Lucas asked.

Mack shook his head grimly. "It looks like the one here in Colorado was deliberately set a couple days after it started in Wyoming."

Olivia breathed out in disgust. "Unbelievable."

"The one in Wyoming we know was from a tanker that went down an embankment and right into where they were conducting a controlled burn. By the time everyone realized the problem, it was already into Idaho. And now it's all the same fire, see? You get what I am saying, here? Call it the drought, call it climate change, or maybe we've just not been doing good forest management. Whatever it is, there's never been anything like this."

Lucas nodded. "I do see, Mack. But we're just talking one building, here—I think we'll be okay."

"Geez, Lucas."

"Mack," Olivia pleaded, "these animals are stuck here through no fault of their own. They've been abandoned or lost by their owners. They're helpless."

"Hey, Mack!" the man driving the big truck called. Mack turned and looked at him. "The National Guard trucks just pulled up. Evacuation is on. We have to go."

"Give me a minute!" Mack shouted back. He turned back to Olivia. I could feel the tension in all of them. "What if you just let them out? The pets, I mean. Wouldn't their instincts tell them to run from the flames?"

"A dog's instinct is to stay with people," Olivia replied softly.

Now all the machines were snarling and the men were busily thrusting them at the trees, which were shaking and then falling. The evergreens were big and bushy and when they landed a cloud of dust joined the smoke and was whisked away in the strong winds.

"Mack!" the driver called again.

Mack gazed steadily at Lucas and Olivia. "You're really staying here? Despite everything I just told you?"

Olivia gestured to where the men were using their loud machines. "They're staying. Diane and her brother are staying. What sort of person would I be if I didn't help a shelter full of abandoned pets?"

Mack looked to Lucas, who shrugged. "When my wife decides something, it's like she sets her emergency brake. And I'm not about to leave her. Here's your radio."

Mack took the phone, staring at my boy.

"I decided a long time ago to devote my life to animal rescue," Olivia added. "It's never pretty, never easy. But we've got help. We'll be okay."

Lucas put a hand on Mack's shoulder. "You go on now, Mack. You're a good man. We've got this."

"Mack!" the driver yelled. "Captain says we got to get back *now*! Hustle up!"

Shaking his head, Mack turned and walked back to his big truck. He stepped up and leaned in and said something to the driver. There was an animated conversation. I watched anxiously—was Mack leaving? Weren't we all going to climb back up on the truck for a ride?

Lucas didn't move. "What's happening now, I wonder?" he murmured to Olivia.

"Looks like an argument. Do you think they're talking about sending the sheriff up here to arrest us? Force us to go?"

Lucas shook his head. "I can't see them doing that."

Mack climbed back down and with a loud blast the big truck rumbled to life and turned in the tight circle of the driveway, going up on the grass and then down and driving off. Mack stood there, watching it go. Then, with a shrug of his shoulders, he trudged back up to where we stood.

I wagged happily because he'd come back.

"What are you doing, Mack?" Lucas asked softly.

Mack shrugged. "If you're serious about this, the least I can do is help you understand the risks you're taking. I told them to give me half an hour, send someone out to get me when they're getting ready to leave. The fire department's always the last to go anyway."

"Thank you, Mack," Olivia said simply.

"I'll say something," he replied seriously. "I'm proud to serve with the both of you. You're *warriors*. But that doesn't mean I agree with your decision-making process, here. You're taking a huge risk. Risk of *death*."

Olivia wiped her eyes. I wagged tentatively, feeling so many awful emotions pouring off these three people. It was this place, I knew, with the smoke and the wind, that was causing them such anguish. I did not understand why we didn't just leave.

Mack slapped his hands together. "Okay, Lucas, I want you with me. These guys seem to be doing the right thing, cutting down the trees that're right up against the structure. Hopefully, they'll have time to get them all."

"What can I do?" Olivia asked.

Mack grinned at her. "From what I've seen, there's almost nothing you *can't* do, Olivia. Okay, the first thing I'd like you to get on is move anything flammable away from the windows inside. Tear down the curtains. Close the windows and fill any container you can find with water."

"In other words, you do the housework," Lucas advised her.

Olivia arched her eyebrows. "Oh, really, you're going to say that to me *now*?"

Lucas winced at Mack. "Oops."

Mack chuckled.

Olivia deliberately turned away from Lucas. "So, why are we filling containers with water? Wouldn't it be smarter just to run the hose and keep the building wet?"

Mack shook his head. "The water's not for fighting the fire. The water's for drinking. I'm gonna guess that we'll lose pressure pretty soon and then the hose will be worthless. It's gonna get hot and we're gonna be thirsty."

"Got it." Olivia turned and went inside and I yawned anxiously, not understanding what she was doing.

I didn't like that she had left, and I didn't like the loud buzzing machines, wind, or the smoke. I didn't like that there was a building full of dogs who were barking in fear.

I pressed up against my boy, trusting that as long as I was with Lucas, nothing bad would happen.

"Okay," Lucas said in serious tones. "Tell me honestly, Mack. What are our chances?"

Mack gazed frankly back. "You want me to be honest? Odds are looking pretty bad. The winds are coming out of the north and they're bringing the fire with them. I appreciate what those boys are doing, but they're fools if they think they can save the town."

Lucas swallowed. "I understand. What about here, though? Can we save the shelter?"

"No."

The two men stared at each other.

Mack sighed. "Can you talk to her? Your wife, I mean. You have to make her see how hopeless this is."

Lucas turned and gazed to where Olivia had gone inside. "I've never met anyone with a bigger heart when it comes to animals. She couldn't live with herself if we abandoned those pets to the fire."

I nosed my boy's hand, but it didn't react. He was upset and I was not able to provide comfort.

"What about putting them down? Wouldn't that be best?"

"I don't know if they have enough humane killer, or even any. And God, can you imagine doing something like that?"

"Well, you know what's going to happen if you can't save the place. Then you and Olivia will have died for nothing."

Lucas was still staring at the building. I glanced in that direction, but Olivia didn't come out. "When you go, would you take Bella with you?" he murmured softly.

Mack gave him a long look.

Lucas met Mack's eyes. "I wouldn't want her to die like that."

"Listen to what you're saying, man."

"I know exactly what I'm saying."

Mack inhaled, then let the air out in an audible whistle. It was a very sad sound. "Tell you what. Let's walk the perimeter, check out your defensive lines, and I'll show you how bad I think it's going to get."

Twelve

I thought we should wait for Olivia to come back outside, but instead Lucas and Mack set off walking close to the building at a brisk pace. We rounded the corner and Mack paused and pointed. "Okay, this is a deal-breaker right here."

"The firewood?"

Mack nodded.

"So, what if I move the logs?"

Mack pursed his lips. "You'd have to remove all of it. Anything flammable. Even pieces of bark."

Lucas nodded. "Where should I put it?"

Mack sighed and turned and looked toward the road. "Take it down and throw it into the woods on the other side of the road, I guess. There, where the trees are sparse."

Lucas bent down to pick up a stick and I watched with interest, even though it was too thick for me to put my mouth around. Mack touched Lucas's arm. "Let's take a look at the rest of the area first. Then we can figure out the top priority."

Mack and Lucas resumed walking, so I got up to follow. They led me around to the back of the building, where I smelled many dogs, although there were none to be seen. Cages extended well out into the yard.

Mack nodded. "Okay. I like this. Nice long kennels sticking out perpendicular to the siding, cement floors, chain-link fence. The only thing that could burn are the doghouses in the individual cages and the grass on the far side of the cement pads. If you dig a trench on the back side of these kennels, pile up the dirt, that should help stop the grass fire from reaching the shelter. The kennels are a nice, big firebreak."

"You're saying this area can't burn."

Mack shook his head. "No, I'm saying it's defensible. Different thing. You need to pull all the doghouses out of here and take 'em down where you're throwing the firewood."

"Got it," Lucas replied.

Mack blinked at Lucas, seeming like he was going to say more, then turned away.

This was an odd walk, with all the stopping and talking, as if we were in a musty room with glass booths and upright dead cats.

We continued around to the other side of the building. Mack smiled at Lucas. "You lucked out. This is a nice big patio, and I like the sand volleyball court. Gives you a huge firebreak—the flames will stop at the edge of the sand pit, and you've got, say, fifteen feet of cement that won't burn either. Plus, you can throw sand on the roof to extinguish embers."

"Okay. So first the firewood. Then the doghouses," Lucas recounted. "Here we've got more than thirty feet of space that's defensible, so we're okay on this side."

Mack nodded. "You'll still want to dig a trench all the way around the building, putting the dirt berm on the structure side, but the kennels in the back and this play area on this side are great. I got to say, if you had to pick one place to try to hold out against the largest fire in U.S. history, this might be it."

"So, odds are good?"

Mack looked glum. "No. It's still insane."

Lucas let me pull him across the wide cement area to a stretch of sand full of interesting odors. Cats had been using this place— this was a giant cat box!

Lucas kicked at it, stirring up more smells. "When I move the firewood on the other side, there shouldn't be any grass growing underneath it. Just dirt. That's another firebreak."

"Sure. But if the trees go up, the air's going to be filled with flaming embers. Along the road you've got thirty yards of dry lawn leading up to a wooden building. Defending three sides won't matter much if the front goes."

"Okay."

I did Sit, but not for a treat. Sometimes dogs do Sit for themselves.

"Even here at the volleyball court, you're going to need to drag the picnic table across the road, and pull the LP tank out from under that barbecue and get it as far away from here as possible."

"All right," Lucas agreed.

We completed our walk by returning to the front. Meat-man and his friends were still attacking the trees with gusto. We strode up to them and they shut off their loud machines, eyeing us expectantly.

"What you're doing is good work, exactly right," Mack informed them. "But you need to drag these fallen trees away from here and down across the road. The road is your natural firebreak and that's where you've got to make your stand." Mack held out his hand. "Mack Fletcher."

The man who smelled like meat pulled glasses off his face, wiped his brow with his forearm, and held out his hand. "Scott. Scott Lansing."

It occurred to me that "Scott" was the name of this man.

"I'll get started on the firewood," Lucas announced.

We left Mack and the others.

What we did next made no sense to me. Lucas would grab an armful of wood so heavy it made him grunt, then nearly run all the way down the hill across the road and into some trees, where he would dump the pile and turn around and run back. He unsnapped my leash and it was fun to gallop alongside my boy, but otherwise I was completely mystified. When we were deep in the woods, dropping the big sticks, I would try to find one small enough for me to carry, but when I did so and trotted up to Lucas, he showed no interest in what I gripped in my mouth. Games are nearly always more fun when a dog participates, but sometimes people don't realize this.

Soon Olivia was playing, too. They didn't run together, but made separate trips up and down that hill, up and down, up and down.

"I'm getting all the cardio I need," Lucas panted at Olivia.

"Maybe you should go in and do housework," she replied with a grin.

"I am so hoping you'll forget I said that."

"We'll see."

Sometimes we passed Scott and Mack and their friends, who would be hauling a felled tree down across the road.

The smell of burning wood was still strong on the gusty wind. And, though my senses told me it was still day, the light was gradually fading, as if night were descending early. When the stack of big sticks was all gone, Lucas and Olivia paused for water and poured some in a bowl for me to lap up. Next, we went inside the house of the barking dogs. The fur stiffened along my back. I couldn't help it, there was so much terror and abandoned loss in the commingled voices of the dogs, because they smelled fire and were in a strange place without their people. The cats were tense, too—they just didn't know how to bark.

We crossed the room, which was different now: all the furniture was in the center, and Olivia and Lucas had to edge around the pile to reach the back door. Then we were outside again, in a place where I could tell many dogs had spent many nights. These were the cages I had seen earlier. Olivia bent over a small dog house and I hoped they were not going to go tell me to Go Kennel into it because it was too tiny.

"You need help with that?" Lucas asked her as she picked it up.

Olivia shook her head. Lucas entered the next cage and lifted a bigger house and half carried, half dragged it through the house of barking dogs, then out the front door and down the hill and back into the woods.

Soon one of Scott's friends was helping us, and he and Lucas carried the bigger houses as a team while Olivia focused on the smaller ones.

After more water, we returned to the big outdoor cat box. Olivia found a bucket, which she filled with shovelfuls of sand. Then, grunting a little, she carried the bucket to the front, where Mack had placed a ladder. She cautiously ascended, getting a firm grip with each rung, hauling the sand up to the roof, where she dumped it. Soon Mack joined her, carrying buckets of his own, up and down, up and down, upending them on top of the house of barking dogs.

I decided there must be a lot of cats up there.

"Lucas! Come up and clean out these gutters!" Mack called down.

I watched anxiously as my boy ascended the ladder. I put my front paws on it, but these were not stairs and I didn't understand how to follow him. The smoke was getting stronger and Lucas and Olivia and Mack were away from me and I couldn't get to them. I did a good Sit and whined anxiously.

They must have heard me because all three people came back down. I wagged, shoving my nose at each one of them in turn, though they did not appreciate what a good dog I had been. They must not have seen my Sit.

They stood close together. Lucas was wheezing. Olivia put a concerned hand on his shoulder and he shook his head at her. "No, it's okay. Just a little winded." He looked at his wrist, then up at Mack. "Don't you need to get going?"

Mack rubbed his face. "I'm feeling cautiously optimistic about our odds."

"*Our* odds?" Lucas repeated.

Mack grinned fiercely. "You think I'm going to let the two of you have all the fun without me?"

"Mack . . ."

Mack clapped his hands together. "You get on the LP tank. I'm going to help these boys here move the remaining trees. Olivia . . ."

"More sand?" she guessed.

"You guessed it. I promise it's going to make a huge difference."

I followed Lucas around to the cement area next to the cat box. He lifted the lid on a delicious smelling metal box. Old cooked meat reached out from inside and tantalized my nose. Lucas wasn't there to cook, though. He pulled a big white metal ball out from underneath it. Then we went for a walk, but this time we marched way, way down the road, to a place where I could no longer see or smell Olivia or any of the men, though I could still hear their angry machines slashing at the trees. Lucas carefully set the tank down on a sandy area on the other side of the road, away from any trees. Then he and I headed briskly back. He was wheezing more loudly, now. It was hotter and darker than ever. He kept putting a hand to his mouth and hacking into it, and I watched him with concern.

When we arrived back at the building, the men from the trucks were using shovels to dig in the front yard. I was intrigued by this, especially when they would pull a shrub out by its roots, carry it down and, of course, toss it in the woods.

Soon the woman named Diane was passing out big plastic bottles full of water. The men were all panting and coughing. They took deep, long drinks.

"I'll get started on digging the trench in the back next," Lucas said.

"How are the animals doing?" the man named Dave asked Diane.

"They're panicking," she replied.

Mack's phone made a noise and he pulled it from his belt. "Fletcher," he told it.

Everyone paused to listen.

"Fletcher, go to channel five."

I heard the odd noise and looked at Lucas; he looked back at me.

"Fletcher," Mack said again.

I sat and scratched my ear.

"Mack, have you lost your mind? This whole area is going up. We're evacuating now. *Get down here."*

"People need me, Captain."

Were we going to stay here? I let my legs fold into nap position.

"Our ETD is twenty minutes. Hear me? Do what you gotta do, but be here in twenty or you will be left behind. Copy? We cannot wait for you."

"Copy. Captain?"

"Yeah, Mack?"

"Good luck to you, sir. It's been . . . I've been honored to work for you. You gave me a chance when I don't think very many others would have."

"God, Mack. I don't know what to say."

"This is my choice, sir."

"Just . . . take care of yourself, son."

For a long moment no one spoke. They all stared at one another, and I felt their fear rising from their skin. Then Scott set his paper cup down. "Okay, that's all the time we can afford, here. Now we're going to go down and try to save as many structures as we can."

"You did good," Mack told him. "It's just grass now, and the tree stumps."

"Thank you all so much," Olivia added.

Soon the men were loading their metal machines into the truck, generating loud clanks.

"Scott, hold up for just a sec, all right?" Lucas called. Scott looked over and nodded, waiting by his truck.

Lucas moved closer to Mack. "Mack, talk to you?"

They took a few steps. I followed. "You know," Lucas advised

Mack in low tones, "you can still get out of this hellhole. Ride down with Scott, get on one of the last trucks. You've got twenty minutes, right?"

"Maybe," Mack grunted. He was quiet for a moment. He was staring off at something. Then he gave Lucas a searching look. "I guess I never really told you all of what happened over in Afghanistan, did I? And this is no time to do it now. But the bottom line is, I wasn't there when the worst of it happened. I had been sent off the line. By the time I got back, it was over. I wasn't there with my buddies when it all went down. That's what still gets to me, if I let it. That's what I couldn't stop thinking about at the VA. I can't live through something like that again. Understand?"

Lucas nodded. "All right, Mack."

Scott had come back up the driveway. The rest of the men were climbing into their trucks. "You staying here, Dave?" he asked.

"Yeah. My sister," Dave replied.

"Okay. We'll come back every once in a while," Scott assured him. "As much as we can, anyway."

I watched the two trucks drive off, their lights diffused by the haze. I wondered if it meant we would soon be leaving as well.

Dave and Lucas and Mack returned to the backyard and took turns digging a long, narrow hole. Olivia came out and periodically used one of the shovels herself. They were all sweating, which made it easier to smell them, but my eyes were watering in the smoke, making it hard to pick them out as night fell.

"Do we need to dig a trench on the south side?" Lucas asked Mack with a cough.

"Don't think so. The volleyball court and patio should be good enough."

"What about the north side, where the firewood was stacked?"

"Yep, 'fraid so. Just beyond where the logs killed the grass."

"Is it my imagination," Lucas asked, "or has the wind died down a little? That's good, right? The wind is as much the problem as anything."

"The fire brings its own wind. It sucks the oxygen to it, strong enough to blow a man over."

"How much time do we have, do you think?"

"Hard to say. But last we heard, it was close, and it's coming from this end of town. We'll get hit here before Paraiso does."

Steadily, like a storm, I could hear a loud roar growing ever more powerful. I kept looking to Lucas to see what we should do and he just kept digging. I dug a little myself but had no real interest in doing so.

Olivia was still going up and down to the roof, building her cat box up there. Mack and Lucas dug and dug, both of them coughing out their exhaustion.

Diane came running out of the back door and up to us. I smelled her before I saw her. She was crying and coughing. "There are these big orange explosions up in the sky!"

We dashed around to the front and down the grassy slope to the road. The woods on the other side of the pavement were filled with a swirling darkness. Occasionally, though, a smear of bright light would flash and I would feel a shock of heat pass over my body.

"We just ran out of time," Mack said.

Thirteen

For a moment, the humans stood facing the road as the approaching roar grew louder. From all of them I sensed fear, though Diane was suffering most terribly, gasping through her tears. Olivia reached over and held my boy's hand. A bright glow penetrated the smoke, and the wind stirred and came alive, whistling down the lawn and into the fire, then blowing hard back out, like an animal breathing. I blinked at the unexpected blast of grit, and Lucas turned away, coughing.

"This is it!" Mack shouted.

Then everyone *ran*. Flaming sticks and pieces of wood rained down out of the night sky. Dave raced up to the building, picked up a hose, and sprayed the bigger chunks, which sizzled. Mack darted forward with his shovel, burying the flaming debris in dirt. Burning leaves chased each other like squirrels out of the trees, across the road and up into the grass, and Lucas jumped on these and stomped them. Olivia scaled the ladder and dashed around up there, tossing sand while glowing particles fell from the clouds of smoke shrieking by overhead.

I stuck close to my boy's side as he stomped and trampled the embers.

I was afraid. Lucas was panting and coughing. Sweat poured off of him and then a new odor rose from his feet, which were smoking. I knew the smoldering pieces of wood and flaming leaves were bad because he was kicking at them so viciously, but there were so *many*. I turned and snapped at my haunches when one stung me near my tail.

"Lucas!" Olivia screamed from the roof. "Stop stomping on fires, you're melting your boots!"

Lucas stared at her and then peered at his feet.

"Here!" Dave yelled. He lunged toward us and sprayed water on my boy's shoes. I crinkled my nose at the chemical smell. "There's a snow shovel in the hall closet!"

I fled with Lucas into the house. I could sense that Diane was in the back with all the barking dogs. My boy grabbed a wide, flat shovel, the kind he used in the winter. He dashed back outside and began beating burning leaves with this shovel.

"We just lost water pressure!" Dave yelled and tossed his hose aside.

I cringed and felt like a bad dog because he was bellowing so angrily.

There was a *crack* and a tall tree, flaming fiercely at the top, fell across the road, the blazing branches flaring in the grass on our side of the pavement.

"Chainsaws!" Mack hollered.

Instantly, Mack and Dave were on the fallen tree with snarling machines. As they hacked out sparking chunks, Lucas pushed and shoved at the burning pieces with his flat shovel, eventually corralling them across the road where the fire was fiercest.

"Lucas! Don't get too close!" Mack warned.

"We should have cut down the trees closest to the road on the other side. If one of them gets to the grasses on our side, we'll lose the shelter!" Lucas yelled back. Now *he* sounded angry.

"There are embers everywhere up here!" Olivia called frantically. The wind stole her voice and whipped it away.

"Do your best!" Lucas shouted back, then crumpled into a cough. I pressed against him in concern.

A piece of flaring branch flew out of the air, landing right next to me, and I flinched. I was scared but Lucas covered it with dirt. "It's okay, Bella," he wheezed.

I felt like a bad dog because I wanted to run, to put this awful place behind me. But I would never leave Lucas.

"There goes another one!" Mack yelled as a flaming tree crashed across the road.

Lucas threw dirt as Mack and Dave cut at it with their machines. I backed away, my tail and ears low. Lucas did not seem to hear me whining.

I tracked my boy back and forth and watched the bewildering, frantic activity, wishing we were doing something else. Occasionally I was conscious of the dogs in the building behind me barking in terror, but mostly I stayed focused on Lucas and Mack and Dave running around, cutting wood and pushing the pieces back across the road. They were all panting and coughing now, and the sharp tang of their sweat mingled with the heavy, oppressive smell of smoke and fire.

Small fires were flaring up in the grass, and my boy was pounding them with his flat shovel. "We're losing ground!" he shouted desperately.

Dave stayed with a felled tree while Mack ran up and helped Lucas fling soil at the pockets of flame.

I could feel their terror, but we didn't get in a car and leave. We stayed in the burning yard.

I heard the sound of a truck before the humans did. I peered into the smoke and saw two lights bouncing their way toward us. Mack and Dave and Lucas straightened and I knew they had heard it, too. The truck roared right up to us and pulled over on the side of the road that wasn't burning. It was Scott and one of his friends. They jumped out and started up their snarling machines and went after trees that were burning and falling across the road.

"We lost the whole Mountain View neighborhood!" Scott yelled over the wind. "But the other guys are still in our cul-de-sac and we're keeping the fire at bay. None of the houses there are on fire yet."

I eventually did Sit because it was the only thing I could think to do. My eyes stung as I watched the humans continue their attack on flaming pieces of wood. They were all stumbling a little now, looking exhausted. But they did not stop.

The sun had long ago left the sky, but it made no difference— plenty of light came from the brightly burning forest across the road. All the sound came from the roar of the fire. All the darkness came from smoke.

I could smell, when Scott wiped his face and held out a palm to me, that his fingers had been singed. I did not lick them, but I did sniff and wag to let him know I was sorry he had hurt his hand.

Everyone was still frantic, wielding shovels and tree-biting machines, dashing from one hot stop to another.

After a long time, Scott, panting, approached Lucas and put a hand on his shoulder. "We'd better get back. Good luck, guys."

Scott and his friend drove away again. Olivia climbed down off the roof and Diane brought buckets of water to pass around. I drank greedily when a dog bowl was placed in front of me. Everyone stopped for a moment, their breath coming slower, their coughing not as frequent. The wind seemed to have lessened, the crackling roar of the fire quieting.

"It's 6 AM," Lucas rasped, holding up his wrist.

"What day?" Olivia replied. She and Lucas laughed—an odd, croaking sound.

Then everyone went silent. I approached Lucas and did Sit to let him know his good dog was right there with him.

"I think we're doing it," Mack observed finally. "Fire across the street was so intense it's already mostly burned itself out."

"I haven't seen any flaming branches or embers on the roof in about forty-five minutes or so," Olivia agreed.

Mack nodded tiredly at this.

Lucas reached for Olivia and pulled her in for a hug. "Man, I'm proud of you for handling the roof all by yourself. That had to be really hard."

Olivia smiled up at him. "Are you kidding? From up there I could see you guys running flat out. I don't know how you did it."

"Could you see the back? Everything okay there?" Mack wanted to know.

"I had a great view. The flames were all directly in front of us. You were right, Mack, the road was a firebreak."

"Well, we got lucky there."

"Glad Scott showed up when he did," Lucas observed.

"That was sort of the hardest time," Olivia agreed.

"Great. . . . ," Mack grunted.

"What is it?" Olivia asked.

"Lost my radio somewhere."

Quite some time later, there was another change as the sun climbed higher in the sky. This time, it was able to cut through the smoke, which was drifting in big curtains. An eerie silence had descended, though I could still smell and hear fires thundering not far away.

Lucas sat down after drinking some more water and I eased my head onto his lap. He placed a hand on my fur . . . a hand that instantly fell still as he slipped into a deep sleep.

We lay like that for some time and then Olivia came and shook Lucas. "Lucas! Mack needs you right away. Now!"

Lucas staggered to his feet. He limped to the place where much earlier he had been picking up the thick sticks and running them all the way down the hill and into the woods on the other side. Mack was there and his shovel was frantically biting into the dirt, making a pile.

Lucas wiped his face. "What's happening?"

"The wind is shifting," Mack explained. "Fire's coming back from this side, now. We got to reinforce this trench before the whole lawn goes up."

I could smell that Dave had gone into the house. Lucas picked up Dave's shovel and Mack and Lucas began digging agitatedly. Olivia used her bucket and clawed out sand from the cat box and poured it on top of a long thin pile of soil next to the trench. The earth smelled cool and delicious and wonderful as it was exposed to the air. Part of me wanted to just climb into the hole they were making and lie down for a nap, but Lucas and Mack and Olivia were so afraid that I stayed with them while they toiled.

Mack wiped his face. "The trees are thinner, and aspens don't burn all that well anyway, so it's just these long grasses we got to worry about. It's gonna blow at us fast, but with enough dirt, it won't get to the wood siding."

There was blood smearing Lucas's hands now, and blood on the handle of the shovel that he held. I smelled the acrid bite of smoke implausibly growing closer. Was this going to keep happening again and again? Lucas and Mack kept digging and Olivia kept piling sand, even as my senses told me fire was coming straight toward us. Soon it jumped out of the sparse, flaming trees and marched quickly across the grass, right to our feet. Coughing, everyone backed away.

Again, burning bits of wood blew at us in strong gusts and the dirt was soon flying from the shovel blades.

Olivia dropped her bucket. "I'd better get back on the roof!"

The heat and fumes were too much and we all retreated until we were pressed up against the side of the house of barking dogs. The flames snapped and the wind gusted and I turned my face away.

"Look! It's not jumping the trench!" Lucas called.

I glanced up at him through watering eyes. I sensed something in his mood and turned and looked—smoke and flames blackened the grasses, but didn't burn the ridge of dirt or the long hole.

"It's holding," Mack agreed. "It's gonna work."

Gradually the fire, seemingly on its own, gave up. I sniffed at the rank and offensive odor of all the grass that had burned, but the smell was receding with the flames.

After a time, Olivia came back down the ladder and walked over to us. I wagged, happy to have her with us.

"It's over," Mack told her. She hugged him, and Lucas and I trotted over to be hugged too.

Mack walked to the long hole and shook his head. "Pretty sure what we just did was impossible."

"That wasn't so bad, this time," Olivia murmured.

"Well, there was a mad minute, but yeah," Lucas agreed. "Not as bad as when it was in the front."

We returned to the inside of the house of barking dogs and there was Dave, asleep, face-up on the floor.

Diane was filling a dog bowl with food. "My brother just collapsed. I thought he was having a heart attack, but I think he's just asleep. I decided in his state there was no sense in trying to get him to get back up." She set the dog bowl on the floor in front of me and I attacked it.

Lucas knelt by Dave and picked up his hand. "Your brother's alive, don't worry. Pulse is fine. Just exhaustion."

"I know how he feels," Olivia replied.

Mack's voice was weary. "I think we should open the windows. We can put the furniture back where it goes. Let's let the dogs take shifts out in the dog kennels."

"I'm afraid the dog houses were across the street and are lost to the fire," Lucas remarked sadly.

"I imagine that's not all that was lost to the fire," Diane murmured.

The heat left the room when they opened the windows. My eyes were not burning as badly now. Olivia and Lucas dragged a couch and put it underneath a window. They sat down on it and Olivia put her arms around Lucas and they were both instantly asleep. I jumped up, circled twice, and lay at their feet. For the first time in a long time, I felt good about things. This felt normal.

Aware of little, I registered the comings and goings of dogs and cats as Diane let them in and out of the kennels in the back.

I noticed when Dave stumbled to his feet and drank some water and sprawled back down. I heard Mack, who had pushed two chairs together and was lying on them, murmuring restlessly, and felt Lucas and Olivia rearranging themselves a few times to be more comfortable. I sensed the sun going down and then coming back up. Diane took me out to a kennel and I squatted gratefully but then I returned to my rightful place with my people.

The air was much clearer the next morning after that, and Lucas and Olivia awoke as soon as the sun's rays filtered in through the dirty window glass.

"Did you get any sleep at all?" Olivia asked Diane.

Diane shook her head. "Just a little. It would have felt selfish. All I did was stay inside and take care of the animals. You fought the fire. You saved their lives."

"It was a team effort, ma'am," said Mack.

"I told Dave not to start the generator while you were sleeping, but now that you're up we'll get it going and I can make coffee. I don't have much in the way of food, but I have some bread and some jam."

"Bread and jam sounds heavenly," Olivia said.

"I'll help," Lucas offered, groaning as he got to his feet.

Olivia and Lucas and Diane were soon in the kitchen opening and shutting doors and I could smell something sweet on the air.

I realized then that something had changed—the frantic, high-pitched barking had died down. An occasional whine or yip emerged from the back hallway, but the dogs had calmed.

I was fed another generous bowl full of dog dinner by Diane, who I was coming to appreciate very much. Then the people sat at the table and ate toast. I did a good Sit by my boy's elbow because, well, toast.

I could smell smoke and was glad that we did not go outside. Everyone napped instead, which was my preference anyway.

I awoke when my body vibrated with a loud, low, and familiar rumble. Mack heard it, too. He eased off of his chairs, went to the window, and looked out.

"Well," he said with a disbelieving shake of his head. "Well, well, well."

Fourteen

Mack was chuckling as he opened the front door. I bounded out ahead of him to see exactly what I expected: one of those loud and gigantic trucks with some of his friends on it. It squealed to a stop in the driveway and men and women jumped off and ran up to Mack and hugged him. I sniffed at their booted feet, wagging, letting them know that if they were in the mood to hug, there was a dog present for that purpose.

One of Mack's friends had what I could definitely smell was some sort of chicken in his pocket. I decided to hang around him for a moment and see if he understood that, generally speaking, chicken treats were usually tossed my way.

Some of the newcomers were familiar to me—even beneath the odors of smoke and dirt, people are, underneath, fundamentally unique and recognizable. On the bed in our home I had a blanket completely covered in my boy's aromas. Though I slept on it and had, over time, covered it with my own scent, my Lucas blanket vividly emitted the smell of my boy.

I realized in that moment how much I missed my normal life. I wanted to do Go Home with Lucas.

Chicken-pockets stepped forward. "Mack."

"Captain."

The man shook his head. Even that small motion sent wonderful chicken fumes into the air. "I honestly didn't think you'd make it."

"We lucked out. Had a lot of defensible space. And a good team." Mack wiped his forehead and looked around. I followed his gaze, but didn't see anything but burned trees and grass. "How does it look? Overall, I mean."

Chicken-pockets shrugged. "Well, not good. Less than one percent contained. This is no longer a state-by-state problem— the whole mountain range seems to be on fire, and the feds have stepped in. Hundreds of square miles have already burned. Paraiso took a pretty bad hit, but there are some sections of town that made it okay. We're going to spend the day putting out spot fires, then we're going to start letting small numbers of people back up. High winds predicted all this week, though. You ready to get back to work?"

Mack grinned. "Yes, sir."

Olivia and Lucas walked up to join us. I wagged. Hopefully now the source of the mysterious bouquet of chicken would be revealed. I did Sit to prepare myself for it.

"You missed the party," Olivia noted dryly.

The people all smiled.

Mack turned to Lucas and Olivia. "I gotta go now. You guys take care."

Lucas hugged Mack. "You be safe, Mack."

Olivia stepped into a hug and looked Mack solemnly in the eye. "Thanks to you, all of these animals are alive."

"Thanks to all of us," Mack corrected softly. He bent down and ran a hand over my head. I wagged. I loved Mack. "You're a good girl, Bella. Thanks for being a good fire dog."

The men and women all climbed up on their truck, and with a loud bellow it started and trundled back down the driveway, taking the man with the fragrant pockets with it. I did not understand why anyone would carry chicken around if they weren't going to give some to a dog.

Scott came a little while later and gave us a car ride. I was in the back seat with Lucas, while Olivia sat up front. Scott turned to look at me just before we started moving. "You guys get some sleep?"

"Eventually, a little," Lucas admitted.

"A lot," Olivia corrected.

"I slept pretty much straight through," Scott replied. "Then I had all-you-can-eat pancakes. I ate more than I could eat."

Lucas and Olivia laughed, so I wagged.

"How is your . . . how is your house?" Olivia asked tentatively.

Scott gave her a sad smile. "It was the last one, at the end of the cul-de-sac, on the edge of the woods. It's the only one on the street we couldn't save. Too many trees."

"That's awful. I'm so sorry," Olivia replied solemnly.

"It's okay. I think we lost more of the town than anyone could have expected. You'll see . . . it's like a bomb went off in some places." Scott's voice coarsened. "The real tragedy is that some people waited too long and got trapped on the road trying to get to the highway. You can't really tell what types of cars they even were before everything was cremated. No way to know who, or how many. . . ." Scott's voice faltered for a moment, and Olivia put a hand on his shoulder. He pressed his trembling lips together for a moment. "I got to say, if I had known what it was going to be like, I wouldn't have stayed, but once I was in it . . ." He shrugged.

"You didn't have time to think," Lucas finished for him.

"Exactly."

"How much of the town was spared?" Olivia wanted to know.

"Well, we didn't lose much of the Main Street district—for some reason, the fire skipped right past it. That's how it went generally: we'd lose three streets, every house burned to its foundation, but then the next street over wouldn't lose a single one. It's . . . This place, it'll never be the same. People are going to be shocked when they come back."

Lucas nodded. "The fire department told us they're going to start letting folks return to their homes tomorrow."

"Their homes," Scott repeated. "Most of them won't have homes to return to."

"We're going to stay for a few days," Olivia told him, "help Diane with the animals."

"You can't get back to Denver anyway," Scott agreed, "unless you go to Grand Junction and take a plane."

"I'm going to see if someone needs the help of a newly minted doctor," Lucas added.

"I'll tell you what," Scott said. "My aunt and uncle's house didn't burn, and their Tahoe is parked in the garage. I know where the keys are. I'm sure they wouldn't mind if we borrowed it. You can even sleep there—beats lying on a cot at the middle school, or even being at the animal shelter, though you got a generator up there and my aunt and uncle don't."

"Your relatives. They got out okay?" Olivia probed.

Scott glanced at her. "We don't know yet."

He drove us to a place where we had been before. There was food and water and people who were dressed like Mack and smelled like smoke. I saw Lucas go into a big soft room and help Mack's friends in odd ways: wrapping cloth around their fingers and arms. Some of them flinched sharply, clearly feeling pain. Later, Scott drove us to an odd stretch of land where everything was ash and burned wood and piles of stone and brick. I had seen big areas of forest that were burned to the ground, but this was different—humans had lived here before the fire came, and an occasional untouched house among the ruins stood as a solemn reminder of what had been lost. We drove past odd patches of scorched ground and then came to a row of houses where trees were felled and torn-out bushes were lining the roads, many with soil clinging to the roots.

Scott gave Lucas and Olivia a rueful grin. "This was the first street we got to after being up at the shelter, when we still had a lot of energy. Cut everything down and hauled it to the street.

That's my uncle's place right there. It's all open—most people don't lock their doors in Paraiso."

I watched uneasily as Lucas and Scott climbed out but left me in the car with Olivia. The two men didn't go in the house; they raised the garage door and went inside. I jumped into the front seat and put my paws up so I could watch. Olivia reached out with a soothing hand. "It's okay, Bella."

I didn't glance at her but continued my frantic vigil. Where did he *go*? I whined.

There he is!

Lucas and Scott walked back out of the garage and when Olivia opened her door, I scrambled over her lap and jumped up on my boy, wagging and licking.

He grinned at me. "Bella! I was only gone for thirty seconds!"

Olivia laughed.

Scott left, which made me anxious, but then we climbed into a big vehicle in the garage. Lucas took us on a car ride back to the area with the large soft rooms. We spent the day there, but when the sun left the sky we returned to that same house, which was nice but smelled of other people.

We didn't go to sleep right away. Olivia and Lucas emptied the oddly warm refrigerator and freezer into trash bags, making faces at all the wonderful odors.

"Ugh, this sure went bad fast," Lucas told me.

I wagged.

When night came, they lit candles and carried them around and we slept in a new bed.

That night, I dreamed I was in the middle of a fire. I was trying to find Lucas, but I couldn't. I spotted Big Kitten, though—she was terrified, running from the flames, unable to escape.

I blearily opened my eyes when I felt a hand on my leg. Lucas bent over me in the dark. "Bella? Are you okay? Are you having a bad dream? You're crying in your sleep." My boy put his arms around me and gently pulled me up, so that I was lying with my head on the pillow next to him. "Good dog," he murmured sleepily.

With his arm around me, I felt safe and loved.

The next day, Olivia and I returned to the house of barking dogs. They were still barking, but more for the sake of barking, not in abject fear. Outside, a squat machine buzzed angrily, but Olivia held me back from examining it. "No, Bella, that's the generator."

Inside, we saw Diane, and Olivia approached each dog and cat and held her phone up in front of its face. "Look at the camera, Casey," she told one. "Hey, Socks, look over here."

I did not know what we were doing then, nor did I understand when we stood by a machine that slowly spat out one sheet of paper at a time. I did not like that Lucas was gone, and I continuously lifted my nose, expecting the return of the flames. I felt anxious and kept glancing at Olivia for reassurance.

I was much happier when Lucas returned and brought sandwiches. I sat dutifully under the table while he and Diane and Olivia ate. Other dogs might be barking, but not good No Barks Bella!

"How's it going? With everyone returning," Diane wanted to know.

Lucas shrugged. "It's not actually everyone. They're only letting folks come up a busload at a time, and they get to spend a few hours in town before they get back on the bus. Mack's one of the firefighters taking people on tours in a minivan. He looks wrecked—I guess it's pretty bad. They're allowed to see what happened to their homes, hopefully make connections with friends and family, and then they have to leave. Anyone with a standing house, the fire department goes in to make sure it's safe, and then they can return in their own vehicles the next day. No electricity, though, and from what I hear portable generators are in short supply."

Delicious odors were up on that table. I sat and stared at Lucas, but he wasn't taking the hint.

"But everyone got out in time?" Diane pressed.

Lucas sighed. "Down by where we set up the medical tent, there's a wall on the side of the library. That's where they are putting up photographs of friends and loved ones that are missing. It's a long list, so . . . we don't really know yet."

"I spent the morning taking pictures of all the animals and printing them out," Olivia told Lucas. "I'll put them up on the library wall next to the people."

"Good idea," he agreed.

Olivia shuffled some papers. She hadn't yet drawn the obvious connection between her sandwich and a good dog, either. "How many pictures are there right now, Lucas?"

Lucas stared steadily back. "The official tally is, eighteen hundred people are missing."

Diane gasped and Olivia lowered her eyes and shook her head.

Soon, we took another car ride back to where all those soft rooms were. I stayed with Lucas while he spoke to various people, and Olivia walked around outside. I soon lost interest—it had been a long time since I had played with anything resembling a dog toy, so I had very little patience for waiting while Lucas stuck sticks into people's mouths.

"Say *ahh*," he'd tell them.

Then he'd pull the stick away and the people would *let him*. People just don't know how to play Tug-a-Stick properly.

"You have to understand," Lucas told one of them, "that it's reasonable for you to be stressed. It's reasonable for you to be feeling shocked. But you're being treated for high blood pressure and we need to get you back on your medication. I know it seems hopeless, but you don't want to stop taking your medication just because you've lost . . ."

"Everything," the man he was talking to whispered. "I lost everything."

I trotted out to see what Olivia was doing, and she was busily affixing sheets of paper to a wall. People gathered around to watch.

One woman gasped out loud. "That's my Trixie!" she shrieked. She put her hands to her face and started to sob.

Olivia walked over to her and gave her a hug. I watched all this curiously, feeling the woman's odd combination of happy and sad.

"We didn't have time, we just left her. I thought she'd be dead for sure," the woman cried into Olivia's shoulder.

"She's at the shelter," Olivia assured her. "You can come any-time and get your Trixie."

"I don't know that they'll let me. We're sleeping at the high school, and my house is gone," the woman replied, wiping her eyes.

"Then when you have someplace to live. We'll take care of Trixie until then."

"Someplace to live . . . when will that be?" the woman asked, her eyes searching Olivia's.

Fifteen

Lucas and Olivia were sitting together on a bench near the large soft-sided rooms, later that afternoon, and I was being a good dog lying at their feet. They both seemed tired—it was evident in the long periods of silence, the occasional sighs, and the way they gazed off as if seeing squirrels, when none were evident to nose or eyes. I did spot a few dogs. My people brightened, though, when a familiar figure approached us.

I jumped to my feet, wagging. *Mack!*

"Hi, Bella," Mack greeted, kneeling and holding out a hand for me to sniff. I found the scent of people and some pungent, sweet food sticking to his fingers. If dogs had fingers, we would sniff them all day.

"How are you two holding up?"

Lucas and Olivia glanced at each other. "We still have a lot of unclaimed animals at the shelter," Olivia answered wearily. "With all the cell towers burned to the ground, there's no way to reach the owners, and even when we have addresses, the houses usually aren't there anymore."

Mack nodded. "It's been tough showing folks where their neighborhoods used to be. They've all been told to expect the worst, but I guess nothing can prepare them for this. What about you, Lucas? You okay?"

Lucas smiled wryly. "I'm no longer the town doctor. We've got more than enough medical personnel onsite, now. I'm not sure what to do next."

"That's why I wanted to talk to you. I've got a new assignment. We're looking for remote areas that might have people stuck in 'em. They might've gotten trapped but survived the burn, or they may be south and think they're safe. We need to evacuate them, bring them to Paraiso."

"*Are* they safe?" Olivia asked.

Mack shook his head. "You didn't hear? Uncompahgre Forest is burning now. Some idiot landowner thought it would be a good idea to put up a firebreak with a controlled burn. In this wind. The Forest Service is throwing everyone at it. Still zero percent contained, naturally. So"—Mack pulled a sheet of paper from his pocket—"they gave me this assignment and told me to see if anyone else wants to volunteer. I'm supposed to get to these fishing cabins down the way, check them out, radio in and evacuate anyone there. What do you say, Doc? They might need medical attention."

My boy nodded. "I'm in."

"And," Olivia added, "they might have domestic animals who need help as well."

There was a silence. "Olivia . . . ," Lucas began.

She held up a hand. "If you think I'm going to let you head off into a fire without me, you have the wrong girl, Lucas Ray."

I looked at Lucas and Olivia, sensing something pass between them. My boy looked to Mack. "What she said."

"Okay, then," Mack replied with a smile. "I've got a minivan."

"I've got a Tahoe," Lucas countered.

Mack brightened. "Better!"

Car ride!

Mack drove and Olivia sat with him in the front and I stayed in back with Lucas. He cracked a window for me and I pressed my nose to it. I smelled smoke and trees but no animals.

We soon passed a large group of Mack's friends standing in the woods by the side of the road, all dressed like him, all holding the loud, snarling machines that brought down trees. I looked for Scott but didn't see him.

"Firebreak," Mack explained as he slowed and waved at his friends. They waved, too.

We drove up a long, long hill, and at the top, Mack eased to a stop. I wagged expectantly, but we did not get out of the car.

"Oh my God," Mack breathed. "Look at it."

"It's black as far as you can see. Is that where we're heading? *There?*" Olivia asked uneasily.

Mack unfolded his paper. "No, uh-uh. The road curves south just ahead. I guess there wouldn't be any sense in searching for survivors to the east. From here to Idaho Springs, everything's gone."

"Look at all the smoke," Lucas observed bleakly. "God, I'm getting sick of it."

We started moving again, and soon were heading downhill, slowing for turns. After a long time, I brightened because the tang of smoke was less invasive on the air. We passed fresh, unburned trees. A squirrel seemed a real possibility, so I remained alert. Soon, we turned on a bumpy road.

"Just up here," Mack informed us.

We turned again and I wagged because I could smell a dog. A cluster of small houses hugged a riverbank. When a door of one of these buildings opened and a dog my size bounded out, black and with no tail, I growled a little, but I was also wagging.

"No barks, Bella," Lucas told me, obviously misunderstanding the situation. I was being friendly and I was not barking.

When he opened his door, I jumped out to greet the new black dog, a female, while an older man stepped out of the same building from which she had emerged. My people left the car to greet him.

I politely sniffed the new black dog while the people talked.

"Your cabins were spotted by the park service drone," Mack

was explaining as New Black Dog and I joined the people. "Is there anyone else here with you?"

The man shook his head. New Black Dog nosed his hand, so I went to Lucas, establishing who my person was. "Just me," the man answered solemnly. "Had a party of six fly-fishers but they took off when the evacuation order came down."

"Are you okay? Any issues with the smoke?" Lucas asked.

"No. It got pretty bad, but Jet here and I just hunkered down."

"Well," Mack said hesitantly, "I need to tell you that there's a new evacuation order."

"Oh. I think I'll just stay here, thanks."

Something was wrong; it was evident in the way the humans all stiffened slightly. Both the new black dog and I reacted to it, looking up at our people.

"Sir . . . ," Mack began.

The man held up a hand and New Black Dog followed it with his eyes. "The first cabin over there was built in 1918. Still standing, and there've been a lot of fires. I think we're going to be okay."

"In 1918 we didn't have the beetle infestation," Lucas pointed out. "Look at all the dead lodgepole pines along here. It'll all go up in a flash."

The man shook his head.

"Sir . . . ," Mack said again.

"What about Jet?" Olivia interrupted softly.

New Black Dog glanced at Olivia, so I did, too.

"Your dog can't make decisions for herself," Olivia continued. "Sir, we've been in the fire. Right in it. When it comes, it's like nothing you've ever seen before. It jumps from treetop to treetop so quickly it's like watching a train go by. If your cabins go, you'll go . . . and your dog will burn with you. Do you really want that?"

The man stared at her. Mack and Lucas glanced at each other.

"Come back with us to Paraiso," Olivia urged. "Please. Just until the fire is contained."

New Black Dog took a car ride with us! Now Lucas sat with the

new man and we dogs sat in the way-back. New Black Dog was
friendly but riding in the back of a car is no place to wrestle, so I
ignored her overtures.

Soon we were back at the grassy area with the big soft-sided
rooms. The new man and New Black Dog seemed tentative as
they climbed out of the car. Olivia guided them over to one of
the soft-sided rooms while I watched suspiciously. Where was she
going with a different dog?

Mack's telephone squawked. He held it to his mouth. "Ten-
four." He looked to Lucas. "Captain's on his way to see us."

"Ten-four," Lucas repeated. They grinned at each other and I
wagged.

With no one sitting next to him, I decided to take the opportunity to leap over and be with my boy.

"Good dog, Bella," he said. I licked him on the face and he
turned away. "Okay! Enough!"

I didn't know what he was saying, but he had said it before.

Before long, a man I knew, a man who still smelled like he
had pockets full of chicken, approached Mack's open window. I
wagged but without much enthusiasm because this man had let
me down before.

"Captain Butcher," Mack greeted.

Chicken-pockets nodded. "Mack." He leaned his head in.
"Hey, Doc."

Chicken-pockets handed Mack a sheaf of paper but no dog
treats. "There's a squad of smoke jumpers south of here, found a
boy's camp they say's got people in it. They've radioed for evacuation. Care to be my eyes on that, Mack? They've given me operational control over the local response. I'd feel better with someone
I can trust. You've proven to be pretty nimble."

"Happy to, Captain."

Lucas leaned forward. "Operational control over the local response?"

Chicken-pockets grinned. "We've got FEMA, state, regional

smoke jumpers, volunteers from Canada, and five county dispatch areas. Kind of hard to keep it all straight half the time." He nodded to the papers in Mack's hands. "Location's right there. Give me a sit-rep when you're ten–twenty-three."

"Yes, sir."

The man left, taking his chicken odors with him. I sat and yawned, more than a little disappointed.

Mack turned and looked over at my boy. "You want to come along?"

"Might as well," Lucas said. "Honestly feels good to get out of here, see parts of the world that haven't burned up. What's ten–twenty-three?"

"It means 'on location.' What about Olivia? Think she's going to want to come along?"

"Oh, you know the answer to that one."

Mack nodded. "Yep, she's a warrior. I met a lot of women like her in the Army. In fact, my division, the 101st, just started enrolling them for combat in 2018. Don't let anyone tell you there's a contradiction in the term *female soldier.*"

I brightened because Olivia emerged from the soft-sided room, talking animatedly to a woman. New Black Dog was nowhere to be seen, though I could still smell her on the air.

I wagged when Lucas lowered his window for me to stick my head out. "Olivia! Time to go!"

Another car ride! I put my nose to the wind and let the fragrances come.

It seemed to me the smoke was more pungent now than it had been that morning. My people did not seem concerned, though.

After some time Mack slowed, and we swayed onto a much narrower road into the trees.

"*Camp Benally,*" Olivia pronounced, "*an Alpine camp for boys.*"

We proceeded a little farther and then Mack pulled over. I peered out ahead of us and saw several cars parked in the narrow road, blocking our progress.

"I guess this is where we get out," said Lucas.

We went for a walk, and it was a nice place to be: nothing burning and the smoke wasn't even bothering me, though I could still smell it, strong and all-pervading. We climbed steadily up a hill and then came out into a big grassy area with sparse trees and some wooden buildings. It was like a town, but with no streets, just footpaths.

Lucas spread his arms. "Welcome to the boys' camp."

A few people were striding in a direction away from us, but a man glanced over and waved. He headed our way and I guided Lucas and Olivia and Mack to meet him. His clothing smelled like smoke and his fingers had a turkey odor. It was an interesting combination.

"Hey," Turkey-fingers greeted us. "Name's Henry Cox. I own this place. Where did you hike in from?"

Lucas and Mack reached out and grabbed the man's hand, then let go. "I'm Lucas Ray. This is my wife, Olivia."

Now Olivia grabbed his turkey fingers. She let go, too. "Nice to meet you."

"Mack Fletcher, Summit County Fire and EMT," Mack said. "We didn't hike, we drove down from Paraiso. Got stuck on your road a couple hundred yards down."

The man nodded. "We were all lined up to go when we got the order to hold in place, and that there were smoke jumpers on their way. They said the fire's coming up from the south."

Mack and Olivia glanced at each other.

Mack frowned. "They said that? The smoke jumpers? We heard it's quite a ways out yet."

Turkey-fingers lifted his eyebrows. "Oh. That's good news, then. The only way to get from here to Paraiso, or to anywhere, really, is to head south and then turn on 765. But you know that, if you just came from there."

Just like that, my tail itched right at the base. I turned and bit at it aggressively.

Mack reached for the phone on his belt. "I'm going to radio Captain Butcher. I'll get an update."

I watched apprehensively as Mack stepped away from us, raising his phone to his mouth.

Turkey-fingers looked at Lucas. "We've got six boys and some staff that we couldn't evacuate before they closed all the roads. Some smoke jumpers on foot joined us a couple hours ago. But if you came down from Paraiso, the roads aren't closed after all, right?"

Lucas shrugged. "We didn't see any cars, though. And everything east is decimated."

Turkey-finger man frowned. "They told us not to leave." He turned to look back at the small buildings. "I wonder if that was a mistake."

Sixteen

Turkey-fingers gazed silently at the small wooden buildings for a moment. Lucas and Olivia glanced at each other. I waited to see what we were going to do next.

"My mother started this camp," the man finally said in the same quiet voice. "I was just a boy. My brothers and I thought it was heaven. They've all gone on to do other things—one's a lawyer in Denver—but for me, all I ever wanted was to stay right here, taking care of things."

"It's beautiful," Olivia told him. "I love all the trees."

Turkey-fingers gave her a rueful look. "I guess now the trees are the problem, aren't they? Well, everyone's gone to the cafeteria. I'll show you the way."

Lucas waved at Mack and pointed. Mack nodded, but continued speaking to his phone.

Olivia, Lucas, and I followed Turkey-fingers across the grass, passing by dense pine trees. I kept turning back to check on Mack. I did not like leaving him behind. Soon we approached a big building from which some nice food odors were emanating, detectable even above the sharp smoke. I trailed behind Lucas up the wooden steps and inside.

The ceiling was high and long tables were lined up in rows. A small clutch of people, including a few boys, were gathered together up at the end farthest from the door. The boys turned and peeked at me excitedly, and I wagged at them. Sometimes I think children exist so that dogs have people who always want to play.

A man held up his hand and people stopped talking. He was one of Mack's friends, I could tell, because not only did they all dress alike, they all carried heavy packs on their backs, and they all smelled like they had been rolling around in ashes. This particular man had white cloth over one eye. When the cloth-eyed man pulled out a piece of paper, I noticed it trembled a little bit. "All right," Cloth-eye began. "First, the bad news. As you probably know by now, we've got fire to the south of us."

People stirred and murmured, and he raised his head and regarded them gloomily with his one eye. "The Rocky Mountains are burning, folks. That's all there is to it. With the winds coming straight at us, the fire is going to sweep right through this camp. There is no time to take out all the trees and try to build a firebreak. I'm afraid you're going to lose all these buildings."

Several people groaned. Turkey-fingers dropped his head and stared at the floor. I didn't see anything to look at, until, moments later, some drops of liquid fell from his face and splatted at his feet.

"We've got a helicopter coming in, should be here in about fifty minutes," Cloth-eye continued. "We'll get all the kids out, and there'll be room for a couple adults. Anybody have asthma or a lung disease?"

A woman held up her hand.

"All right, you're on it. Who else?"

The people began speaking amongst themselves. Lucas turned to Olivia. "I think you should take the helicopter."

"Oh, for God's sake, Lucas." She sounded angry. My boy bit his lip.

I turned at a familiar scent and wagged, relieved. It was Mack. I strained at the leash to get to him, nosing his lowered hand.

"He's saying a helicopter is coming for the boys and a couple of vulnerable adults," Olivia told Mack. "He hasn't said what the plan's going to be for the rest of us, though."

Mack gestured grimly with his phone and spoke in a low voice. "Just spoke to Captain Butcher. He says they were shown the wrong aerial photos before he deployed us here. Now they think the fire has cut us off from the south. We're trapped."

"Wait, what? We just *came* from that direction," Lucas objected. "How can we be cut off all of a sudden?"

Mack shrugged. "It's the latest intel, Lucas."

"Let's get back outside, wait for the chopper, and make a plan," Cloth-eye told the group.

I did not like it when Mack left us to go speak to Cloth-eye, especially when everyone else trailed out of the building. I stuck close to my boy, doing Heel without being asked, because I could sense the agitation in the humans and it made me uneasy.

I perked up when some boys came over to see me. There were no treats but I was hugged several times. Turkey-fingers petted me, too.

"Are you okay?" Olivia asked him.

He cleared his throat. "I guess the important thing is to get the children out."

Cloth-eye came out with Mack and the friends who were dressed like Mack. "Do you have a swimming pool?" he asked Turkey-fingers, who shook his head.

"No pool, no."

"Show us around your camp, will you?" Cloth-eye turned and looked at the anxious, gathered people. "Folks, we're going to work this out. Henry's going to give us a tour so we can see where to set up our lines of defense. I suggest you all take a seat at the picnic tables. We've still got some time."

We wandered over to some outdoor tables and the people sat, but there was no food. I tracked Mack and his friends leaving with Turkey-fingers.

A man and a woman came and sat with my boy and Olivia.

They did not seem to notice there was a dog. The woman had long hair and she kept touching it.

"Did you just get here?" the man asked.

Lucas nodded.

"How?" the woman demanded. "They say the way is blocked by fire."

"I guess we were dispatched with bad information. Now they've got photos showing the fire closed off the road out of here."

"Did you drive through fire?" the man challenged.

"No."

The man looked at the woman. "I say we go for it."

She touched her hair.

"Whenever the fire department has told us fire was coming, it's always come," Olivia advised.

"And we already tried outrunning it in a vehicle," Lucas added. "You can't."

The man and the woman stood and walked away. Lucas reached out and held Olivia's hand, but not in a happy way. I wondered what I could do to provide comfort.

I did not know why we just sat there for so long. I did not know, if this place made my people so tense, why we didn't just take a car ride and go back to where New Black Dog was probably being fed cheese.

I did register Mack and his friends returning after their long absence, but they were talking to other people and didn't approach our table.

I glanced up sharply when a loud pounding noise emerged from out of the cloudy sky and drifted over us, eventually resolving itself into a large machine that was so noisy I looked to Lucas for reassurance.

Whatever it was, it dropped slowly toward the ground, swung back and forth a moment, and then touched down.

As it stopped making so much noise, Cloth-eye announced, "Okay. Time to go."

Suddenly there was a lot of crying. Everybody wanted to hug the children but not the good dog who was right there in front of them. Then the children and some adults ran across the grass to the still-loud machine. A big door slid open and a man stepped out and waved at them and they began climbing into the big machine the way I sometimes jump into the back seat of Olivia's car.

As the loud machine beat the air with its thumping noises and rose straight up and tilted and flew off into the haze, the few people who remained with us went to stand closer to Cloth-eye. Only adults surrounded me, now. I had not gotten to play with a single child.

"All right," Cloth-eye said. "So we're going to get the pump going and get some water. I want us to wet down sheets and blankets from the bunkhouse. Carry them all to the basketball court."

Olivia raised her hand. "What's the plan?"

Cloth-eye turned and gestured at something. "The basketball court is a firebreak. The cement can't burn. We don't have time to take down the trees near it but they're very sparse. We're gonna get under the wet cloths and the fire will do a burn-over."

The man with turkey fingers stirred, looking worried. "I just thought of something. The basketball court is close to the propane tank."

The man on the steps looked at Mack's friends.

"On it," one of them said.

"Count me in," Mack added.

Lucas and Olivia and Mack and a few of the other people jogged with us across the field, stopping at a big, smooth metal object almost the size of a car.

Mack took a hard tool off his belt. "Let me disconnect the hose." He wrenched at a metal pipe that snaked out of one end of the big object. He finally managed to pull it off.

"How full is it, do you suppose?" one of Mack's friends asked Turkey-fingers.

He shook his head. "Not very. We called last week to have it refilled, but they haven't been out yet."

Lucas and Mack and the rest of them began pushing on the big metal object. Soon it was rocking, and with every rock back and forth, the motion increased. I jumped in surprise when the big thing toppled off of its perch and landed with a huge *thump* on the ground. It immediately began rolling downhill but did not go far before it ground to a halt against some trees.

Lucas reached out and touched Olivia's arm. "You okay?"

Olivia nodded. "Somehow I'm not as afraid this time. I sort of know what to expect, you know?"

I lifted my nose. I could smell that the fire was coming back now. And I could hear it, hear the noise that had been filling my senses since the day after we saw the not-Big-Kitten in the room with the glass booths.

Mack came over to us. He was sweating and not smiling. "Wish we could have gotten that tank farther away." He set down his pack and rummaged inside it. "For some reason when I saw Bella in Frisco, I decided to pull one of these and put it in my pack. It's an air filter for dogs. Forgot I had it until just now. Sorry, Bella."

I heard my name and heard the word *dogs* but did not sense that a treat would be forthcoming. Not only was I right about that, but, worse, Mack took what appeared to be a wide and deep plastic dog bowl and fit it over my face. I wagged because, though I did not know what he was doing, I knew that Mack loved me and would not harm me.

Once the dog bowl was over my snout, I noticed something new: the awful smoke that had been in my nose for so long was suddenly much less intense. Instead, while I could still smell fire, I could also detect the taste of cleaner air. I inhaled deeply, noticing as I did so that some people were bringing wet, dripping blankets and dropping them in a pile in the middle of a large, flat area that looked like a piece of road. They were moving quickly, twisting away from one another to cough. Smoke was curling around us. I expected that at any moment Scott and his friends would arrive.

"We're going to be okay," Lucas said to Olivia. They clutched at each other desperately. I did not wag.

"Let's go! Let's go!" someone yelled.

"Everyone to the middle of the basketball court!" someone else called.

All the people shuffled quickly onto the flat cement area. A lone metal pole poked up toward the sky at one end. I could smell that a male dog had recently marked at the base of the pole and wanted to investigate, but Lucas snapped his fingers at me. "Bella, come!"

We were in the center of the flat space.

"Get down low," Cloth-eye instructed.

Mack and his friends began picking up large wet blankets. Lucas and Olivia knelt down on their hands and knees next to each other, but not to play with me. Soon Mack and his friends were the only ones standing.

"Okay, folks, I'm not gonna lie," Cloth-eye announced. "This is going to be scary. The fire will be in the tops of the trees, and it will be hotter than anything you can imagine. But there's nothing on the basketball court to catch fire. Hopefully, the embers won't ignite these wet blankets. If they do, yell out and we'll try to stomp out the flames."

"Hold the cloth to your face and breathe through your nose," one of Mack's friends said as he handed people more wet blankets.

"How long before the fire gets here?" Olivia asked.

Mack turned to look at her as she huddled next to Lucas. Lucas put his arm around me and I lay down next to him.

"Now," Mack said. "It's here now."

Seventeen

H ands and knees, everybody!" Cloth-eye yelled. "Firefighters, flashlights on!"

"Huddle as close together as you can and stay low," Mack urged. "That will stop the hot air from getting in between you. Picture the wet sheets like they're the roof of a tent—we want to keep us all in the same space, inside the tent!"

He and his friends pulled out short metal objects and waved them, and beams of light illuminated the people's sweaty, panicky faces.

I felt terror and dread pouring off everyone as they shuffled close to each other. I did not understand this and wanted to flee from it, but humans decide where dogs go. None of them were running, so I wouldn't run either. There was scarcely room for me, but Lucas, coughing, pulled me between himself and Olivia and held me tightly there.

With his arm around me I felt protected. I wanted to give his face a lick, but I was still wearing Mack's dog bowl. I panted with apprehension, but my boy and Olivia needed me. Their faces were contorted with fear and I could feel their galloping heartbeats, even above the wind. I also heard the whimpering and sobbing of the others.

"Get ready!" Mack shouted hoarsely.

"Oh, Lucas, I don't want to die," Olivia moaned.

"You are not going to die!" Lucas whispered fiercely. "Olivia, look at me."

She focused on his face, her eyes wild.

"We've been through worse. Remember what you saw from the roof? We're going to make it, I promise."

Weeping silently, Olivia nodded.

The wind brought with it the now-familiar shriek, the one I associated with unbearable smoke and heat. It was mere moments before the sound totally engulfed us, sucking the very breath from my lungs. I felt the blanket above me getting warmer, getting hot. Everything was too hot! Several people starting talking, crying. I could tell they were in distress, but this was not a time for a good dog to go comfort other people because Olivia and Lucas were stiff with dread.

"Oh God. Oh God. Oh God. Oh God. Oh God," one woman cried loudly.

A man turned and threw up.

"No!" someone howled. "Please!"

The scorching wind blew hard over us and some of the blankets whipped off and were gone. We were battered by a roar more terrible than any thunder. Lucas's grip tightened even further. A woman screamed and kept on screaming, screaming even more loudly than the wind.

Olivia's face was tight with terror. "Lucas! I love you, Lucas!"

"I love you, Olivia!" Lucas and Olivia reached for each other's hands, their arms still wrapped around me.

"Hold on!" Cloth-eye cried, his voice stolen by the blast of searing air.

"It's on top of us!" Mack bellowed.

Now, almost all the people were screaming. No words, just tortured sounds.

It was impossibly hot. I blinked, blinded. My breathing hurt my throat.

Then, just as the noise was growing so oppressively deafening that I thought there could be nothing louder, a huge bang filled the air and concussed us with a powerful force. It was like being kicked and I flinched in pain, but Lucas and Olivia held me fast.

"That's the LP tank!" Mack yelled.

The light in his hand criss-crossed its beams with the lights that his friends held, cutting through the black smoke that was moving so quickly past us it was whistling. My eyes were stinging and I was choking and I felt myself losing control. Every instinct told me to run.

I struggled to my feet, straining against the hot blanket covering us, but my boy yanked me down. "Stay, Bella!" he snapped.

"Is anyone hurt?" one of Mack's friends yelled. "Anyone get hit by any metal from the LP tank?"

"We're all going to die!" a voice wailed. The man who'd spoken threw off his blanket, leapt to his feet, and began struggling to run away. "We can't stay here! We're going to burn to death!"

Several people answered this with harsh shouts and screams.

"No!" Mack jumped up and struggled past people and tackled the man, and they crashed down onto the pavement. "Get down! You can't outrun the fire! You will die!" Mack climbed atop the man and pinned his arms.

People were gagging and choking now. Lucas and Olivia were pressing their blankets to their faces. I retched inside my dog bowl, drooling uncontrollably. I shook my head, trying to free myself from the dog bowl. I needed air!

"The worst is past us!" Cloth-eye bellowed. "It's already blown by . . . hang on, hang on! Not much longer!"

I could not imagine a worse moment.

And then I felt something. A small lessening. With every choking, smoke-filled breath, the heavy blast of heat and ear-piercing wind diminished.

Mack focused on the man he still had pinned. "You okay, now? You won't try to run?"

The man shook his head.

Mack patted him on the arm. "Good man." He began crawling under the blankets from one person to another. He had a plastic dog bowl on a tube and he began handing it to people as they coughed. "Three breaths!" he shouted above the noise. "Take three breaths!"

The fury was fleeing now, heading away from us. The wind decreased and the smoke began clearing. It was a subtle change, but I could sense the fire had done what it could and was moving on to terrorize people somewhere else.

The cement was hot, almost too hot, beneath my feet. I hoped that whatever we were doing, we were not going to be doing it much longer. I felt like a bad dog for not wanting to do Stay.

Mack crawled under the remaining blankets to Turkey-fingers and handed the dog bowl to him. "Here, Henry."

The man nodded gratefully and put it on his face. He breathed and when he pulled the dog bowl away, he wasn't coughing. "How come you have an oxygen tank and the other firefighters don't?" Turkey-fingers wheezed.

Mack shook his head. "It's not oxygen. It's compressed air. Smoke jumpers don't wear them, but I'm regular fire department. You're going to be okay, sir."

Turkey-fingers handed the dog bowl back. "I hope so. But for a moment there, I didn't believe it."

"I hear ya, brother."

"I think we can get out from underneath these blankets," one of Mack's friends said. "It's like a sauna under here."

Cloth-eye climbed to his feet. "Agreed, we're good. Let's ditch the blankets."

Everyone stood up and pushed away the blankets. Now I could see much more clearly.

Mack picked his way to each person in turn and let them put the dog bowl on their faces. When he made his way to Olivia and Lucas, his light flashed across my eyes briefly. Mack offered the dog bowl to Olivia, who wearily shook her head and pressed the dog bowl to my boy's face. "He's coughing worse," she explained.

Lucas nodded, taking breaths and barking them back out, his chest contracting. Then he reached up and pulled the dog bowl away and handed it to Olivia. "I'm okay," he croaked.

A woman was crying, the same woman who had been saying, "Oh God. Oh God. Oh God." People were wiping their eyes and coughing and looking around.

I shook. It felt as if dirt were falling from the sky. I looked at Lucas, who was hugging Olivia. He held out a hand, palm up. "Watch for the embers, some will be hot!" he warned loudly.

"Here." Cloth-eye and his friends produced knives and began shredding blankets, passing the rags to people. "If you feel something on your head or shoulder, brush it off with these."

Things had changed. The trees were gone—now there were just blackened, mostly fallen trunks. Here and there, a few remained on fire, still standing. Across the field, every building was burning, billowing black smoke into the air that was less intense with the dog bowl over my muzzle. Everyone was hugging everyone else so I wagged. I understood little, but the relief flowing over people was pushing the fear away, and I knew it meant that the danger brought by the fire had passed.

Lucas began moving from person to person, reaching out a hand. "Are you okay?" he asked each one. They were all coughing and spitting. One man was wheezing so badly he couldn't answer.

"Mack, air tank, please?" Lucas called.

Mack handed my boy the dog bowl, and he pressed it to the man's face.

"We'll get you looked at, but I think it's just smoke inhalation. You don't have any lung condition you know about, do you? Asthma?" Lucas prodded.

The man pulled the dog bowl away, shaking his head. "Nope."

"Are you a smoker?" Lucas pressed.

The man shook his head again. "But I smoked for twenty years."

Lucas nodded. "That's it then. Just breathe."

Gradually, the hot surface under my pads released its heat. When gusts of wind came at us, they brought less smoke, not more.

"Let's all just catch our breath here for a minute," Cloth-eye suggested.

Turkey-fingers turned and smiled sadly at Lucas and Olivia. "Those cabins down there, my dad and I built one summer, just the two of us. I've always been able to remember him, anytime I went into one of them. And now they're burning. I can rebuild, but I won't be able to look at the window frames he hammered into place or the center beam and think of him putting them there."

Lucas nodded sympathetically.

"Sorry for your loss," Olivia murmured.

Eventually we all sat on the ground. Lucas reached out and unstrapped the dog bowl on my face and I licked his cheeks gratefully. He and Olivia were no longer frightened, even with fires audibly burning nearby and smoke still wafting in the air.

Lucas raised a fist to his mouth and coughed. Olivia touched his shoulder. He nodded at her. "I'm okay," he rasped. He wiped his face.

What I picked up from the people around me was a dismal sort of exhaustion. Some of them lay down, bunched blankets under their heads, and slept. One man snored. I put my head in my boy's lap.

I awoke with a start when I heard something: a big loud engine. Then there was a crashing sound like two heavy things coming together, metal things, that reminded me of when we went for a car ride in the Jeep to the lake. The impacts were so loud I could feel them. Olivia seemed to understand that I was uneasy and reached down and stroked my head.

All the people looked in the direction of the loud noise. I yawned anxiously. There was another huge *bang,* and another.

"I think that's going to be the truck," Mack told the group.

Then I saw what was making the noise—the big, long truck

that Mack liked to ride around in. While I watched, it slammed a parked car aside with another crashing *boom,* clearing the road so it could move forward. Some people began to run to it.

"Stop!" Cloth-eye yelled. "It'll come to us. We don't want to walk on the ground just yet."

With smoke swirling behind it, the truck rumbled over and parked right on the cement where we were all still standing.

A man climbed down off the truck and went to Mack and Mack's friends; they hugged and hit each other on the back, all grinning.

I noticed that the face of the man from the truck was sweaty and black with smears. "What do you want to do?" he asked Cloth-eye.

"I don't think we want to stay here, the smoke's too dense," Cloth-eye replied.

The driver of the big truck leaned over and spat into the dirt. "Well, there's only the one road and it leads straight to the center of the whole thing before you can hook north on 765. It might get hairy, we decide to head that way."

Turkey-fingers stepped forward. "It's the only way to get to Paraiso."

Mack and his friends looked at one another. Cloth-eye shrugged. "What choice do we have?"

We climbed onto the big truck for a car ride, but this time Olivia and Lucas stood with Turkey-fingers in a small space in the middle and some other people got to ride with Mack on the roof in back. There was no room for me to lie down, so I did Sit at my boy's feet.

People were sad and afraid, which I did not understand because we were leaving the hot cement place. Olivia put the dog bowl back on my face, as if determined to make the car ride even worse.

Two of Mack's friends passed out dog bowls, each with a hose attached to a metal object that clanked. "Share, okay? Share the masks," Cloth-eye called from the front.

The truck rumbled as it drove, and I felt the smoke as much as smelled it—burning my eyes, clogging the air. The roar of the fire grew steadily louder. It seemed to me that we were driving directly toward it. I whimpered inside my face bowl.

Lucas passed his dog bowl to Turkey-fingers and coughed, his hand over his mouth. Olivia's eyes were streaming as she reached out to touch his arm. "I'm worried about you, honey. Are you sure you are all right?"

Lucas nodded and coughed again as Turkey-fingers passed Olivia the dog bowl. I anxiously pressed up against my boy's legs. Now I felt heat, great gusts of it on currents that were growing stronger and stronger. I didn't understand what we were doing.

"How far?" Lucas wheezed at Turkey-fingers.

"Not far. Maybe another mile until we can turn on 765."

Olivia gestured. "Another mile into all this smoke—I don't know how we're going to make it."

Both Olivia and Lucas were coughing. I was drooling inside my face bowl and felt sure I was about to vomit again. I could see nothing, smell nothing but black smoke.

"We have to go back!" a woman cried shrilly.

Lucas shook his head. "We can't!" His voice was a croak.

"Hang on, folks," Mack called. "Almost to the turnoff!"

Eighteen

The acrid bite of burning wood was on my tongue and in my nose, more intense than anything I'd ever experienced. I panted, my throat aching. Lucas bent over, his hands on his knees, and Olivia stooped down and pushed the dog bowl at him. The woman who had been screaming collapsed and Turkey-fingers knelt and they vanished in swirling blackness. It was dark as any night.

Then the truck leaned over and everyone grabbed for handholds. I skittered across the metal floor, digging in my claws. I could no longer see Lucas, but his hand snagged my collar, halting my slide.

"That's it!" Mack shouted, his voice strangling into hacking and gasping.

People cheered, so I wagged, but I didn't understand. The big truck surged beneath our feet, and I was pressed into Lucas's legs by the force of it. The vibration from the engine was louder than the fire, drowning everything else out. I glanced up and I could see my boy's face as he spasmed a cough into his hand.

Then smoke began whistling past my ears. I looked at Lucas, who was wiping his eyes now and spitting out onto the road. With each passing moment, his form became more visible in the black haze, which was breaking apart. He sucked on the dog bowl, then, nodding, handed it to Olivia. He gave her a weak smile.

Even within my dog bowl, I could smell that the fire was lessening rapidly. We were leaving it behind. My vision cleared even further, and the roar and the heat receded. Lucas reached down and took off my face bowl and I blinked away the water in my eyes.

"Pretty much ready for life to get back to normal," my boy rasped.

Olivia coughed and then smiled. "Remember when you asked me to marry you, and you promised you would make every day interesting? Well, you've sure delivered on *that*." Swaying, she reached for my boy, who held on to a rail with one hand while he pulled her to him with the other. They kissed, and I wagged and pushed my face in between them because they were doing Love and I knew they wanted me to be part of it.

Every moment brought better air. Soon the car ride on the big truck became even happier when we slowed and I smelled a place we had been before: it was the town with the big soft rooms in the grass.

That night, Mack gave us a ride to our new home, but I spent most of the next several days at the house of barking dogs. All the other animals were in kennels in the back rooms or in the yard behind the building, but I was permitted to lie on a dog bed on the floor near Olivia because I was a good dog. I wasn't allowed on the couch, though—I wasn't that good.

I greeted the people who arrived in groups or as individuals, and they were always glad to see me. When Diane or Olivia went in the back of the building and emerged with a dog or a cat, the new people would laugh or cry or yell in joy and the animals would be so glad to see the humans . . . though it wasn't easy to be sure with the cats.

I thought I understood why the people were so happy: life is just better with a dog. Cats are not dogs, but they're pretty good.

The male dog who had so briefly been in my pack, Gus, left on a leash held by a tall man, and Trixie went out the door with a weeping woman. If I had understood that they each had their own person, I would not have been so suspicious of their motives.

Sometimes, instead of remaining with Olivia and Diane and all the animals, I was taken to the outside area with the big soft rooms with Olivia and Lucas and all the people. More and more cars drove on the streets and humans walked around, and a lot of them were sad and needed to pet me and give me hugs. I saw children and, every so often, a new dog. The children and the dogs did not seem sad.

The next afternoon, Lucas was inside one of the soft rooms talking to people—I could smell him—and if I concentrated, I could separate his voice from the buzz of conversation going on all around me. I was sitting under a long table at Olivia's feet. She was not eating, but I did a good Sit anyway because there had been treats before at this very same table.

Sometimes friends, known or unknown, would sit and talk to Olivia and I would sniff them from under the table, smelling the one thing they had in common—they all still carried the odor of smoke.

At one point, Olivia straightened up sharply. "What's happening?" she asked a man who was sitting across from her.

They both stood up, so of course I got up, too, thinking we were going to take a walk or at least maybe get a sandwich.

"I don't know," the man told her. "Something, obviously."

"They've got guns. Why do they all have guns?" Olivia asked.

I sensed the alarm in her voice, but could not see or smell anything that would cause her to be upset. Many things that happen to people are not really detectable to a dog.

"Scott!" Olivia shouted. She looked both ways and ran across the street to where our friend Scott was in his truck. I followed closely on her heels.

Scott rolled down the window. "Hi, Olivia."

"What's happening?" Olivia asked him. "Why do these men all have guns?"

"You didn't hear?" Scott replied. "There've been a couple of mountain lions spotted inside city limits. They must have been driven out of their territory by the fire and now they're here in town."

"Well, you can't just shoot them," Olivia protested. "They're probably scared and just need to find a way out of here. They're not here to *hunt*, for God's sake."

Scott shook his head. "We just can't take that chance, Olivia. You remember what the district wildlife manager said: predators out of their territories are unpredictable and aggressive. We've got kids coming back to Paraiso now . . . kids and dogs and other pets. We can't have cougars running around."

"This is wrong, Scott. You're overreacting. It can't be legal and it sure isn't moral. Let Animal Control handle it."

"Yeah, well, I wasn't supposed to stay and help defend the town either," Scott reminded her. "Sometimes you got to bend the rules because of the situation. If they want to arrest us, they're welcome to try."

"And you really think it's a good idea to be shooting rifles in town? You said it yourself, you've got kids and pets here."

Scott frowned.

"Could you just wait a bit? I saw that wildlife manager a little while ago. Can you hold off until you speak to her?"

Scott sighed. "Okay."

"Thanks!" She turned and ran off. I started to follow, but Scott leaned down out of his truck. "Hey, Bella, good to see you, girl. Want a little turkey jerky?" He held out a delicious treat and I delicately took it from his hand. This was the second person I had met with turkey fingers! It was wonderfully chewy, and as I crunched through it, I was aware that Olivia had vanished into the gathering of soft rooms.

Normally I would chase after her, but Scott held out another treat.

A truck pulled up close to us. I could smell the two men inside through their open windows. "Scott! Someone spotted them out by the Safeway. You coming?"

Scott glanced pensively toward where Olivia had gone, then nodded. He tossed me another treat. "Good dog, Bella. Go home."

I gobbled the small morsel. I did not understand why Scott had just told me to do Go Home. Go Home meant find Lucas, and I knew exactly where he was.

When Scott drove off, I was alone in the street. I wandered around, noting where a female dog had deposited a pile. I sniffed it with interest.

Then I saw a squirrel! It was digging in the dead grass at the base of a black tree. I lowered my head. It took a few hops. It didn't see me! I stalked it. It raised its head. *Yes.* I burst into a run and it turned and scampered up the burned tree. I put my front paws on the trunk and stared up at it, and it stared back.

I waited for it to come back down for another try, but after a moment passed, it jumped from the branch, sailing over to another tree, and scaled it. Squirrels often leap from tree to tree and I find it very irritating.

I searched with my nose for signs that the squirrel was coming back down for another fun chase, but there was no trace of it. And then a subtle shift in the wind brought me something on the air besides smoke . . . besides fire. It was an animal smell, both wild and familiar. I couldn't help but wag as I turned in that direction. I knew that scent as well as I knew my own. There had been a time when I breathed in that scent every waking moment, and many of my sleeping moments, too.

It was Big Kitten.

She was close by.

I had not been told Stay by either Olivia or Lucas. With a guilty glance behind me, I trotted down the street in the direction of my long-lost friend.

I made my way briskly past piles of charred wood and blackened brick buildings, turning a rubble-strewn corner and descending down a wide dirt road into a low-lying grassy place. I could smell a small stream, and this area was refreshingly unscorched, with moist grass and leaves fluttering in the breeze. I saw no houses nearby—the space felt like a dog park, and I could smell that several male canines had treated it as exactly that. There were big boulders and some trees in this area that had been spared by the fire. And it was here, my nose told me, that I would find my friend Big Kitten.

Her feral scent was strong now, but I did not attempt to track her down in the rocks and shrubs. I knew she could see me; I was standing out in the open in the short grass. I stood, wagging, unsure if she would even remember me after such a long time.

And there was something else: I could smell that there were other big cats with her.

After a moment I spotted some motion and Big Kitten slipped out from behind thick foliage and stood and stared at me. I took a few hesitant steps forward, still wagging, and stopped. What happened next was up to her.

When she stalked out into the sunshine, I play-bowed to greet her. It was so wonderful to see my friend again.

Cats don't wag, they don't sniff butts, they don't really act friendly toward dogs or even each other. But there was one thing Big Kitten did . . . one thing I knew would show she still remembered me. I wanted to leap around and wrestle with her, but I stood motionless, only my tail moving, waiting as she carefully picked her way toward me. She stopped, facing me, her nose twitching ever so slightly. And then she did it: she lowered her head and rubbed it against me, making that deep rumbling sound in her chest.

Oh, yes, Big Kitten remembered me.

I could smell the other big cats—they were still hiding in the rocks. I looked curiously in that direction.

Big Kitten turned away and glanced back over her shoulder in a way that I had learned long ago meant that she wanted me to follow her. I trotted behind her, eager to meet these new friends.

I was shocked when we slipped into the dense bushes and I saw who was waiting there for us: two kittens!

They were not little, actually; though they were smaller than the wild cat with the rabbit, they were larger than any other cats I had ever met except Big Kitten. But they were smaller than Big Kitten had been when we first met while I was doing Go Home to Lucas.

There was a Boy Kitten and a Girl Kitten. When I approached them, they both scrambled to hide behind Big Kitten. I wagged and bowed but they just stared at me. Finally, I flopped down and rolled onto my back as if inviting a belly rub.

Girl Kitten was the braver of the two and finally advanced, tentatively sniffing while Big Kitten watched impassively. But when I jumped up, Girl Kitten retreated rapidly, eyes large. She apparently was not interested in wrestling with me, nor was her brother.

Big Kitten had become a mother cat. These were her cubs, and I hoped that they would all follow me back to see Lucas. He would be so surprised!

When she was little, Big Kitten loved to play one particular game. I decided to try it now and, when I darted away as if to flee, I turned to see if Girl Kitten followed, but she didn't budge. She didn't want to play Chase Me.

I looked up when a fresh animal scent touched me. It was the monsters: the great hulking beasts we had seen before everyone got busy playing with dirt during the big fire. The huge brutes were plodding slowly along the street, plainly visible now because there were no houses, only ashes on the ground. They would soon be passing by the wide dirt road that led down to this dog park.

Beyond them, a truck was rattling down the street. It stopped abruptly behind the pack of gigantic animals, who completely ignored its arrival. The doors flew open and men stood up on either side, pointing what looked to be big sticks at the cats and me. I wagged tentatively. The two cubs were playing with each other and not paying attention, but I saw that Big Kitten was alert, watching the big monsters and the men standing on either side of the truck.

I saw a flash and some smoke and heard a very familiar *crack* slap at my ears. Big Kitten stiffened. The other man's stick made the same noise and I was surprised when a clod of dirt near Girl Kitten spat into the air.

Big Kitten and I met eyes and I wondered if she was remembering the same noise, the same smell, from the day we met. The day her mother died in the dirt. And then we both turned because of something else: with the two loud bangs, tension had rippled through the herd of monsters and suddenly the big bull at the front pivoted and ran right down the wide road toward where we were playing! Instantly all the other huge creatures were running, too, following this huge animal. The entire pack was thundering straight for us.

Big Kitten fled and her kittens followed suit. I ran as well, pursuing Big Kitten, who swiftly left me and her cubs behind. We were running hard over rocks and grasses, dodging boulders and foliage. I could smell my friend, but she was very fast, and soon I could not spot her in the dense growth.

Big Kitten would not want Boy Kitten and Girl Kitten to be trampled by the monsters who were still behind us. But she was afraid, and the fear was leading her to abandon us.

I decided to stay with the kittens.

Nineteen

We were falling behind in our pursuit of Big Kitten. She had sprinted so far ahead, only my nose could find her now—the cubs seemed to be following me as much as tracking their mother. Somehow, in these changed circumstances, they were no longer suspicious of this dog who was friends with their mother.

These kittens were not a responsibility I would have wanted, but I instinctively accepted it. Big Kitten and I were part of a pack—long separated by time and distance, but a pack. I would return to Lucas, of course, but for now, following my friend felt natural and instinctive.

Big Kitten was fast, but my nose told me we were not trailing too far behind her. We ascended a grassy hill, where some fallen trees, the sort Big Kitten could clear in a single leap, slowed us down.

The big beasts were no longer charging us, and the men were far behind, but Big Kitten didn't seem to realize this—she was still on the move. And moving unnaturally. The cat I knew covered ground in sprints and dashes, moving from one hiding place to another, as if she considered herself prey despite being one of the fiercest creatures in the mountains. But what I found with my nose now was a straight path. Big Kitten wasn't running to something, she was running *away*.

Concentrating on Big Kitten's scent, I could smell her hunger, I could smell smoke from her skin, and I could smell her fear.

Big Kitten had never seemed afraid before, not since she was
a baby cat.

The cubs and I caught up to Big Kitten at the top of a fire-
blackened ridge, far from where we had started. I picked my way
through a field of rocks and joined her. We were all panting. Big
Kitten's eyes seemed larger than normal, and she didn't greet me
as if she knew me, didn't bend down to her cubs, who sidled up to
her, craving reassurance. Her ears pressed back on her skull, her
fear plain and frantic.

Down below, at the base of the ridge, I could see and smell a
huge fire charging up a mountainside opposite us. Big Kitten was
terrified of this fire. I couldn't tell her that when there's fire, Lucas
and Olivia and the other humans throw dirt at it and put blankets
over us and make it safe for everyone.

Though she seemed exhausted, Big Kitten turned and fled yet
again. I had no choice but to follow, as the cubs struggled to keep
pace with their mother. She moved more slowly now, making it
easier to keep her in sight. She was no longer in a mindless panic,
but she obviously wanted to be far away from the threat of fire.

There had been many times in the past when I sensed that Big
Kitten knew where she was taking me. Her self-assurance was
clear and evident in her purposeful stalking.

This was not one of those times. I knew she wanted to flee
the fire, but the fire was everywhere, sending her in a variety of
directions. As we ran, I would smell it getting stronger, and then
we'd change course and head a different way until a wall of smoke
hit us, and we'd change direction again. She was running in bursts
now, always moving but only occasionally breaking into a sprint.
The way she was behaving frightened me; she seemed heedless of
her cubs struggling to keep up, unaware of my presence, focused
solely on the urgent need to escape danger.

At one point, I smelled water and deliberately broke away from
Big Kitten, who sensed I was changing direction and turned to

look at me. Girl Kitten followed me, and Boy Kitten ran to his mother cat.

I found a small stream and, ignoring the bitter taste of the burned wood floating on the surface, lapped it up gratefully. Soon I was joined by my cat family.

With some water in her belly, Big Kitten seemed less panicked. I wondered if she understood, now, that everything was burning all around us, and that the smartest thing to do would be to find people to take care of us and give us a car ride back to Lucas.

The sun was lowering to the horizon, oddly looking more like the moon through the haze of smoke painting the sky.

We could not keep fleeing. Even refreshed by water, the cubs looked exhausted. I knew I needed rest, and the dull sheen in Big Kitten's eyes told me she was drained as well.

She allowed me to guide her, and we soon found a safe-seeming place by some fallen, blackened trees. Big Kitten nudged her kittens with her nose, forcing them to take shelter. They went rigid with alarm when I climbed into the hollow space with them, but then Big Kitten joined us, and that seemed to decide things for them, and they relaxed. I had met many other kittens in my life and it usually went like this: mistrust and fear, followed by acceptance when they understood what a good dog I was.

We slept, but Big Kitten soon roused herself in the growing gloom.

I knew what was coming, and as night fully descended, Big Kitten stared at me for a long moment, then abruptly departed into the darkness. This was her pattern: Big Kitten hunted at night, which made no sense. Dogs know the time to hunt is when the prey can be seen, but cats don't really pay attention to the things dogs can teach them.

I was tired and ready for sleep but Boy Kitten and Girl Kitten decided it was time to play. They wrestled with each other while I looked on tolerantly. I was drowsy, but every time I was about to slip into luxurious sleep, one of the cubs would pounce on me. I had apparently been accepted into the cat pack.

I wearily bore their assaults because with their mother out prowling, they were my responsibility. It was what Big Kitten would have wanted, and what Lucas would have wanted. Lucas and Olivia often took care of cats.

The kittens were sprawled against me and the sun was just barely giving light to the morning when Big Kitten's scent arrived on the smoky air. I wagged, because I could smell that she had brought a meal.

When she emerged from the gloom, she had a small deer clamped in her jaws.

At the scent of blood, Boy Kitten and Girl Kitten roused themselves and we shared that meal, just as Big Kitten and I had done so many times in the past. The little cats seemed unsurprised to be feeding next to a dog, though Girl Kitten paused from time to time to sniff curiously at my face.

I was not surprised when, after we had all eaten our fill, Big Kitten dragged the carcass over near the boulders and began scratching at dirt, covering the kill the way she always did when we were finished eating. Another cat tendency that made no sense to me.

Boy Kitten and Girl Kitten watched their mother raptly. I wondered if they were as perplexed as I was at this behavior. I had no way of letting them know that it was simply what Big Kitten liked to do.

I knew what would happen next: we would spend a few days right there, feeding on the deer, remaining out of sight during the day and hunting at night—well, Big Kitten would hunt. This was the pattern of behavior we had long ago established. But now, of course, I would stay with the family, because the kittens seemed too young to leave alone. Which meant I would not be doing Go Home to Lucas on my own—the cubs would have to come with me. I knew he was probably calling for me, but I could also sense that the fire had descended from the mountains and was separating me from my humans. I would not go toward flames without Lucas guiding me.

All of this made me confused and anxious. Every decision was too hard for me to make. I needed my person to tell me what to do.

Several times during the next day, I heard a loud *crack*, followed by the booming rumble of a tree falling suddenly. It was as if, having been consumed by fire, the trees no longer had the will to remain upright. Many that remained erect lost the strength in their limbs and dropped heavy branches to the ground in a shower of black, cold embers. The cubs always jerked and stared at the noisy trees.

Big Kitten's nocturnal forays were unproductive for the next several nights. We were running out of food, and I was beginning to feel desperate. This wasn't merely a matter of my own hunger—the kittens were young and needed to eat frequently.

My nose sensed that the flames that had threatened us were weakening, losing their grip on our area. Even though I knew the fire was still out there, it felt safer now. I could smell that many places had become like the forest of dead black trees—no longer hot and burning, but smoldering and passable.

So I could do Go Home now, I thought, find my way to Lucas. But not while my kittens were starving. I had to be sure that Big Kitten could take care of them.

I lay panting in the heat, wind whipping, bringing me scents of the rising and falling of the flames in trees near and distant. I longed to be with my boy again. I wanted to eat at his hand, to be a good dog doing Sit.

If Big Kitten could not find food, I wondered if she'd follow me back to the town where Olivia and Lucas waited. Would she understand I was leading my cats to a meal?

Night fell and I prepared myself to stand vigil over the kittens, both of whom seemed to develop a reckless wanderlust whenever the sun went down. I had learned to keep them from straying too far by going to them and prodding them with my nose, just like

Big Kitten. Occasionally I found it necessary to growl at them a little, a sound they seemed to find fascinating. When I did it, their eyes widened and they stared at me as if in amazement. But they understood, especially when Girl Kitten seemed determined to leave her brother at the den and go for a long walk by herself. I always scampered after her, got in her way, and barked. That startled her, and she'd turn and flee back to the den, where her brother would pounce on her.

At night, I was Boy Kitten and Girl Kitten's mother cat.

Thankfully, Big Kitten finally hunted successfully, returning at sunrise with prey. Rejuvenated and no longer hungry, we all played together. Big Kitten and I wrestled as we always had, and when I tumbled, the kittens pounced. I was so happy to have a full belly and to be rolling around with cats!

Afterward, I napped with Big Kitten and the cubs, thinking this would be my last full day with them. They had food now. I could return to my humans knowing the kittens would be all right. I was sorry I could not remain with my cat family, who must have come very far to find me. Just as I had long searched for Big Kitten, she had been looking for me. But perhaps if I did Go Home, Big Kitten would return to wherever she lived now.

Back at the house where Olivia lived with Lucas and me, there was a woman across the street who had cats. Lucas called her the "cat lady" and I liked to go over and visit her. I hoped Big Kitten was living with someone like that. She distrusted humans in general, but so had my original mother cat, back before I went to be with Lucas, and now my mother cat had a woman who took care of her. Cats can always find a person to love them, though it's much easier for a dog to do so.

Girl Kitten yawned as we lolled together, and the sight filled me with peace and love. It would not be easy to say goodbye to her and her brother. When I left Big Kitten several summers ago, she had become an adult. These kittens had not, but I had stayed away from my boy for too long.

As usual, the presence of a new food supply made little difference as far as her habits—Big Kitten would still hunt that night. As she left, she turned and stared at me, and I wondered if she knew I had decided that I would leave her and the kittens the next morning.

When she slunk off, I realized how much I would miss the three of them. We had been through so much together. But I'd made my decision.

I awoke the next morning to a fierce wind and the realization that Big Kitten had not yet returned. The wind forced an eye-stinging smoke upon me—somewhere fairly close, a large gathering of trees was being devastated by flames. The kittens remained huddled in the shade, snoozing, while I restlessly prowled the area, lifting my nose for a sign of Big Kitten. I could not feel her or smell her. She must have gone far away.

I thought back to her mindless retreat the last time she'd felt threatened by fire. If she had ended up near this new outbreak, she could be fleeing in any direction.

I was concerned. This was not a good time to be away from her cubs.

There was no sign of Big Kitten all that day, and she did not return during the night. Boy Kitten and Girl Kitten seemed anxious and pressed closer to me than usual, trying to lure me into reassuring play. Boy Kitten rubbed his head against my shoulder and made a rumbling sound in his chest, exactly as his mother would do.

When the sun came up the next morning, I woke with a start, thinking I had heard Lucas calling my name. There was no sign of him on the wind, though—just the ever-present smoke. The cubs were peacefully slumbering. I shook, stretched, and stepped out of our den.

There was still no sign of Big Kitten.

She was gone.

Twenty

A desperate fear and loneliness settled over me as I watched the kittens sleep soundly at my feet. Their faces were undisturbed. They didn't know anything except the peace of being with the good dog who was taking care of them.

But I knew other things. My previous time with Big Kitten had taught me the mountains were a dangerous place. Predators would see the cubs, and even a solitary dog like me, as a meal worth hunting. But such attacks were far from the only threats. The fire was still out there, claiming what it could. And then there was hunger, which could sap our strength and destroy our will to survive.

I only knew how to hunt from the hands of people, or indirectly through large bins that contained the remains of human dinners. But such opportunities had been thinned by the fire. Now, when I sorted through the scents on the air, I found no people, only smoke.

We were utterly alone.

A helpless whimper escaped my lips. The humans might never come back, now that there were flames everywhere again. But I couldn't possibly protect my kittens without them.

The only thing to do was to do Go Home to Lucas. He would know what to do with Boy Kitten and Girl Kitten. He would take care of us, love us, and give us each a t-i-i-iny piece of cheese.

The thought of food ignited an insistent hunger within me.

There was little left of the carcass of Big Kitten's kill. I nuzzled the sleepy cubs awake and demonstrated that it was time to eat. They accepted my guidance, and we ate what I knew would be our last meal in that safe place.

The scent of their mother was faintly overlaid across the surface of the carcass, and I wondered if it provided the young cats any comfort.

Lucas felt far away—it would take some time to reach him. I resolved to depart that morning.

I hoped Big Kitten would soon return to this den and find us no longer here and follow us. I had the sense that a mother cat could always find her kittens. In any case, I couldn't wait any longer, so we set off.

But I was not able to be a good dog and do Go Home, because the fire seemed determined to stop us, pushing us to take another direction. I could smell it constantly now; sometimes the sky would grow dark during the day when our path took us too close to flames. Desperate to get back to Lucas, I kept up a steady, hard pace, moving as fast as the little cubs could tolerate. At night, they collapsed in a heap, too exhausted to pounce or wrestle.

I was depleted as well. We found water; there were streams and ponds, some tainted with the now-familiar taste of fallen embers, but all drinkable. Still, we were hungry, and I could tell after two days that the kittens were running out of energy.

We needed to find food or they would not survive many more days like this.

They trusted me, but they didn't understand fire. They didn't seem afraid of the encroaching danger, only hungry and tired. Whenever I halted to allow them some recovery time, they would paw at me, not in play, but in a frantic attempt to communicate their need for food.

I was very afraid. When the cubs were curled up against me for the night, their warmth and the tiny sounds of their breathing stoked a love within me as powerful as anything I had ever felt for Big Kitten. I sometimes lowered my nose to their soft fur, the better to breathe in their scents. I was desperate to take good care of them, but I was failing.

As was true of Big Kitten, they were wary of a road when we came across one. They gingerly approached this new surface, sniffing at it, probably distrusting the human and machine odors embedded in the gravel. But for me, a road made for an easy path away from the fire. We struck a compromise, the kittens and I, walking along the edge of the road and staying as hidden as possible.

We hadn't traveled very far when I came across an odd sight: items I recognized as being human in origin. I found bags, a small shovel, and other objects strewn along the side of the road. It was as if several people were walking through here and suddenly decided to drop their belongings. The scent of humans was still strong on everything—the objects had only recently been abandoned.

The most interesting of these was a big backpack exactly like the one that Lucas often carried. It was lying on the ground next to the road and was yawning completely open. The kittens were alarmed when they saw me approach it, and they bobbed their heads and flinched when I thrust my face into the opening, but I could smell something edible in there. I tore out some cloth items and tossed them aside and dragged out a big pouch, which I ripped open with my teeth. I was rewarded by succulent dry meat, along with something crunchy. I greedily gobbled it down while Boy Kitten and Girl Kitten watched me in what appeared to be astonishment. They reacted with more interest, though, when I tugged out a long and hard tube of what turned out to be a spicy meat. I let the two of them share this and they pounced on it with such eagerness I felt a stab of shame—I had let them come so close to starving.

I pulled out more packets, and Girl Kitten needed no encouragement to approach one and eat the contents. Boy Kitten wouldn't do this until I ripped it open and shook it violently as if it were a pair of Lucas's socks. Food chunks scattered everywhere, and Boy Kitten pounced and gobbled up the small morsels, crunching on the dried meat.

Everything edible I shared with the kittens. They had no interest in a spongy cookie infused with a deliciously sweet honey flavor, so I ate that myself. Even when famished, cats will often turn away from treats that dogs are smart enough not to ignore.

Invigorated by the snack, we proceeded at a brisker pace, eventually leaving the road when it became apparent that it was curving back around in the direction of the heaviest smoke.

Big Kitten had trusted me to take care of her kittens, and I was doing my best. But I was dismayed to realize my best might not be good enough. I still felt that I could sense the direction I should take to find Lucas, but we were not headed that way at all. Instead, we were stuck fleeing the fire.

At one point we emerged from a scorched forest into a meadow with green grass unaffected by flames. There were horses in this field, their noses down. They appeared to be eating grass, something I might do from time to time but never with the enthusiasm that these big creatures showed for it. Boy Kitten and Girl Kitten were fascinated by the horses, staring at them, and then, in a move that surprised me, slinking down to their stomachs and creeping slowly toward one of the smaller ones. The horses lifted their heads in unison and stared at this spectacle. The kittens jerked when a horse took a single step forward, though they continued their low-belly advance when that same horse put its head back down to the grass.

I had a bad feeling about this. I did not know what the two kittens thought they were doing, but their movements clearly had caught the horses' attention. The grass-eating creatures were big and powerful and their feet looked dangerous. And since they weren't running, I assumed that they weren't the slightest bit afraid of the approaching kittens.

I eventually realized what the kittens were up to: they were stalking, with motion and manner similar to how I hunted squirrels. But these were not squirrels—they weren't about to bound away and dash up a tree. I knew that if I allowed them to continue their hunt, they might be killed. I couldn't let that happen!

So, I barked.

The effect was electrifying. Both kittens turned and gawked at me in shock. The horses, on the other hand, were now staring at *me* intently. I barked again, charging forward with bared teeth, and one of the horses turned its head and began trotting away; and with that, all the horses suddenly galloped across the field.

Girl Kitten sprang to her feet as if to give pursuit, and I barked several times in warning; it was enough to halt her in her tracks. I trotted up to the cubs and nosed them to let them know I loved them and wasn't angry, but we should not spend time chasing horses. The horses might decide to chase us back.

It was as hard to communicate this message to the kittens as it would be to another dog, but I thought they understood from the wag of my tail and the way I deliberately turned away from the direction of the horses that I was ready to move on and that they should follow—which they did, though Girl Kitten kept stopping and staring back in the direction of the horses.

A day after finding the backpack on the side of the road, hunger had returned and was carving away at my insides. I was plodding dully along a human trail, registering that it had twisted me away from my intended direction and finding it difficult to care, when I detected a tendril of succulent meat odor drifting on the wind. I quickened my pace and the kittens, lethargic and weak, struggled to keep up.

They reluctantly followed me into an area where the ground was black, clearly afraid of the lingering scent of fire. The trees in this burned place had no limbs and were pointing sharply skyward and had been completely scorched. I made my way steadily toward what smelled like someone cooking meat and the two cats warily stayed close on my heels, clearly unsure of what I was doing or where I was going.

Cats, I had long ago decided, didn't recognize obvious odors the way dogs do.

We eventually found the source of the tantalizing smells. We were in an area where some rocks formed a natural barrier to further progress. At the base of these rocks, there was a gathering of large, four-legged creatures, some kind of big deer. They had died from the flames and had been cooked where they fell.

The kittens were unsure about this offering with its burned meat, but I had no such compunctions. I dug in and, observing the gusto with which I was enjoying this long-delayed meal, they joined me, taking a few tentative bites, then ravenously attacking the carcass. It was as satisfying to hear the quiet munch of their little teeth as it was to fill my own belly. When Boy Kitten raised his eyes and gazed at me, I felt sure I was seeing his gratitude.

Sated, I decided to explore along the base of the wall of rocks. As happened so often, we emerged from the scorched area into a sandy place with sparse, unburned grasses.

The kittens wanted to nap and I tolerantly let them climb on top of each other at the base of the rocks. Sniffing around, I found a pool of water that was fed by a tiny stream coming from a crack between two boulders. There was barely space for me to squeeze past the boulders, but that's what I did, finding a small cave just past the entrance. Water dripped from a wall covered with black moss, the drops joining to form a small basin that flowed out between the two boulders and into the sun.

I turned and saw the kittens following me into the cave, concerned that I had left their side. When I curled up for a brief nap in a soft, sandy patch of earth, they came to me instantly, purring and rubbing their heads on me before they, too, began to slumber.

For the first time since their mother abandoned us, I felt that I was doing a good job of taking care of my kittens. I thought about

Big Kitten and anxiously hoped she wouldn't wind up like the cooked deer, trapped by fire.

It was day outside the cave when I awoke. The kittens were still asleep. I wandered out away from them and back down to the herd of burned deer. After eating a meal, I seized one of the large creatures with my jaws and pulled it, stepping backward. I couldn't drag it very far before the ache in my jaws forced me to take a moment to recover, but I kept at it, thinking that if I could draw it to our new den, it would entice the kittens to stay put for a time, and perhaps their mother could find us. Our place seemed safe for now, as I could smell no new smoke on the air.

As I was resting from my efforts, a motion caught my eye and I whirled.

Fox.

Twenty-one

The fox was staring at me with light-colored eyes, its sides heaving. I stared back. It opened its mouth and I braced myself for an unnerving scream, but the rows of wicked teeth were on silent display for only a moment before the jaws hinged shut. We kept our eyes locked on each other.

A growl stirred within me at this unexpected threat, and I gave it soft voice. I was larger—attacking me would not be wise. But desperate animals will make bad choices, so the fur was up on my back, my gaze unwavering.

I did not like foxes. They were feral, with fierce fangs, and not friendly to dogs or humans. I had chased a few and they were nimble as they fled, but I never really wanted to catch one, not the way I lusted to catch a squirrel. I did not wish to find out what a fox's bite might do to my nose.

This fox could harm the kittens and would see them as prey. Though they were nearly the size of the fox, Boy Kitten and Girl Kitten still moved through the world with the vulnerable innocence of the very young. They needed my protection. If that meant engaging this fox in battle, I would do it without hesitation.

Yet even as I girded for a clash, I reconsidered. I could smell the fox now, and I could sense that it was terrified of me, and that it was starving. The corpse I was dragging lured it forward even as its fear of me held it back. It didn't know what to do: take on a larger foe in hopes of food, or withdraw without trying to steal a meal?

We were still staring at each other, the fox and I. Though not a dog, the small predator before me was clearly communicating a real desperation. Especially since I had recently eaten, I was much stronger, yet it still was challenging me because I had food. I felt the tension leave me, my back fur relaxing from its upright ridge. This creature, I realized, wasn't evil; it was just trying to survive in a world gone mad with fire.

The meal the fox so frantically coveted was on the ground between us. I backed away, offering the burned deer. The famished creature approached cautiously, timidly, flinching if I so much as moved. With its eyes on me, it lowered its head and urgently fed on the carcass. I watched and did nothing.

Having spent many days eating with the relatively dainty kittens, I was struck by the forcefulness with which the animal before me dove into its meal. A fox, I realized, was more like a dog than a cat, despite its ears and cat-like body. Still, I had never seen a fox on a leash. I could only assume that they envied dogs for our connection to people.

The fox managed to separate a hunk of leg from the carcass and, with a last look at me, scampered off with it.

I tracked the small predator by its scent; when I was satisfied that it had gone far enough away, I relaxed.

Evening was approaching, and the cubs would soon be stirring. I bent to continue the work of dragging the burned carcass and suddenly smelled the kittens. I looked up and saw them approaching at a run. I was not able to suppress a wag at the joyous manner in which they were scampering toward me. I was glad, though, that they hadn't found me when I was face-to-face with a predator.

They sniffed me and the deer and, when I lowered my mouth and put my jaws on it and began dragging the deer, they watched alertly, eyes bright with interest.

Before long, Girl Kitten reached a decision and darted forward, pouncing and seizing the deer's body with her teeth. She began backing away, joining me in lugging the food toward the den. Hesitantly, Boy Kitten followed his sister's example. Between the three of us, we were able to make good progress, and soon we were there at the mouth of the cave. We managed to wrestle the deer into the den, and I watched contentedly as Girl Kitten threw sand and dirt over it while Boy Kitten observed as if learning a lesson. Then they bent their heads together to lap at the water pooling from the drips trickling down the moss wall.

I knew now that I had found a safe place to await Big Kitten's return. The two of them would not be leaving this food supply until it was gone. They would rest and feed and play, never straying too far. It was how their mother had behaved when she was their age.

So, I had created an opportunity to try to range farther away and pick up Big Kitten's scent without worrying about my kittens.

I set out to do exactly that the next morning. I left behind the familiar smells of the territory around the den and crested a rocky ridge and started downhill through loose rocks to a stand of trees well below me. I was feeling happy. My stomach was full and my cat family was safe in the den. We might remain here until we had fully regained our strength, and then, with or without Big Kitten, we would resume our trek to Lucas, whom I could sense was now at a considerable distance—the fires were closer than he was, so I would need to be careful when we were back on the trail.

I indulged my nose when I picked up traces of rabbit, though I didn't find one. A small patch of unburned grass and flowers attracted me for the sheer joy of the fresh, moist dirt. A large shadow flickered past and I peered up at an enormous bird clutching a small rodent in its talons. The mountain creatures were already recovering from the trauma of the fire.

I was midway down the hill when an updraft brought me the unmistakable smell of canine. Not dog, though. Not any dog-like creature I'd ever encountered. I slowed, concentrating, peering into the wooded area below me. When I saw a shadow flit between trees, I was startled. I had learned that the animals I considered to be small, bad dogs were called coyotes, and they were feral and they would hunt me, but they were small, smaller than I. Only as a pack would they be a threat. But these hunters carried a different scent, and from brief glimpses, I could see they were larger than I was.

They weren't dogs, but whatever they were, I could see several of them. I wasn't sure if they had detected my presence. I needed to get a good head start back to the den if they had.

I turned around and was shocked to see Boy Kitten and Girl Kitten romping down the slope toward me, as if we were out for a neighborhood walk with Lucas.

I panicked. Surely the predators in the woods would see these small cubs as an uncomplicated meal. I didn't dare turn to see if they were coming up the hill at us. I wanted to bark, wanted to warn the kittens of the danger, but I kept silent, hoping we had not been spotted. Panting, I dashed up to the kittens and, to their astonishment, ran right past them toward the den. I looked over my shoulder and saw them racing after me, clearly sensing my urgency, if not the threat we faced.

We had covered most of the ground back to our cave when I sensed that the big hunters had grown near. I glanced back and saw them, pursuing us steadily. They were cloaked in light bushy fur, with bright, dark eyes atop long snouts, and tails that were not wagging. They were chasing us with deliberate and deadly intent.

Any one of those animals would be a formidable opponent. A pack of them would tear me and my kittens to pieces. I pictured it, how they would move to encircle us, falling on me in numbers while the kittens were easily picked off and carried away. The last thing I would hear would be Boy Kitten and Girl Kitten's frightened cries.

To protect them I needed to divert the attack toward me, give the cubs time to escape. I lagged slightly, ignoring my rising terror. The cubs did not pause to see why I had slowed, but continued to flee toward the den. My fear had somehow communicated to them the urgent need to make themselves safe.

I sensed the predators gaining ground. They were not only larger, they were faster. They were going to catch me.

Ahead was our den. I saw Girl Kitten slip into the crack, followed by her brother. Panting, I put on a burst of speed. I knew the pursuing predators were coming closer and closer. Now I could not only smell them, but also hear them. I could *feel* them, right there, and it wasn't until I reached the crack in the rocks that I glanced back and saw that I was mere steps ahead of the closest predator.

It was a female, clear determination written in her gaze. She hesitated, though, at the entrance to the cave, which gave me an opportunity to slide into the narrowest part of the passage and turn around.

My lungs heaving, I growled.

The female was joined by the rest of her pack and they milled about outside, taking turns peering through the crack into the dark cave. I had no doubt they could smell us. Certainly, they could hear me. I didn't bark, I just kept my growl low and continuous, my lips drawn back from my teeth.

Behind me, the kittens bobbed their heads and sniffed each other anxiously. They saw the danger now.

The big canines probably could squeeze in here, but there was no room for them to maneuver, so they would not be able to attack as a pack. It would cost the first one dearly to try to take me on face-to-face, wedged between boulders, with nowhere and no way to turn. And whatever damage I inflicted on the first one would be a lesson to the next.

Try to come in here and you will learn what a dog's teeth can do to your snout.

Whatever happened, whatever I had to do, I would protect the kittens.

When I nuzzled Boy Kitten, I could feel his heart racing inside his rib cage. Whenever I moved, the cubs darted to a new position, always directly behind me.

The big female hunter put her cold eye to the tight entrance. I eased forward, showing her my fangs. She wanted my cubs. I would not let her have them.

I was no longer afraid.

That night, the predators vented their frustrations in a mournful wail. The sound of it was chilling and unlike anything I could remember hearing before. It rose up into the night sky, and not long after I heard an answering howl from somewhere far in the distance.

We had food, we had water dripping down off the moss, and I was determined we would not leave the cave until Big Kitten returned.

The next morning, the sharp, oily tang of the hunter canines was gone from the air. I cautiously emerged into the sun, suspiciously peering around, but I did not see our would-be killers. I could smell where they'd spent the night, huddled right here, hoping I would come out and lead my kittens to them, but they'd grown impatient. Surely there were easier meals to be had than one they could reach only by fighting their way through a narrow crack in the rock.

To be safe, I remained inside with the cubs that day and that night, restlessly sniffing for the scent of the predator pack. If I concentrated, a faint trace came to me, but it was like so many other odors drifting on the air, thin and distant, never strong enough to indicate threat.

When I decided it was safe, we emerged into the fading light of a sunset. The kittens and I spent the rest of the daylight dragging the final carcass from the burned-out area of the woods, across the charred ground back to the den. As we did so, one of the tall trees suddenly snapped at the base and fell to the ground with such a roar that the two kittens fled in terror. I watched them, thinking their reaction was silly. It was just, after all, a big stick.

Eventually they returned to me, led, of course, by Girl Kitten. The three of us worked together and managed to get that deer all the way back to the cave.

Now, I knew I could leave the kittens here and they would remain safe, watered, and well-fed for many days.

It was a good den. The tiny stream was enough water, especially where it pooled.

I resolved that I would range farther to see if there was any trace of their mother on the wind. With her hunting at night, we would have food to keep us strong while we did Go Home to Lucas. But I did not know if Big Kitten was even still alive.

I left with the sunrise and made steady progress, keeping the fire to one side as a frame of reference. I mostly followed trails, which made the journey easier.

No sign of Big Kitten. No trace at all. I lifted my nose and inhaled the air, concentrating, separating out all the odors, searching for hers.

And then, because I was so focused on finding individual threads in the vast jumble of smells that were the mountains in the summer, I was jolted by the faintest whiff of a familiar scent.

I knew where I was.

Twenty-two

Every dog carries a unique scent, just like people. And, again like people, some dogs smell nicer than others. (Dogs who've just had a bath smell the worst.) When I know a dog well, I can remember their scent without having to use my nose. I'll find it in my dreams, and meet other canines on walks with similar bouquets that remind me of the original dog. So, when the wind brings me even the faintest trace of an old friend, I know exactly who it is.

Several winters ago, when I was making my way back to Lucas through these same mountains, I was separated from Big Kitten and met a big, shaggy dog named Dutch. For a time, I lived with Dutch and a man named Gavin and another man named Taylor. Precisely how this happened was something of a mystery to me, because people decide where dogs live, and where they walk, and what they eat. One moment I was doing Go Home to Lucas, and the next there was a leash on my collar and I was with Gavin and Taylor and Dutch. I soon came to understand that both Dutch and I were new to the two men, because we both laid down fresh dog scents when we first arrived. (Astoundingly, Gavin and Taylor did not already have a dog!)

A good dog obeys kind people, so I felt guilty that, despite the affection lavished on me by the two men, I was always looking to escape and get back to doing Go Home. Dutch, on the other hand, loved Gavin and Taylor, Gavin especially, and accepted them as his pack. Which was why Dutch was so surprised when I seized my first opportunity to leave and head back into the mountains.

Dutch followed for a time when I departed, because we were a pack, but eventually he broke off to return to his new home. He did not know about Lucas, and there was no way for me to explain. But I never forgot the big, shaggy dog or the two men with the tender hearts who took me in and gave me human love and a warm bed to lie in.

It was Dutch's smell coming to me now, as clearly and uniquely him as any other canine I'd ever been acquainted with.

Even better, his scent was recent. It was on the air and not drifting up from the ground. Dutch was not nearby, but he was out there, and I was instantly consumed with a need to find him. I pictured jumping on his back and wrestling with him and, in that moment, there was simply no urge more important.

I felt the tug of the kittens I'd left behind. I had tied myself to them with an invisible leash. But they had food and water and a defensible den—they would be safe for a time. So I dashed straight toward the source of that wonderful canine bouquet.

Before long, other familiar smells were calling to me. I had been on this trail before! Soon, I lunged across a small stream I remembered wading with Dutch. Now I was panting as much from excitement as exertion. If I was tracking Dutch, I was also tracking Gavin and Taylor. When dogs live with people who love them it makes for a bond never broken. Dogs never stop loving the humans who have taken care of them, even if they wind up living with someone else.

Next came a gravel road running in a crooked line across the landscape. I had walked this road, leashed to Gavin and Taylor. I sniffed the air, then followed a sharp smell. Dutch had recently lifted his leg on a rock, which I stopped and examined carefully. I could tell he frequently marked this rock, though to me there was nothing special about it. My trot became a headlong sprint, ignoring all protests from my tired muscles.

This whole area was marvelously unburned. Leaves were out and lush, grasses hummed with small bugs, and an occasional larger-animal scent reached out to me from the woods. I turned confidently up a rutted driveway, crested a small rise, and there it stood before me: one of the two houses in which Gavin and Taylor lived with Dutch.

Their other house was far away, down a lengthy stretch of pavement that had hummed under our tires. Gavin and Taylor called that place "home" and this place "the cabin." As I approached, I could tell that the wooden fence had been freshly rebuilt in the backyard, its scent strong with the tang of new lumber. I could also tell that the two men and my old friend Dutch were all inside the cabin.

I joyfully mounted the front steps, clawed at the front door, and barked impatiently for someone to open it.

My summons was immediately answered by a reply bark from Dutch. He did not know who it was, but he recognized another dog when he heard one, and was letting everyone in the house know there was a trespasser on the front porch.

I could sense him on the other side of the door. His nose was pressed to the crack at the bottom, and he was inhaling in great, shuddering gusts. When he whined, I knew he'd recognized me.

"Okay, hang on," grumbled a familiar voice.

Gavin opened the door and I wanted to greet him joyously, but Dutch lunged out, whining, and immediately tried to climb on my back. He was as huge as I remembered, so much heavier and stronger than I that he knocked me over. I leapt up and spun around, play-bowed, and then managed to dodge his affections long enough to get to Gavin.

Gavin's eyes were wide and his mouth open. He was staring at me as I went to him and rose up and put my paws up on his chest. I wagged and licked and ignored Dutch, who was prancing around, crashing into me, wanting to play.

"Bella?" Gavin blurted in disbelief. "Bella? Bella! You came home?" He turned and looked into the house. "It's Bella! Oh my God, Taylor, she's here. Bella came back home!"

Because I was on my hind legs, Dutch joined me and Gavin staggered under the combined weight of our front paws, falling back into the house and landing on his butt. I smelled and then saw Taylor stepping calmly around the corner. He held a cloth in one hand and a glass in the other. "Are you sure?"

"Am I sure?" Gavin answered, a burbling laugh in his voice. "Am I sure? Look at her! It's Bella!"

Gavin remained sprawled on the floor. I tried to reach his widespread arms, longing for his embrace, but Dutch muscled me out of the way to take the hug for his own.

Dutch was always Gavin's dog.

I turned and trotted over to Taylor, who squatted and reached out a hand for me to sniff. Taylor's hands were dark and his hair was gone from the top of his head. He had a bright smile and a friendly, deep voice. Taylor's unflappable approach to things had always struck me as being more like my boy Lucas than Gavin, but for some unknown reason, Lucas and Taylor were not yet friends.

"Are you Bella?" he whispered to me.

I wagged and licked that hand. I was so happy to see him again, and to hear him say my name.

"How do we know this is the same dog?"

"Bella!" Gavin called sharply. "Come to your daddy!"

I knew "Come" and went over to Gavin.

Taylor's knees produced a snapping sound as he stood back up. He cocked an eye at Gavin. "Daddy?" he repeated.

"Can't you see? She got lost but made her way back to us," he gushed. "Oh Dutch, you are so happy to see your sister. The family's back together!"

Taylor nodded. "Sure. The family."

"This is the happiest day of my life. Bella, want a treat?" Still sitting on the floor, Gavin reached into his pocket. Dutch and I both snapped to attention. He brought out a chicken morsel and fed one to each of us. Dutch swallowed his without seeming to chew, but the wonderful flavor of that chicken deserved some crunching, in my opinion, and I took my time.

"What's it say on her collar?" Taylor asked after a moment. "On the tag."

Gavin reached out and snagged my collar. "It says Bella, of course," he responded triumphantly.

Taylor nodded. "Mm-hmm. Does it say anything else?"

Gavin fumbled with my collar some more. Something happened then, a settling of his shoulders and a slight whiff of sadness. Dutch leaned forward and gave a comforting lick to Gavin's face. "It's got a name and a phone number here. Lucas Ray," he admitted reluctantly. "Denver area code."

"Ah," Taylor replied knowingly.

"We're pretty far from Denver." Gavin struggled to his feet, pushing Dutch away.

I am bigger than most dogs, but Dutch is broader and has huge forelimbs and a lot of bushy fur. His nose doesn't stick out as far as mine, but his muzzle is far thicker below his black eyes. I speculated momentarily that if Dutch wanted to keep Gavin pinned to the floor, Taylor would have to come over to help him up.

"Far from Denver," Taylor prompted. "And?"

"You know what, Taylor? Our dog finally returned home. Remember how heartbroken we were when we lost her? How hard we searched? Before you start looking for the dark cloud, can't we just take a moment to be happy?"

Taylor threw up his hands. "I'm not saying we can't be *happy*. I'm glad to see her, too. But she belongs to this Ray guy. Probably belonged to him when she first met us."

Gavin shook his head. "She was *starving* when she met us. Remember? She looked worse than she does now, even. If she was living with the Ray family, they weren't feeding her. Someone like that doesn't deserve a dog. You said so yourself."

"I didn't say that," Taylor responded. "When did I ever say that?"

"What matters is that Bella is home and we need to feed her dinner."

Dutch and I looked up sharply and with approval at that word.

"Okay," Taylor agreed. "Then what?"

"Then we should celebrate. Open a bottle of champagne."

Taylor grinned. "I'm okay with the champagne part. But then we should call the phone number on her collar and see what the story is. Right? You're not saying we shouldn't call."

"Well, first, let's feed her," Gavin said stubbornly. "She's almost as skinny as she was when we first found her. Because obviously this Ray guy isn't taking good care of her."

"I do get that's your point, Gavin."

Dutch and I were each given bowls of food. I could tell by the less-than-frantic way Dutch went after his meal that he had been fed recently, but for me, this was the first real dog meal in a long time. Somehow, a bowl of food laid down by a person's loving hands tastes better than even a wild deer that has been cooked in fire.

After we had eaten, Gavin let us go out in the fenced-in yard. Dutch marked, lifting first one back leg and then the other, and I sniffed carefully at his distinctive smell. I needed to squat as well, and then we both turned and trotted back to the sliding glass doors, just as we had done many times before.

Though it was wonderful to be out in the yard with Dutch, the excitement and agitation of the men compelled us to run back inside and be with them.

"All right," Taylor declared. "Let's call Lucas Ray."

Twenty-three

utch and I enthusiastically tagged behind Gavin and Taylor as they made their way to their table and eased into chairs. We did Sit, anticipating that plates of people food would appear, but the only thing between the two men was a phone. Dutch glanced at me to see if I understood what was happening, then snapped his attention to Gavin, sensing the same tension from him that I was. As usual, Taylor seemed calmer. Gavin touched his phone, and then an odd noise filled the air.

I heard what sounded a little like a human voice. *"Hello?"*

Taylor and Gavin looked at each other and Taylor leaned forward and cleared his throat. "Hi. We're looking for Lucas Ray. Is he there?"

More than once, they had said the name "Lucas," which puzzled me because there was no sign of Lucas anywhere. Not painted into the dusty smells in the corners, not embedded in the rug or the furniture, and certainly not on the air.

"I'm Dr. Ray, may I ask who's calling, please?"

"My name is Taylor," Taylor replied hesitantly. "Taylor Patrone."

Gavin leaned forward. "And I'm Gavin Williams. We have you on speaker."

"Okay. . . ."

There was a short silence. Taylor nodded at Gavin, who nodded back and leaned forward again. "We're wondering, Dr. Ray. Do you have a dog named Bella?"

"Yes! She got lost in the mountains. We were separated by the fire. Did you find her? I mean, do you have my dog or did you, God, did you just find her collar?"

"Uh . . . ," Gavin started. He looked up helplessly at Taylor.

"So, perhaps you could tell us a little bit of how Bella came to be in your possession," Taylor suggested.

There was a pause. "My possession. I guess I don't see how that's even relevant."

"Humor us?"

"Okay. . . . Sure, if that helps. I adopted Bella when she was a puppy. She lived across the street from us under an abandoned house with a bunch of feral cats. When she was not very old, I sent her to friends outside of Durango, down south. Do you know the area?"

Both men said, "Mm-hmm."

Dutch was still doing an admirable Sit, but I was growing less optimistic. Sometimes people will gather at a table, but that doesn't always mean they're planning to eat.

"Pretty place," Taylor observed. "Right on that river, there."

"Fort Lewis College," Gavin added.

"Sure, right. I guess my point is that it's practically New Mexico. It's a long way. But I had no choice. Bella was banned from living in Denver for being a pit bull. They had breed-discriminatory legislation, even though everyone hated it. The city council overturned it, but the mayor vetoed it. He's not a real bright guy. So the people petitioned to put the measure on the ballot and overwhelmingly overturned the pit bull ban."

Gavin reacted instantly. "Oh!" He grinned at Taylor. "Okay, then. See, this is not a pit bull. She has brown and tan markings. And the most beautiful brown eyes. You look at them, you just melt."

Taylor smiled and shook his head.

"Right, that's the thing. In Denver, a dog didn't used to have to be a pit bull to be classified as one. It's really strange, but it just took like, a vote by Animal Control and then no matter what breed your *dog actually was, it was condemned. They'd pick it up and declare it a pit bull, you'd pay a fine and they'd let you have your dog back. If they caught her a second time, they'd euthanize her. It was insane. That's why my wife and I moved to Golden, where they've never had a breed ban. Before we did, though, we sent Bella away, and one day she jumped the fence to make her way back to us."*

Dutch glanced at me, finally realizing that even this pair of masterful Sits wasn't getting us any treats. I flopped down on the floor, giving up.

I sleepily thought about the kittens. Should I lead them here, to be with Gavin and Taylor and Dutch? No, I decided, I would have one more dinner in this house and then return to the den and continue to do Go Home to Lucas.

"From Durango? On foot?" Taylor asked dubiously.

"I know. When she showed up . . . you can imagine what that was like. It was a miraculous day. So . . . I think you can understand why I am pretty tense here. It sounds like you've found Bella. Do you have her?"

The phone was making sounds that were a lot like my name. I still was uninterested in whatever that was about. Dutch agreed and joined me, sprawling on the floor.

Taylor was regarding Gavin with a sad smile. Gavin nodded reluctantly. "I guess so. It sure sounds like your dog, anyway."

"Oh my God! That's great! This is the best news I've ever had. You have no idea what we've been going through. I missed a lot of work because of the fire, so I've had to pull double shifts, but every single chance we've had, I've gone up with my wife looking for her. We've put up all these posters. Did you see them? Olivia says there's not a telephone pole in Colorado without Bella's picture on it."

"Hang on a sec," Taylor said. He picked up the phone and turned toward us.

Dutch and I both raised our heads, but then dropped them when he swiveled back to continue to sit pointlessly at the table. "I'm sending you a picture of the dog right now."

"Okay, let me look. That's her! Man, you have no idea how happy this makes me. I'm so glad you found Bella."

Taylor nodded. "So, my husband is a novelist and I think he wants to tell you a story. He has this look that he gets."

"Right, sure, of course."

Gavin cleared his throat. "We found Bella in the mountains. This was, gosh, four years ago? She was trying to dig a guy out of the snow. He'd been buried in an avalanche. There were two dogs, one named Dutch and yours. Bella didn't have a collar back then, so we didn't know her name. Dutch was easy, it was on his tag."

Dutch perked up at his name, then put his head back down with a weary sigh.

"So, we helped the guy who was trapped in the avalanche. We figured because, you know, both dogs were there digging, that they must belong to him. He had some kind of crazy name."

"Kurch," Taylor supplied helpfully.

"Yeah, Kurch. Like 'church' with a hard K. He was a real . . . let's just say he was not a nice person."

"Putting it mildly," Taylor observed.

"Did he hurt the dogs or something?"

Gavin shook his head. "No. Well, kind of. He obviously didn't know who Bella was, but he didn't want Dutch. I mean here we are with his dog, in his bedroom, and he's lying there in a cast, and all he's doing is swearing at Dutch, who was just so happy to see his person. You know? Dutch didn't understand what was going on, but the guy wouldn't take his own dog back. It was . . . it was one of the most awful things I've ever seen."

Now Dutch and I were both staring at Gavin because his voice had become tight with sadness. Taylor reached his hand across the table and put it on Gavin's.

Gavin tremulously smiled at Taylor. "Anyway. So then we had Dutch, who's this gigantic Bernese, and your dog, who isn't exactly tiny."

"I wanted a cat," Taylor observed dryly. "We guessed she was called Bella because it was the only name she reacted positively to. We tried everything, even 'Blanche.'"

"Blanche was my mother's dog's name," Gavin explained, "and Taylor seems to think that's the most offensive thing that has ever been uttered by a human being before."

Taylor chuckled. "You need to meet Gavin's mother."

"Anyway," Gavin continued, "Bella stayed with us that winter, but in the spring, when we came back up to the cabin, we let the dogs run off leash, and that was the last time we saw her."

"By 'her' he means Bella," Taylor elaborated. "Not Gavin's mother. We've seen plenty of Gavin's mother."

Gavin rolled his eyes. "Anyway, we did the same thing you're talking about. Put up posters and posted to social media. We assumed the worst had happened to her, got attacked by a mountain lion or something, until today, when Bella just shows up out of nowhere. She's lying here now as if she never left."

Dutch cut his eyes in my direction to check my reaction to hearing my name spoken so much, but I was drowsy and didn't feel like moving.

"Well that's it, then. Bella was missing for a few years. She ran off from that family all the way down by Durango, and I don't know how she did it, but she found her way back to me. By then I'd moved to Golden, but I still worked in Denver. It must have been with the help of people like you that she survived. I am so grateful. Bella is the most important thing in my life, except for my wife, Olivia."

There was a short silence. Dutch rolled onto his side, and it took no effort at all for me to slide over and put my head on his chest, where I had laid it so many times in the past.

Gavin sighed. "Well, I guess that means that you should come get your dog."

"Okay, yes, of course. Could I ask if maybe you could watch

her for a couple of days? I've got to arrange my schedule to get a day off. Where are you, anyway?"

"Well," Taylor answered, "we're at our cabin in the mountains right now, near Elk Knob Peak outside of Buford."

"What? Buford? I've always wanted to go Jeeping up around Elk Knob. Bella's there? She made her way on foot?"

"I guess. She just showed up," Gavin replied.

"Wow. That's amazing. We were in Summit County camping, and then the fire came, and we fled as far as Paraiso. That was the last time I saw her. You had any fires there in Buford?"

Dutch and I glanced up because Taylor and Gavin were exchanging tense looks.

"Uh," Gavin answered, "not yet. But that's one of the reasons we're here, to grab anything we'd hate to lose. They're saying the fire's not contained enough to know for sure if it's coming this way or not."

Taylor added, "But we're headed back home to Glenwood Springs the day after tomorrow."

"I just can't wrap my brain around a time line that takes my dog from outside Durango to Glenwood Springs to Denver."

"Well," Gavin replied, "she's a very special dog, our Bella."

"That she is. Hey, speaking of that, there's something you can do. Bella loves when you take a small chunk of cheese and ask her, 'Bella, would you like a t-i-i-iny piece of cheese?' She'll go absolutely hypnotized. Then you let her have it and she'll act like you gave her the greatest gift ever."

Gavin smiled. "We'll for sure do that. All right then. Bye, Dr. Ray."

"Call me Lucas, please. I'll call when I know I can come get her. Probably day after tomorrow."

"Sounds great," Gavin agreed.

Taylor got up, put a hand on Gavin's shoulder, and then went into the kitchen. "I think the champagne's still a good idea, so let me fix you something to eat," he suggested. "And I'll let the term 'our Bella' go by without comment."

"Yeah, well, you actually didn't let it go without comment," Gavin said with a grin. He leaned down and I knew he wanted to touch me so I sat up. He grabbed my head in his hands and leaned forward and looked into my eyes. "You're going to go home in a few days, Bella."

I wagged at the tender voice, which held a note of sadness. I thought I knew why—Gavin loved me, but he knew I always remained with him only briefly before resuming my Go Home to Lucas, this time with two kittens in tow. I would be sad to part with this pack, but I was the mother cat to Boy Kitten and Girl Kitten.

"What is it, Gavin?" Taylor asked softly.

There was a long silence.

"I was just thinking, when Bella got lost—not the first time, but now, today—she came to us. She barked at our door. Because she trusts us."

Taylor shrugged. "I suppose." There was another long silence. "You have something on your mind. Are you regretting that we called Lucas Ray? I mean, you know we had to."

I twitched an ear at the name of my boy. I had long learned, though, that people will say all sorts of things that don't necessarily have anything to do with dogs.

"Oh, not really," Gavin replied. "That's not it."

"Not . . . really?" Taylor repeated dubiously.

"I don't know, it's just that when I saw her, I felt like our family was back together again."

"You seemed pretty happy," Taylor admitted. "And then it turns out Bella already has a family." There was another long pause. "Are you thinking you want to get another dog, maybe?" Taylor probed. "Someone to be a friend for Dutch?"

Dutch lifted his head momentarily when he heard his name.

Gavin shook his head. "No, it's just that I realized when we were all together, you know, before we made the phone call, that I'm a good dog daddy."

"That you are."

"And you are too, Taylor," Gavin continued. "Maybe I get a little more emotional than you do, but kids need that steady hand."

"Kids."

"What?"

"You said kids."

Gavin was silent.

Taylor sighed. "What are we really saying here, Gavin?"

Twenty-four

Dutch and I both watched alertly as Taylor ambled over to the refrigerator, and our noses twitched as he produced rustling sounds in there. *Bacon, perhaps?* Then we *really* reacted when Taylor returned to the table and handed Gavin something we both recognized. *Cheese!*

We scrambled into best-behavior-style Sit. Taylor bent toward Dutch with a hand extended, while Gavin smiled at me. "Bella? You want a t-i-i-iny piece of cheese?"

I was being so good I was trembling with the effort. I licked my lips, scarcely breathing. When that chunk of deliciousness was within reach, I lifted it ever so delicately from between his fingers. Dutch slurped his own morsel with a great deal of noise, glancing over at Gavin as if expecting to share *my* treats, which I was not about to allow.

I was not surprised that Gavin knew about *t-i-i-iny piece of cheese*. Humans know everything.

Taylor and Gavin straightened up and away from us, but Dutch and I remained in Sit position because the tantalizing redolence of that cheese still danced in the room.

"So. Kids," Taylor prodded.

"You never said anything about a cat."

Taylor arched his eyebrows. "So, the author dissembles on the question."

Gavin chuckled and nodded. "Well, okay. Yeah, kids, like we talked about before."

"Talked about. Yes, and I said that if you really wanted that, I would never deny you the experience of being a father. And you've always said you didn't think you had it in you. What's changed?"

Gavin stood up and went into the kitchen and poured himself something. Dutch and I both tracked his motions, though nothing was pulled out of the refrigerator. He didn't even reach for the handle! If I could open a refrigerator, I'd sit there and stare into it all day.

"Well, I kind of was following the thread that you were talking about." Gavin handed Taylor a glass. "That maybe we should adopt another dog, so Dutch would have someone to play with. There are so many dogs out there who are lost and need families. We could get any breed we want. I mean, a sister for a Bernese would probably not be a Maltese or a Papillon, but maybe a dog the size of Bella. And then I started thinking about how these huge dogs like Dutch don't live all that long, so would we get one his age? Or a puppy? And then I realized, that no matter what the age, we would wind up burying both of them, someday. And I haven't been through something like that since childhood, when Blanche died."

"I still have trouble processing the name Blanche."

Gavin laughed softly.

"Okay," Taylor prompted. "If we got another dog, we'd outlive it. And?"

Gavin agitatedly turned away and sat down in the living room and Dutch struggled to his feet. Sensing the same disquiet that I detected, he put his head in Gavin's lap. Taylor left the table and joined Gavin in front of the fireplace. Taylor put a hand on Gavin, so I reluctantly left the kitchen table and all its possibilities to join them.

"Gavin. You're crying. Tell me what's going on."

Gavin wiped his eyes. "So, say we adopt another dog. And another, sure. Or even a cat. But then I started thinking, there are also children out there who are abandoned. Children who could use a pair of daddies. And I'm not just being selfish. It isn't only that our kids would bury us instead of the other way around, it's that we would make as big a difference in their lives as we have for Dutch, and especially as we've done for Bella."

"I see." Taylor nodded.

"I got to say, for me to make a statement like what I just said, and for you to say 'I see,' makes me feel like this whole time when you've been saying we could adopt kids if I wanted, that what you were really saying was you knew that I'd never want to," Gavin complained.

"How is that fair?" Taylor objected. "I've always meant it. I just didn't know you were having these feelings."

"Okay."

"It's a huge step, Gavin."

"Bella came back and I thought our family was back together again, but she has to leave, and her leaving makes me want what we don't truly have. A real family, with children. Is that so wrong?"

Taylor pulled in a deep, thoughtful breath. "I have to admit, when you first said Bella was home and I saw her, I was so happy."

Gavin raised his eyebrows. "Right? Something about having her walk in that door changed everything."

"Maybe not everything. But I see your point. Two dogs and suddenly we're not just a married couple with a pet."

"We're a family," Gavin finished for him.

There was a long silence. Dutch lifted his head and gazed up at Gavin, who no longer seemed sad.

"So, would being a human daddy mean you could no longer be a dog daddy?" Taylor asked lightly.

"Oh, no, I will always be a dog daddy."

I was hearing the word 'dog' a lot, but with no food out in the open and the cheese gone from everyone's fingers, I simply couldn't maintain my focus on the people. I sprawled on the floor and closed my eyes.

Next, I believed, Gavin and Taylor would take us for a quick walk in the trees. While Dutch lifted his leg, I would head out into the night and get back to the kittens.

Except that didn't happen. We were allowed out into the fenced-in backyard, and then we returned through the sliders.

Though it felt good to be sleeping with Dutch, I was disturbed by the implications of my situation, especially the next morning, when Gavin and Taylor took us for a walk *on leashes,* and then returned us to the backyard.

Gavin and Taylor were making no move to let me out so I could return to my duties as a mother cat. It was clear, suddenly and completely, that they intended to keep me at their home with Dutch.

I loved Dutch, I loved Gavin, and I loved Taylor. But I had to protect the kittens. I remembered the big predator canines circling outside the den. Would they show the same restraint if I weren't there and it was only the two cubs in the cave?

I was too agitated to lie down with Dutch while my kittens were defenseless without me.

I could still smell smoke, but it seemed far away. Also far were Boy Kitten and Girl Kitten—their scents weren't present on the wind at all, but I knew in what direction they lay. I needed to get back to them.

Gavin was gone most of the morning while I paced restlessly in the backyard. Dutch watched me lazily, seeming to understand my distress, if not its source. We both alerted, though, when we heard Gavin's vehicle pull up the driveway. Taylor slid the back door open for us so that we could bound inside and greet Gavin at the front door. I thought that would give me my chance to escape, but Gavin was carrying a big box that intimidated me and I did not seize the opportunity to dart between his legs. Taylor shut the door firmly behind him.

"Happy birthday!" Gavin announced.

"Well, it's not my birthday, that's one thing, and another is I have never before in my life asked you to get me a chainsaw. Is this about the neighbors? I know you don't like the guy's politics."

Grinning, Gavin set the box on the floor with a loud *thump*. Dutch and I both sniffed it curiously, but could detect nothing of note. He straightened. "Okay, I know they say the fire isn't likely to reach up here, but they've been wrong about it this whole time. *Nobody* thought copycats would keep setting new ones. According to the experts the one thing we need to do is cut down any trees that are up next to our house."

"The experts are not saying *we* need to cut down anything. They are saying the *experts* need to cut them down."

"Sure, great, but it could take weeks to get someone up here. They're pretty busy—I don't know if you've heard, but the whole state of Colorado is burning. So we've got that big dead ponderosa . . . that one *has* to come down. Then all those lodgepole pines on the south side are like a ladder coming up the mountain and directing the flames straight into the heart of our home."

"Spoken like a true author," Taylor observed dryly. "What you really mean is you thought this would be fun."

"Sure!" Gavin replied brightly.

Taylor smiled, shaking his head. "I don't want to be a lumberjack. I've never wanted to be a lumberjack. I don't like plaid. I don't know how to work a chainsaw. I don't even know which end you're supposed to hold."

"You're killing me. Which end." Gavin slapped the box. "How hard can it be? This baby is top-of-the-line. The guy at the hardware store told me we could cut down the whole rain forest with it."

"You meet the most interesting people in the hardware store. I wish you would never go again."

Gavin and Taylor exited out the back door together but left Dutch and me in the house. Dutch was anxious and cried a little bit. He jumped up on the couch and stared out the back window, watching as Gavin and Taylor opened the side gate and slid through. Dutch was a good dog to his people.

Dogs know that humans sometimes leave us by ourselves, which makes no sense—why go anywhere without a dog?

After a while, we heard what was to my ears a very familiar, harsh, mechanical snarl. I wondered if it meant that soon trees would be catching on fire. That would be bad and it reminded me yet again that I needed to get back to my kittens.

Now I was as anxious as Dutch.

Or did the loud noise, which I associated with Scott and Mack and Dave, mean *they* were coming? I raised my nose—no, they weren't here yet. But if they did arrive, would they take me back to Lucas? My thinking had been to lead the cubs to Lucas, not the other way around. How would I make my boy understand what we needed to do?

Dutch and I watched without any real comprehension as the big old tree next to the house suddenly shuddered and began moving. It was falling, just as trees had fallen when they had been burning. Dutch and I looked on in concern as it came down toward us, faster and faster, crushing through the wooden fence of the backyard and smashing with tremendous violence into the roof right over our heads. The whole house echoed with the impact. Broken glass flew everywhere. Dutch yelped and we scrambled to get away. Dust filled the air and we cowered, not comprehending any of this. *What was happening?*

"Dutch! Bella!" Gavin called urgently. The back gate burst open and he came running across the backyard to the sliders. He opened them with a *bang*. "Hey! Stay away from the glass! Come dogs, come!"

Dutch and I meekly obeyed, running to him with our tails and ears down. He clearly wanted us out in the backyard, so we went.

Once outside, we relaxed—the danger seemed to be indoors. Dutch lifted his leg as a way of returning to normal. I looked up as Taylor sadly shut the back gate behind him. He put his hands on his hips and shook his head. "Well, that was more fun than I would've thought."

Gavin seemed angry. "We did everything it said on the box. We cut it perfectly. It should have fallen the other way."

"Well, let's call the chainsaw company and complain. Maybe they'll fix the roof and the window and everything destroyed in the cabin, which looks to be our bedroom, at a minimum."

Inside smells were wafting out into the backyard.

Gavin stared mournfully at the tree as it lay in the crease it had created in the house. Both men seemed upset with what had just occurred, which led me to wonder why they had done it in the first place.

"We have to keep the dogs out here until we've cleaned up the broken glass."

Taylor shook his head. "No, I don't think so. I guess I'd rather go down and hang out with my lumberjack buddies at the bar. Throw darts and listen to Garth Brooks. While I'm gone, would you mind getting the tree out of the living room?"

"Okay, fine, I'm sorry!" Gavin replied testily. "I was just trying to do what they say to protect our home."

Taylor laughed. "Oh, you did an excellent job at that! No self-respecting fire is going to show up now. What would be the point? The place is already obliterated."

The two entered the house through the sliding door and closed it firmly in Dutch's face. My friend came over to me, nosing me and putting a playful paw upon my shoulder. Now that Gavin and Taylor were in the house and the machines were quiet and trees had stopped toppling over, he was a much happier dog.

I examined the big tree, looking at how it had plunged through the fence, smashing a whole section. Right where the fence and the tree met, the debris from the fence formed something of a step for me, and I cautiously ascended until I stood on the tree trunk. Big Kitten had taught me how to stride confidently on big, fallen trees. As if she were leading me now, I carefully walked along the trunk over the flattened fence, until I could leap down safely on the other side.

I was out.

I loved Gavin and Taylor and Dutch, but I could not stay here. I had to protect my kittens. As bad as I felt about leaving them alone, I would feel worse if I did not go back to my cat family and lead them to safety with my boy Lucas. And convincing Boy Kitten and Girl Kitten to follow me here would not be a good idea— Gavin and Taylor would simply shut the cubs in the house, taking them for walks on leashes, never letting any of us do Go Home.

I trotted briskly back the way I had come the day before, my nose leading me unerringly up into the mountains. I had not gone far before I heard an unmistakable sound behind me and turned to look over my shoulder.

Dutch was following me.

Twenty-five

I knew exactly how to retrace my steps back to the cubs, and did so at a rapid pace, driven by my worry. I pictured Girl Kitten growing impatient and leading her brother through the tight crack and out into the world. Would they try to find me? How long before some predator spotted them? I remembered the gigantic bird with a meal gripped in her sharp talons. Danger like that could descend from the sky without warning.

Dogs understand that sometimes they are running together, even if only one of them knows the destination. Dutch unquestioningly clung to my flank as I made my way uphill. After a time, he seemed to be lagging. I reluctantly slowed my own pace because we were a pack.

When I caught the first scent of the kittens, I worried they had, indeed, wandered out into the open.

Dutch was panting and probably a little confused. He was a big dog and the long run had been hard for him. I slowed as we approached the entrance to the cave, letting him catch up. He nosed me in concern. Both of us could smell that there were animals on the other side of the crack in the rocks, but only I knew that they were a pair of harmless kittens.

Dead animals emit a different odor from living ones. Carefully, I sorted the commingled scents in my nose.

They were alive.

I yipped softly, letting the cubs know I had returned. Within moments, Girl Kitten came springing through the narrow opening right at me, jumping up and seeking to wrestle the way I had taught her. Moments later, her brother joined the fray. Their play contained a certain urgency—they had clearly missed me.

Dutch's reaction was to shrink back when he saw the cats. I did not blame him. Though they were obviously kittens, they were unusually large. In fact, I've met many dogs smaller than these two cats. Dutch even growled a little, which halted their playful assault on him before they even launched it. They could tell that this dog was not friendly, not like me, their mother cat. They stared at him and Dutch stared back, the fur rising in a ridge behind his head.

I attempted to break the impasse by playfully pushing at Boy Kitten, but he remained fixated on the large canine in front of him, fascinated but also fearful. I turned my attention to Girl Kitten, who was far more willing to ignore what was, after all, just another dog. Dutch watched silently as I threw Girl Kitten on her back and nuzzled her. She wrapped her legs around my head, but her claws were safely sheathed.

There are some dogs who simply cannot resist fun play and I knew Dutch was one of these. His tail wagged as he watched us wrestle, an involuntary reaction. Soon he had tentatively joined us in the scrum. Boy Kitten backed away, but Girl Kitten jumped up at Dutch without hesitation, despite his intimidating size. I had demonstrated to both of them how to properly play with dogs, and Dutch quickly recognized that this was exactly what Girl Kitten was doing. Thankfully, he understood that there was nothing to fear from these babies.

I kept my eye on Boy Kitten, who was bobbing his head. Finally, he couldn't resist any longer, and when he joined in, we played until we all fell down in exhaustion.

I occasionally focused on Dutch, wondering if he was feeling the pull of Gavin and Taylor, if he now considered himself part of this strange pack. Would he stay with us or do his own version of Go Home?

Having accepted the new dog, the kittens would have tussled all day, but Dutch's head whipped around and I knew he had caught the odor of the cooked deer floating through the crack in the rocks. Understandably, he couldn't comprehend how the rocks were emitting meat smells. I led him into the space, wriggling through the tight turn just inside the entryway. For Dutch, this passage was particularly challenging, as his bulk nearly became stuck between the rock walls. But the smell of the meal lured him forward until, with a grunt, he was standing beside me in the cave, watching, probably perplexed, as I dug industriously at the sandy dirt where the deer was buried. Soon I had exposed a leg and Dutch lunged at it with considerable enthusiasm. That I was able to unearth such a large meal did not seem to surprise him— one of the things I liked most about Dutch was his complete willingness to accept anything that was happening.

The kittens decided it was mealtime and silently joined us, though they were less interested in eating than they were in watching Dutch consume his meal.

Dutch and I employed different approaches to eating. I would eat until I was full, and then maybe a little bit more. Dutch seemed as if he could keep eating as long as there was food. Eventually, though, he tired of it and left us to go outside to squat and then mark the rocks around us as his territory.

I think he was a little surprised that I didn't follow him, and eventually he returned to the den.

The sun was setting and I was weary, and Dutch watched in bafflement as I circled around and then sprawled out with my back against the wall. Then he seemed to decide this was what we were doing now, and collapsed with his head on my hip. The kittens joined us, purring. Though it was evening, normally the time of increased activity for them, they seemed exhausted.

There was too much kitten scent in the area outside the lair for me to tell whether the cubs had, as I feared, ventured outside in my absence. No matter, I was here now. And with Dutch by my side I was confident that if the large canine predators showed up again, they would be even more reluctant to attack us in our den.

I was conscious of Dutch's restlessness all through the night. He kept getting up, turning in circles, and lying back down. At one point, I think he made the decision to abandon us and this strange place, but after he slipped outside for just a bit, I smelled him returning and he squeezed back in with us.

The next morning, we fed and explored the ridgeline. I was feeling restless—knowing we would soon be back on the trail to Lucas. He would be so surprised to meet the cubs and Dutch!

I watched Dutch, who was as cheerful as ever despite being away from Gavin and Taylor. Did he now think of himself as a dog who slept in a cave with enormous kittens? Meanwhile, the cats were as approving of Dutch as if he were their father cat, though they never bothered to examine the places where Dutch lifted his leg. Cats don't always know the proper way to behave.

They did, however, know to follow their canine friends. I lifted my nose, focusing on feeling Lucas, and set off to find him.

We wandered down into the trees, pausing constantly because Dutch seemed determined to mark every single one. We had just come upon a small pond and were drinking when something hit me with the force of a slap. Dutch raised his head at precisely the same moment, though the kittens seemed entirely unfazed. A dank, feral, dangerous smell had reached us. Some sort of creature was nearby, something between the den and ourselves.

The kittens were oblivious, but Dutch and I immediately communicated our anxiety to each other by lolling out our tongues. Tension and fear arose in me. What we smelled now was an animal I had once sensed before. I was immediately taken back to a strange night, when fire danced in a black sky and I growled at an enormous beast standing in shallow water. This was not the same individual, but it was the same type of beast, and Dutch and I could tell it was a meat-eater.

Some thin, unburned trees lined the grassy area around the

pond. Dutch and I stood absolutely still, focused on the trees, waiting to see what would emerge. We both reacted with alarm when we saw a huge, lumbering creature come out of the woods. It was black and walking on all fours, kind of like a dog does, but when Girl Kitten scampered around, trying to induce me to chase her, the animal stood up on its rear legs and held its nose to the air. It was as tall as a man, broad and covered with coarse black fur. . . .

Bear. Lucas and Olivia had called the dangerous animal a bear. When it dropped back down and lowered its head, I knew it was coming for us.

It lumbered toward us slowly but with deadly intent. The kittens now saw the predator and instinctively gathered behind us.

It was too late to run. The bear was hunting the cubs and did not consider the two dogs shielding them any sort of threat.

Though there were only two of us in the pack, Dutch and I reacted with pack instincts. Dutch, his fur up and his teeth bared, seemed ready to do battle with the bear. He stalked off to the side while I planted myself directly in front of the cubs to protect them. We both growled loudly.

The bear slowed. It peeled its lips back in a snarl, and I saw that it had claws like a cat, like a Big Kitten cat, menacing and deadly. I had never been this close to such a powerful animal. I realized I was panting with fear, but Dutch had gone from being an affable, happy dog to one who was threatening a killer several times his size. I noted his technique as he stealthily worked his way around to flank the predator.

The bear ignored Dutch, and it and I both made the same calculation—that I was no match for this hulking threat. The great animal tensed, preparing for a charge.

I could smell hunger on its breath, see its eyes focusing on the cubs. It felt as if the carnivore were looking through me.

I changed that by snarling and barking as ferociously as I

could. I would *save* these kittens! I would stand here and keep them from being hurt.

The bear hesitated, startled by my viciousness. Dutch came up fast behind the creature in a silent rush and bit the thing on its back leg. The bear kicked him away and stood up on two legs, bellowing.

As it went after Dutch, I attacked, reaching it before it could reach Dutch, who scrambled desperately back. I closed my jaws on a leg and tumbled when the bear whirled back to face me. I scrabbled back as it raised its front paws, and as it was preparing to swipe at my face, Dutch went at it again from behind.

Astoundingly, Girl Kitten darted forward, claws out, lips pulled back in a spitting snarl. She stopped well short of the bear's reach but the distraction gave me time to slide to the side.

In a flash, Boy Kitten had joined her, two fanged mouths now hissing at the huge creature.

Surrounded by such a fierce pack, the bear halted its assault and glared at us. Dutch was barking, I was snarling, and the kittens had their ears back and were ready to fight for their lives. The bear gnashed his teeth at the air, teeth banging together, loops of saliva flying. It pounded the soil with its front claws in fury, then twisted quickly around to growl at Dutch, who was moving up from behind.

That was my opening. I leapt forward.

But the bear had had enough. With a few loud snorts, it abruptly turned and lumbered back into the woods, as if it had grown weary of us and could no longer be bothered. Dutch charged after it, but only for a few steps, withdrawing his pursuit when I didn't join him.

When he returned to me, wagging, Dutch was transformed back into the carefree canine I knew so well. I would not soon forget, though, the ferociousness with which he had gone after that bear.

Boy Kitten and Girl Kitten swarmed me, pushing against me, needing physical contact. Dutch lowered his immense head and they both rubbed against it, their chests rumbling.

When I was sure the danger had passed, I led Dutch and the kittens back to the den. I think we all took comfort from the sheltering cave and the meal we had after our encounter with that fierce creature. The den felt like home, and we needed to reassure ourselves that all was safe.

It was the middle of the day and the two kittens were ready to settle down for an afternoon snooze. Dutch watched them lying there, and I wondered if he was feeling what I was feeling: we were taking care of these kittens now. They were part of our pack. Instead of fleeing, they had stood with us when we confronted the bear.

But when Dutch lifted his head to stare at me for a moment, I knew that he had made a decision. He turned and squeezed through the passageway to the outside. I followed him and we stood under the sun in the grassy field. Dutch and I touched noses. I understood what was happening—we were saying goodbye, because Dutch needed to be with Gavin and Taylor. That was his home.

I would soon do Go Home to Lucas myself. That was where I belonged. But it wasn't as easy to get to him, to follow the pull of his invisible leash, as it would be for Dutch to return to his people.

For a long moment Dutch and I silently regarded each other. I think he was picturing being fed by his people, and how easily I had rejoined them after being gone so long. Why would I give that up for a couple of ridiculously large cats? But Dutch had never met Big Kitten and didn't understand.

At last, Dutch turned and trotted off back in the direction of Gavin and Taylor. When he reached the line of trees where he would disappear from sight, he turned to gaze back at me, his tail twitching just a little bit. His ears were down, his lips were loose; we shared a long stare.

It was how dogs say goodbye.

And then, as I watched, my friend and favorite member of my dog pack turned his head toward home, slipped into the woods, and vanished from sight.

Twenty-six

The fire was no longer everywhere, surrounding us, threatening at any moment to force us up against some rocks and cook us. I was so accustomed to its biting presence in my nostrils that the lessening of the peril led me to question whether it had gone away completely. It hadn't—a shift in the breeze, which had also weakened, gave me a sense of where trees were burning the hottest. Now the mountains around us were much like the forest of dead trees where we'd found the charred deer—different, altered, perhaps forever, but not as dangerous.

This meant I could stay on a course more or less straight to Lucas. Once I made this decision, I didn't hesitate, and set out just as the sun, an odd, flat disk in the hazy sky, rose above the sharp edge of the nearest peak. The cubs followed me unquestioningly, though I knew it made them uneasy to be out in daylight, particularly on trails trod by humans. I smelled almost no people now, though. The fire had forced them away in the same way it had separated me from my boy.

The kittens were strong and confident, their bellies full. When I glanced at them I saw no distress, just a singular trust in my leadership. If they wondered what had happened to the big shaggy dog who had helped save them, they gave no sign.

I loved Boy Kitten and Girl Kitten as surely as I loved their mother, as I loved Lucas. The fierce instinct to protect them from harm was as omnipresent as the smoke. I adored how, whenever

I paused to get a bearing on my boy's location, find the invisible leash, Girl Kitten would bat at me playfully, inviting me to give up the serious task of doing Go Home and frolic with her on the path. Moments later her brother would leap on her, and then the two of them would tussle together.

That first full day passed with no pause in our journey. My cubs were content to collapse into a deep sleep when I found a suitable den in the grasses. It pleased me to still catch a subtle trace of Dutch's scent on their fur. It left me with the feeling, as I slipped into slumber myself, that my good friend was with us still.

In my dreams, Dutch and I encountered a snarling, hulking monster in Gavin and Taylor's backyard, and held the creature at bay.

By remaining high up in the rocky, often treeless terrain, we were able to watch for predators, but I saw and smelled none; there was only the smoke, growing or weakening at the whim of the wind. Water, though, was unavailable along the ridges, and by the middle of the next day I reluctantly turned downhill, where my nose told me we would find something to drink.

The descent was easy, down a slope of rocks and plants. On one side, the fire had destroyed the vegetation and blackened the boulders; on the other side, it had shown mercy and the plants waved healthy branches in the gusts.

I smelled blood and, curious, halted at the base of a lone tree. There was nothing to see, yet the dirt at the roots was infused with the unmistakable odor of a fresh kill.

I looked up and was surprised to see one of those enormous hunter birds looking down from a high perch. It tilted its head and winked a cold eye at me. Its talons clutched both the top tree limb and a small prey animal of some kind. I wagged, unsure what I was seeing.

At my feet, the cubs, unaware of my reason for halting our descent, were pouncing on each other, rolling in the dirt.

The bird stabbed down with its sharp beak, tearing at its kill.

It was sloppy in its work, and a small piece of meat fell and landed nearly on top of Boy Kitten, who jerked back in surprise, rolling away.

Girl Kitten was first to realize what was happening—food from the sky!—and gobbled up the treat. Boy Kitten stared at her in amazement.

Untroubled by our presence at the base of its tree, the bird continued to feed. I wondered if it might drop another treat and did Sit to encourage this. The kittens remained unaware of what was happening above, but they weren't wrestling anymore. They were watching to see if I could produce another miraculous morsel.

They were soon rewarded. It was almost as if the hunter in the tree deliberately tossed down a chunk to land right between them. Again, it was Girl Kitten who got to it first. Boy Kitten gave me a hurt look, as if I were favoring his sister over him.

We remained at the base of the tree for some time while the bird alternated between eating and throwing food down for the cubs. I watched tolerantly, thinking that Girl Kitten was the better hunter of my two kittens. Her reactions were always faster, though the raptor apparently decided to compensate, because a few of its gifts landed in front of Boy Kitten's nose.

I sensed what was coming when the bird, with a lingering look at the cat pack below it, spread enormous wings and dropped from the tree. The air resounded with the percussion of her wingbeats, and the remains of the carcass fell from the tree. I pounced, conscious as I did so that the bird was flying up and far away.

There was little left of the kill, so I let the two cubs have it. It reinvigorated them, and they now seemed ready to play for the rest of the day. I turned back to my descent, following my nose toward water.

We made it to the bottom of the steep hill and found ourselves in a broad, flat area untouched by fire. The wind was cooler on my tail than on my face, making it difficult to get a reading on which direction to take. The water, when I caught its scent, was far ahead of us, so I led my kittens steadily through the waving grasses.

The cubs were sensitive to how I moved along the trail, so they slowed when I did. I was still headed toward water, but now I sensed something else . . . something dangerous.

More than just a stream lay ahead. My nose filled with the commingling odors of the same brutes I'd seen plodding slowly down roads like a line of cars.

Though they were not meat-eaters and would not hunt us, I proceeded cautiously. The beasts were large and powerful enough to be a menace to anything.

We soon drew close enough to see them. A large herd was feeding placidly on grass by a wide, slow-moving river. They were between us and the water, enough of them that a path forward wasn't immediately clear. Anything *that* huge was best avoided. Downstream, however, the waters narrowed and rollicked in dancing rapids before twisting into an area of thicker trees. I far preferred the placid areas of the stream for drinking.

Girl Kitten's reaction to the immense grass-eaters was to flatten herself to the ground, and Boy Kitten immediately followed suit. I could see her focusing on a couple of lighter-colored babies, as if the offspring of these monsters weren't larger than Dutch.

That was Girl Kitten—if she couldn't bring down a horse, she'd settle for one of these giants. The two kittens slunk toward the pack, which had thus far ignored us.

I had seen the cubs stalk small rodents this way, hunkered down and creeping forward, finally to pounce with utter ineffectiveness. A dog knows the only way to successfully hunt is to run flat out. I had employed this technique with squirrels many, many times, and was always very nearly successful. I glanced around now, thinking how happy I would be to see a squirrel bounding through the grasses. I could show the cats how to go about catching one.

Thinking about squirrels led me to remember days at the dog park. My boy would laugh at how close I came to nabbing my prey before it scampered up a tree and chattered down at me. After, he'd throw a ball for me and I could *always* catch one of those, no matter where it bounced. Then he'd snick a leash into my collar to take me home, where he would feed me a t-i-i-iny piece of cheese and I would sleep on my Lucas blanket. . . .

I watched indulgently as my two cubs crawled toward their would-be prey. In a moment, I would need to bark a warning not to get too close. We would have to move upstream, past all the beasts, before we could drink.

Suddenly I snapped to attention. A shadow in the trees downstream had moved. I turned and faced the woods, aiming my nose in that direction. What had I seen?

There it was again. A flicker of movement, a dash from one tree to the next, furtive and cunning.

Something was hunting.

I concentrated on the hidden figure, ignoring the kittens for the moment. Though the breeze was behind me, it was slack and inconsistent. Now that I was focused, I separated a new odor from the strong aroma of the huge beasts and the clean smell of flowing water.

The scent was familiar. It was not Big Kitten, but it was something like her . . . a giant, feral cat.

An instinctive wag started and died at the tip of my tail. I loved most cats, and always enjoyed watching them hunt, but the elusive movements of this one felt directed at *us*. Somehow, I knew that this enormous cat had been stalking the calves of the four-legged animals munching grass by the riverbank . . . but now it had spotted easier prey.

My kittens.

Girl Kitten and Boy Kitten were so in tune with my thoughts that they both turned to stare at me. They clearly didn't smell the danger, but they could tell something was wrong.

The cat in the woods made another move and now there was no doubt. If it had been hunting the youngest of the monsters, it would have advanced to a thick stand of trees closer to the giant beasts, but instead it had darted to a new position nearer to us.

The huge, horned animals were seemingly oblivious to our presence, even when I slowly took a few steps in their direction. The cubs, not understanding, rose from their bellies and scampered to join me.

My eyes were on the trees. The big cat was hiding effectively, but my nose was tracking it and could tell it was a male.

I had spent many days wrestling with Big Kitten. When she was young, it was as easy to topple her onto her back as it was to dominate either of my two cubs. When she was grown, though, if I managed to knock her over it was only because she fell down willingly. Without deploying any strength at all, she could send me tumbling with a single thrust of her forepaw. In a fight, claws extended, I would be no match for her.

If this male came out of those trees after us, it would kill me and then kill the cubs.

Not long before, I had been happily remembering Lucas at the dog park. Now, we were in mortal danger. I had never in my life missed Lucas so much as I did in that moment.

Every cat I had ever known was inclined to pounce when something darted away from it, but showed restraint if its prey moved more slowly. With deliberate control, I limited my next steps to careful, easy strides, despite my terror. The cubs fell in line behind me, mimicking my slow pace. We eased toward the water and away from the big cat, as if unaware we were being watched.

Something I knew from roaming the mountains with Big Kitten—predator cats did not like deep water. If we could make it to the opposite bank, my kittens would be safe.

Positioned between us and the waters, however, and blocking our way, were the monsters.

Twenty-seven

I couldn't tell if the massive creatures along the river were aware of our approach. They were ponderous and impassive and unperturbed by the slow and careful advance of a dog and her two kittens. When one raised a horned head and tossed it, I froze, feeling the cubs behind me pausing as well. They didn't seem to have the sense to be afraid of the huge animals in front of us, and weren't alert to the danger at the edge of the woods, but they had learned from their mother to mimic adult behavior.

For a moment, at any rate.

Boy Kitten soon became bored with our slow, creeping advance and dashed a joyous circle around us, his gait the silly, bouncing scamper of a young kitten having fun. It was precisely the sort of darting motion that could lure a hunting cat. Terrified, I glanced back and saw exactly what I dreaded: the male predator eased away from the tree, out in the open now, eyes cold and staring, elongating his body, sinking low. I could *feel* his muscles gathering themselves for the attack.

I glanced helplessly at the milling giants in front of us. A kick from one of those hooves would kill, as would a gouging from one of those horns. Every instinct within me told me not to risk getting any closer.

I turned and locked eyes with the big cat and it seemed to know we were trapped. It uncoiled and sprang forward, frighteningly fast. I looked at the kittens, still unaware, and knew if I didn't do something, I'd lose them. So I bolted in the only direction possible, straight at the pack of beasts. The two cubs, confused, tumbled after me, but too slowly.

The male cat was streaking with impossible speed across the grassy flats, cold eyes on his prey. Boy Kitten uncertainly trailed Girl Kitten as I darted for a narrow gap between two of the monsters, but the killer was right behind us, closing in.

He's going to catch Boy Kitten.

I halted, turning back to face the big cat. Girl Kitten stopped at my feet, looking up at me for guidance.

In that instant, the monsters became aware of the predator, swinging their enormous heads around. Even as Boy Kitten dashed toward me, fearing abandonment and moving as fast as his little legs would take him, the creatures stepped past us to face the approaching hunter. Mindful of their horns and hooves, I led the cubs into their midst until we were in the middle of the milling pack.

The male cat pulled up short as an implacable wall of horns faced him.

I lay down.

It was the only gesture I could think of to let the monsters know that we were not there to hunt or harm; we were friendly, passive, small animals crawling on our stomachs.

I looked anxiously to the cubs. If they darted around in their usual fashion, the enormous beasts surrounding us might well stomp them to death, though for now the herd was focused on the predator, heads lowered.

The male cat turned and retreated ahead of the mass of monsters advancing on him with clear intent. There was something in the panicky speed of the cat that reminded me of Big Kitten frantically trying to escape the fire.

Snorting, the monsters halted after just a few steps. They did not pursue the killer into the trees.

The big creatures were clearly anxious and disturbed by what they had seen. I thought briefly of the way they had charged into the dog park. If the herd bolted now, I knew we'd be trampled.

Fighting my fear, I lay as motionless as I could, panting but otherwise still. I intended to remain that way. Boy Kitten pressed up against me in fright, while Girl Kitten stretched out in the grasses, her eyes tracking calves so many times larger than she. That was my girl: here we were, moments from being crushed under the hooves of these beasts, and she was back to hunting.

When the larger of the creatures lowered its head to continue feeding, the other beasts followed suit, a new calm flowing through them. More than any other animals I had ever encountered, these brutes seemed to think and react as one.

I kept an eye on Girl Kitten, ready to stop her if she began stalking forward. But after a time, she seemed to tire of her vigil—the animals were moving too slowly to entertain a cat—and she relaxed.

I did not relax. They seemed passive now, but I knew what they were capable of if something startled them. And the big male cat was still skulking beyond the tree line—I could smell him, furtively biding his time, waiting for us to lose the protection of our new pack.

The horned beasts continued to ignore us as I watched and waited. The kittens became drowsy, lying there in the sun, while I tracked the herd as it moved slowly upstream. Gradually, there were fewer and fewer of the creatures gathered around. Our accidental guardians were abandoning us.

The male cat had to be very hungry. From what I had learned of Big Kitten's patterns, they preferred hunting prey during the night. But he had been stalking the beasts in the daylight, and when we came along, he hadn't hesitated to shift targets.

I rose to my feet. The cubs did the same. Tentatively, I took a few steps toward the river. The beasts ignored us. I moved more boldly, the kittens practically underfoot. Finally, we found ourselves at the banks, and we drank gratefully.

Soon the sun would dip down behind the mountains. I did not want to be out in the open with that cat prowling.

I assessed the river. It was cold, and when I took a few steps forward, I knew that it was deep enough for me to need to swim to make it to the other side.

I looked to the two cubs, who were watching me for an indication of what was coming next.

I plunged into the water. As I suspected, my paws soon lost their purchase, and the current pushed me gently downstream. I swam powerfully, compensating for the flow, aiming for the opposite bank. Behind me, I knew, my cubs would be paddling frantically, determined to keep up with their mother cat.

I pulled myself up onto the shore and turned to check on the pair's progress.

They were still on the other bank.

Boy Kitten, more anxious than his sister, put a paw in the water and then snatched it back as if burned. He opened his mouth in a silent plea. Girl Kitten simply stared at me as if demanding an explanation for my actions.

I didn't want to bark, for fear of scaring the monsters or alerting the male cat. But my kittens were clearly not willing to take to the water, not even to stay with me.

Frustrated, I whined, then play-bowed. Could they not understand what was expected of them?

They weren't moving.

Finally, I resigned myself to going back into the water. It felt even colder on the return trip. When I emerged, dripping, onto the sand, Boy Kitten greeted me by scampering around and jumping on me, swatting me with a playful paw. Girl Kitten was more aloof, disgusted at my behavior. She would be the most problematic.

So, she would go first.

I closed a gentle mouth on the back of her neck, as I had so many times before. She waited passively to see what sort of game

I was playing. As I gripped the loose fold of skin, she relaxed and went limp.

She stiffened, though, when I pulled her up off the ground, the way I had once been lifted when I was a puppy. She was heavy, but I kept my head high as I turned and waded back into the water.

Girl Kitten yowled in protest when I began swimming, half her body submerged in the river. Her legs flailed ineffectively at the surface, splashing it.

When I climbed up the opposite bank for the second time and dropped her to the sand, she darted away from me, climbing up higher and then turning to stare down at me with angry eyes. Then she licked her front paw in a way that seemed to be deliberately disdainful.

I looked back across the stream. Boy Kitten was frantic. He was leaping into the water and then scrambling back from it, his ears down and his mouth open in silent distress.

I glanced up at his sister, who seemed entirely unconcerned with her brother's fate, and waded back into the river.

Boy Kitten seemed to understand what was coming, because when I emerged from the water, he retreated from me anxiously, fleeing up the bank. I caught up to him and the moment I put my mouth on the nape of his neck, he flattened and went still. He was a motionless weight, lighter than his sister, when I picked him up by his scruff. He flinched but otherwise did not protest when the cold waters enveloped us.

When I deposited him on the opposite bank, he ran to his sister in anguish, but she turned from him and padded away, as if prepared to abandon both of us. I got in front of my cat pack, though, and led them into the dark of the night, unwilling to halt until a rock formation rose up in the moonlight, offering deep shadows and crevasses where a hidden den could be made.

Exhausted from the events of the day, we were soon asleep in a pile.

When I roused the kittens the next morning, I realized that

sometime during the night I had become confused about my signal. All at once, I wasn't sure where Lucas was, exactly—my unerring sense of the invisible leash was no longer pulling me in a firm, clear direction. He was out there somewhere, but where?

As if they sensed my disquiet, Boy Kitten and Girl Kitten came to me, seeking comfort and reassurance. They climbed on me, they tried to tussle with me, engaging me with their quick paws and willingness to tumble onto their backs when I nudged them with my nose. We played, briefly, and then I decided it was time to move. I led them away from the den, unsure which direction to take.

Utterly lost and disheartened, I finally found purpose when, after some time, I picked up the smell of food. Since heading toward a meal is never the wrong thing to do, we followed the scent and soon came into a type of area familiar to me from other times in these mountains—a set of tables, some structures, a nearby stream and, most tantalizing, large metal bins that had been set aside with food for dogs.

The cubs were too small to do what I could, which was to leap up and, scrambling with my front paws, pull these cans over to allow their contents to spill out on the ground. They watched, learning this new hunting technique from me, which I was happy to demonstrate.

The first such bin provided little more than paper, but the second one was a bonanza of chicken bones and sandwich meat. Though slightly rancid with age, it was still edible, and we patiently sorted the food out from the rest of the trash and gobbled it. After a drink in the cool stream, I found a place on the bank where the grasses were long and some fallen logs formed a natural den. When I sprawled down in this safe area, the cubs gladly joined me and were soon sound asleep.

Cats, especially predator cats, were not like dogs—that was clear from the way the big male had targeted Boy Kitten and Girl Kitten. A dog might have a surly personality, but I couldn't imagine one hunting a puppy for food. This meant that, while I could trust Big Kitten, I could not trust any other cat I might encounter. Big cats meant danger.

I slept a little bit myself, and when I woke, the cubs were piled on top of each other and still slumbering. The sun was high, so sleeping now came naturally to them. I followed the stream for a while, watching carefully for fish. Big Kitten could leap into water and grab a fish, something I had never been able to accomplish.

I realized after a time that I was wandering for the sheer joy of it, for the luxury of breathing in unburned grasses and fragrant flowers. It was like taking a walk with Lucas and Olivia off-leash, my nose bringing me all the delightful odors of a late-summer forest. My wanderings took me uphill, following the trees until they thinned. I remembered standing with Big Kitten and looking down into the enormous forest fire. I was thinking of her so intently that when I crested the ridge, it was almost as if I could smell her.

And then I realized, I did—I *did* smell her.

I ran down the hill, bursting out of shrubbery and racing across a flower-filled field. At the other end of this flat area, I could see some men walking along, struggling to carry something. It was from them that the scent of Big Kitten wafted so strongly, though that made no sense. As I approached, the men, each holding a corner of what looked like a thick sheet, set their burden on the ground, obviously tired.

What I saw in the middle of that sheet shocked me: it was Big Kitten.

Her eyes were half-lidded and sightless.

She wasn't moving.

Twenty-eight

My reaction to what I was seeing was based on fear and rage—fear that these men had killed Big Kitten, just as other men had killed her mother; and rage that they would do anything to harm her. I rushed across the field, seething but not making a sound, not even a growl. I had no thought except to get to the men.

I had time, though, to reconsider. I could not attack a group of people, no matter how enraged—I had been raised by human hands and would never bite one. I slowed, less sure, while the people stood and gazed down at my friend on the ground between them. The men did not notice me approaching. I could not hear them yet, but they were talking to one another.

Big Kitten still sprawled insensate in the middle of the sheet.

But my nose told me something: despite appearances, she was not dead. The scent reaching my nose was warm with life. She was sleeping, flopped out loosely in a manner almost ridiculously unnatural.

This should not be happening—she was afraid of people and always ran from them. I could not possibly comprehend what I was seeing—how could Big Kitten be so comfortable among humans that she fell asleep at their feet?

When the men squatted and, grunting with effort, hefted their load back up, I realized I had to act.

I ran straight for them, a warning growl building in my throat.

They all seemed to hear me at the same time and turned their heads sharply in alarm.

"Yikes!" one of them shouted.

I reached the two men at Big Kitten's head and snarled and snapped at them, and they dropped her to the ground. She tumbled lifelessly into the dirt, and the other men dropped their end of the cloth as well.

They all backed away from me, holding out their hands.

"No! No, dog, *no!*" one man warned.

I did not feel like a bad dog.

Another man reached to his side and pulled something out and pointed it at me. "Should I shoot her?" he asked tensely.

I inched forward, my teeth still bared, and they retreated, glancing at me and each other, fear and anxiety pouring off of them. I thought Lucas would approve of my actions—I was protecting a cat, which was something my boy did as well.

Another man in a big floppy hat shook his head. "No, don't shoot. She's a pet, can't you see? She has a collar."

"She might be rabid."

"No," another man objected. He wore glasses like some of Lucas's friends. "This is not rabid behavior. Something's going on here."

Once I reached Big Kitten, I sniffed her carefully. Though her head was lolling unnaturally, and her tongue protruded through her barely opened mouth, she was breathing steadily and seemed uninjured. Yet she didn't wake up . . . not even when I pressed my nose to her face.

The men were staring at me with wide eyes. "Andrew," one of them asked softly, "you have any more tranquilizer darts?"

The man with the floppy hat shook his head. "No, we used them up. She was moving so fast. I was lucky to hit her at all."

"Well," the man with glasses said slowly, "the truck's only a quarter mile away. Why don't you get more?"

The man in the floppy hat nodded and turned and left at a

brisk clip. Watching him go, I was disappointed he didn't take his friends with him. I wanted them to leave now . . . leave me with Big Kitten so she could wake up when they were gone.

The man with the hairy mouth rubbed his chin. "I've got some food in my bag. I'll get some for the dog." I watched apprehensively as Hairy-mouth moved slowly toward me. I was not fooled by his careful advance. I could see him right there, and I knew he was coming to do something to me and perhaps Big Kitten. I began barking loudly so that he would know I did not intend to allow him to touch me or my friend. Whatever was going on, I knew Big Kitten would not want to be carried around by men.

Hairy-mouth backed away from my warnings. "Well, that's not going to work."

"Maybe you shouldn't have dropped your backpack," the man in glasses observed mildly.

Hairy-mouth turned and put his hands on his hips. "Hey, the dog was coming for me, not for you. I had to think fast. And you're the one who always says if you're attacked by a bear, you should drop your pack and run."

"I think the operative word there is 'bear,'" the man with glasses replied. "This look like a grizzly to you?"

I barked again, because the tension had built up within me and barking felt like a release. They were responding exactly as I had hoped, maintaining a good distance, their hands loose by their sides. They were still afraid of me and that was good. As long as they kept their eyes on me, nothing bad was going to happen to Big Kitten.

They didn't know I wouldn't bite them.

I was impatient for the situation to change, but when it did, things just got worse.

I smelled them before I saw them: Boy Kitten and Girl Kitten, probably drawn by my barks, were making their way toward us. I didn't want them to come any closer, but they were only kittens and didn't always understand a warning bark. Within moments, they emerged from the tree line, bounding innocently across the field toward where we stood.

I stopped barking.

"Look!"

The men took another few steps back, which was good. It was also good that the cubs slowed down as they converged on me, instinctively wary of these new creatures and unsure what I was doing so near them.

Someday, I realized in that moment, the cubs would be adult cats—Big Kittens in their own right. They needed to learn that while humans were mainly kind to dogs and some other animals, they posed a threat to a Big Kitten. If they didn't kill the cubs, they still might make them take a deep, unnatural nap on a blanket.

"Can you believe this?" the man with glasses exclaimed. "They've got to be her cubs!"

"You don't know that."

"Why else would they be here? Where is their mother, otherwise? No cubs would willingly approach any other mountain lion, not even a sleeping one, except their own mother. I'm telling you, these are her offspring. That's the only logical explanation."

The kittens slowed their advance with each step. They glanced back and forth between the humans and me.

"Step back. Let's see what they do."

I watched approvingly as the men walked back a few paces.

"Well, if you're right and these are her cubs, we've got a real problem."

"Exactly," Hairy-mouth man agreed agitatedly. "Her tag shows that she's way out of her territory. If she encounters another cougar, she, and now her cubs, could be killed."

"Right, that's what I've been saying."

"So, what's the solution?"

The kittens were still uneasily edging forward, eyes on me, with flickering glances at the humans. Neither one of them had yet noticed their unconscious mother, though her scent was heavy on the air.

The man with the glasses spread his hands. "I don't think we're going to be able to do anything. The dog won't let us near the stretcher, and now we've got two cougar cubs to worry about."

Both kittens alerted to their mother at the same instant. All else forgotten, they burst past me to leap on her. Big Kitten lay unresponsive as they climbed all over her, sniffing and purring and rolling against her. Their joy was unmistakable, even if they could not bark or wag their tails like dogs.

I turned because Floppy Hat was working his way back up the trail.

The man with the glasses held up a hand. "Hang on!" he shouted. "There's been a big change in the situation."

Floppy Hat slowed and approached cautiously, and I moved slightly so that I stood between him and Big Kitten, still keeping my eye on the cubs, who were relentlessly crawling on top of their mother, trying to get her attention.

After a time, all the humans gathered together in a tight bunch a respectful distance away. I stood protectively between them and the cats.

The man with the glasses turned to the man with the floppy hat. "Hey, Andrew," he said suddenly, "you've got some food, too, right? Don't you have some beef?"

The floppy hat bobbed. "Yeah, I've got dried beef and some bison jerky."

"Try giving it to the dog," the man in glasses suggested.

I heard the word "dog" and watched alertly. Moving slowly, the man in the hat, his eyes never leaving mine, stooped down and reached into his bag.

My attitude about the entire situation changed when, with the unmistakable plastic rustle of a bag of treats, he reached into a package and pulled out some meat pieces, whose succulent odor came to me at once. He moved his arm, and I tensed, but then several pieces of food sailed through the air and landed close to my feet.

I gobbled one up instantly. And then, knowing the cubs were not going to leave their mother's side, I carefully picked up a few of the delicious treats and carried them over and dropped them. Famished, the cubs attacked the meal, chewing vigorously.

The man with the glasses took them off and wiped his face and put them back on. "I have never seen anything like this in my life."

"I'm not sure what we're looking at. It's like the dog is their . . . ," Floppy Hat trailed off.

"Nanny?"

"Right. She's taking care of the cubs like she's friends with them."

"And the mother. Why else would the dog be so protective of a darted mountain lion?"

More treats came out of that bag, and I gladly accepted and shared them with the kittens.

Boy Kitten and Girl Kitten then decided that since their mother was taking a nap, they should do so as well. They sprawled out on her, clinging to her, desperate for contact. I sat but did not cease my vigil, watching the men who were watching us.

A short time later, I noticed a change in Big Kitten. Her cubs were still sleeping, but their mother's muscles were beginning to twitch and her eyes flicked wide open and glanced blearily around.

The men became alert.

"I guess this is it," Hairy-mouth said.

"She looks good. She's going to recover just fine."

"We'd better leave now. I don't want to be here when a mother mountain lion is able to stand up and defend her cubs. We'll come back for the stretcher later."

"You guys get some pictures of all this?" asked Floppy Hat.

"Oh, yes," another man said.

"Good, because I don't think otherwise anyone would believe us."

"But no social media, okay? I want to write this up."

I watched the men turn and walk away. They were nice. They had given me treats to share with Boy Kitten and Girl Kitten. But they had done something to their mother, and I did not know what would have happened if I had not arrived. So I stayed and did what I was supposed to do, which was protect the cubs and their real mother cat.

When Big Kitten awoke, it was with a jolt that startled both of her kittens. Looking alarmed, she stretched out her claws and pulled herself into a standing position, her back legs splayed and helpless behind her. She sniffed Boy Kitten and then Girl Kitten, and then turned and looked at me. She tried to walk to me, but her back legs didn't seem to want to work. I trotted up to her, wagging, and she did what she always has done, which was to lower her head and rub it against my shoulder.

The sun had dropped a little farther in the sky when Big Kitten's strength returned enough for her to be able to move, albeit in an odd, sideways-slipping gait.

We were back together as a pack, but I knew we needed a rest. I led the cats back to the small depression by the stream where I'd left the cubs earlier.

We all found a place to lie down. I put my head on Big Kitten's chest and drifted off to the soft sounds of the nearby creek.

Big Kitten seemed her old self the next morning—whatever the men had done to make her so sleepy was no longer affecting her. She drank water and let her cubs climb on her. Girl Kitten broke from all the cat-wrestling at one point and came to me as if worried I was feeling left out. I played with her but didn't try to jump on her mother. The memory of the big male cat streaking across the grass had left me uneasy about her strength and claws.

We spent a lazy day together, and then, that night, something occurred that I hadn't seen for a long time.

Rain.

Twenty-nine

My experience of rain in the mountains was that its approach was similar to that of fire: first a distant roar, building force, then an approaching scent, initially faint, then ultimately obliterating. It was all so recognizable, tying my memory back to other storms on other nights. I could not help the homesickness that touched me in that moment, the ache of loneliness that comes from being a dog without people.

Big Kitten was out hunting while I remained with her cubs. I hoped she would find prey; the treats tossed to me by the men had not gone far in abating my hunger, which was gnawing at my insides.

All of this—the almost desperate food craving, the sense of Big Kitten out in the dark stalking a meal, the feel of spending the night in the mountains, away from my Lucas—was all too familiar.

I was back to being a dog lost.

I detected the dramatic change in weather long before the kittens, who were absorbed in nighttime play and happily oblivious. They didn't hear the faint rumble, and didn't lift their noses to the fresh odors. In their utter lack of awareness regarding the obvious sensations of the world, cats are much more like people than dogs.

Presently, the characteristics of the smoke that had plagued us for so long changed completely. Charred wood reacted strongly to being painted with wet. Now I could *taste* it, an odd, thick, tongue-coating presence somehow made more powerful by the misting rain.

The cubs finally caught it and stopped playing and stared out into the night, alert and curious. It occurred to me that in their short lives, they had never seen anything like this.

In moments, the showers gained strength and began to fall with more force. Big Kitten soon returned to the den, looking disgusted. She did not appreciate being soaked by the clouds. She licked herself, smelled me, and then settled down next to us. The kittens were excited to see her, but Big Kitten gently swatted at them with her enormous paw, and they settled down.

In the morning, the downpour was still a steady drumbeat on the ears and a wet, welcome presence on the air. Rocks and trees gurgled with flow. I strolled out into this new clean environment, and the cubs, accustomed now to my diurnal ramblings, automatically followed. Big Kitten grudgingly brought up the rear. I knew she did not like the showers, but for me they brought back a pleasant set of memories of being with my boy, Lucas, on walks near our home when the rainwater would stream in the streets and patter off the rooftops.

Something else brought my boy to mind: a town was nearby, or at least a large assemblage of people odors—machines and oils and cooking food. I steered my cat family in that direction, following air currents, ascending a long, rocky slope speckled with the twisted remains of burned bushes.

Before long I crested a hogback. Spread out below me was the small town I had detected with my nose. I had been to similar places, where a few larger structures were surrounded by well-spaced houses. To one side of the clutch of taller buildings, a steep, looming mountain, completely blackened and stripped of all vegetation from the fire, dominated the landscape and sent its powerful tang of scorched earth and rocks and wood into the air. Down below, in the town, I could see people stepping rapidly, some of them carrying umbrellas against the steady downpour.

Olivia liked umbrellas. Lucas preferred hats.

Big Kitten joined me at my perch on the ridge, glancing impassively at the activity in the streets below. The scurrying movements of the people caught her attention. Big Kitten had no use for people, but darting motions by any creature fascinate cats. The kittens didn't seem to notice anything at all; they were busy pouncing on each other.

I felt an urge to climb down to the town because I could find food for the cat pack there. Perhaps a kind hand would feed me.

Big Kitten, of course, had no interest in following me when I descended the hill, and her cubs remained with her, watching me curiously, waiting on my return.

I was soon walking through an area of dead trees, and the occasional gust of wind brought with it the crack of one of these lonely spires collapsing exhaustedly into the wet cinders on the ground.

At the edge of the town, I noticed something unusual: it seemed as if everyone were carrying things out of houses, throwing the objects into their cars, and driving off. I saw people wearing wet, slick coats standing in places where roads met, waving their arms, lights in their hands. "Go! Keep moving! Go!" one of the coat-wearers shouted. Cars zoomed past these people. The whole scene conveyed a sense that everyone was in a dramatic hurry.

Humans often seem driven by purposes that a dog cannot understand.

Every so often one of the people would turn and stare up at the black mountain. I saw many of them pointing at it and shouting things to one another. Vehicles with bright, flashing lights were moving from house to house, and people jumped from these cars, ran to houses, pounded on the front doors, and often opened them and stuck their heads inside for a moment.

I remembered witnessing this same sort of frenetic activity when we decided to stay with Scott and Mack in the house of barking dogs, the day when the smoke and heat were nearly unbearable. People had been dashing around in fearful agitation before the flames arrived, driving and honking. I had even seen a car with goats sticking their heads out the windows, a sight I probably would never forget.

The same thing was happening here, the same frantic energy and commotion, the same line of cars moving swiftly away, only with no goats. I felt a rising anxiety watching it all.

But there was no fire advancing upon this town. If there had been I would easily have smelled it, even with the drenching torrent pounding scents flat. Something else was happening, something that frightened the people of this town.

When people are fearful, dogs should be, too. Part of me was so unnerved by all the disquiet, the agitation, I wanted to retreat back up the steep slope to Big Kitten. But hunger has a way of overriding apprehension.

I was smart enough to stay away from the road as the cars growled past, throwing up great sprays from their tires. No one was willing to stop for a wet dog in need of a meal, which was another sign that something was seriously amiss.

I tracked along the edge of town, constantly shaking the water out of my fur, searching for someone who might be eating dinner outside, or cooking something on a hot metal box. I would do a perfect Sit, or a Lie Down—I pictured being handed a treat by a gentle person, and it made me wag in anticipation.

I had no luck. Not only was the deluge making it difficult to track food by scent, I had the sense that with every passing moment there were fewer people in the town who might take pity on me. I could feel their dwindling presence even as I heard their departing cars.

When I wove my way between buildings to a big, rain-flooded road, a man was standing there with a light in his hand yelling, "Keep going, keep going, keep going!" Raindrops flared in the beam as he waved it. The line of cars diminished, each individual vehicle moving faster, and I noticed that every one of them splashed some water up on the man's pants. He did not seem to care.

The sound of cars approaching him faded as traffic lessened. Soon there were few sloshing vehicles anywhere. I wondered what would happen if I went to the scared man and tried to offer him comfort. I wasn't only a dog who roamed the mountains with a giant cat family, I was also a good dog who could help calm people in distress. Whatever was sending the inhabitants of this town into a panic was afflicting Wet-pants with a desperation that I heard in his voice and saw on his face.

I curiously watched as a car with a brightly flashing light on the roof drove up and stopped. The driver's side window was rolled down, and a woman stuck her head out. "Time to go!" she shouted urgently.

What was terrifying everyone?

The man with the light opened the back door, then turned and stared up at the big black mountain for a moment. Finally, he ducked into the back seat, and my opportunity to help him drove rapidly away.

I decided that there was no sense in continuing my search for friendly people. Everyone in this town was more interested in taking car rides than they were in stopping to see if a good dog was hungry. I had seen some dogs, their noses to the cracks of car windows as they sped by in the downpour, but they didn't bark at me, and I didn't bark at them. I wondered if they were reacting to all the tension, because it was very unusual, in my experience, for dogs *not* to challenge my presence, especially when they were on a car ride and I wasn't.

I turned back in the direction from which I'd come, deciding to return to Big Kitten and wait out the storm. Perhaps the cars would come back once dry weather returned. If not, we would all keep moving to Lucas.

The town's sounds had gone oddly quiet, now that the vehicles had all driven off. The thunder of the rain was the only dominant noise. My senses told me the houses had emptied out. It was as if everyone, all at once, had decided to flee, though I could discern nothing dangerous.

I was listening so intently I was startled at the blast of a motor, starting up fairly close to me. The air filled with a familiar rumble, one I associated with the truck that Mack liked to ride around on with his friends. I wagged, remembering going for a car ride on the top of Mack's truck. I watched alertly, feeling the vibration in my chest as the loud noise moved slowly my way, coming at me from down the street. I wagged again when a pair of lights blinked on at the front of the approaching vehicle.

I instinctively inhaled, searching for familiar odors from the big truck.

But instead I smelled something completely different, a scent from back up the hill where I had left my cat family.

Alarm jolted through me.

I knew that smell.

It was another cat, a cat like Big Kitten. The large, vicious male who had hunted my kittens was up there. He had found us, and I had no doubt what he planned to do.

The fur rose on my back as I remembered the intensity with which the male cat had pursued us, his focus on Boy Kitten, *my* kitten, his prey.

At the same moment, I heard my name being called.

"Bella!"

I snapped my head around, startled, as the big truck drew up next to me. It came to an abrupt halt, its tires biting the loose, wet gravel. A man swung down from the open door, his boots making twin splashes as he landed.

Mack!

"Bella!" he called again. "Is that you? Come here, Bella!"

I stared at him, then turned and looked back up the hill. I was torn. A man was calling me and clapping his hands together and a good dog would go to him. Mack was my friend, and I knew Lucas would want me to obey.

If I trotted over to Mack, he would praise me and offer me treats and take me on a car ride on the roof of his big truck. He would deliver me to Lucas, and I would be Go Home. I would no longer be a lost dog, I would be a good dog with a Lucas blanket and a soft place on the bed. It was everything I wanted.

But that would mean leaving Big Kitten and her cubs behind to face the certain threat of the big male killer who was stalking them.

That was the choice facing me now, a choice so stark it hurt. I could not leave my cat family to face the predator alone, which meant doing something unthinkable: I turned my back on Mack and ran, cringing at the implications of my decision.

"Bella!" he shouted at me. "Come!"

I kept running.

Thirty

Mack's cries echoed in my ears as if he were still calling to me, though once I scrambled up the wet, slick slope, he stopped shouting my name. Lucas wasn't the only person who had an invisible leash on me—anyone, any person calling my name, pulled me as surely as if I were tethered to the end of a rope. If a person knows a dog's name it means they have a right to use it.

I felt like a bad dog.

But I couldn't turn around and go back to my good human friend. I could not honor his command to do Come because I was sliding and stumbling, finding treacherous footing as I climbed the slippery rocks. I was focused on the unmistakable scent of the predator cat, now commingled with Big Kitten's. I had left Big Kitten alone to deal with the deadly threat of the larger animal. Panting, I desperately followed my nose up the rain-drenched, blackened slope.

A loud snarl ripped through the air, and it was not Big Kitten. The battle had already begun. I crested the ridgeline, dedicated to nothing less than finding and saving my cat family.

I dodged around an enormous boulder and skidded to a halt in the mud. Before me, in a tight but open space in front of a jumble of rocks, Big Kitten was making her stand. She stood with one paw lifted from the ground, her lips pulled back from her teeth. Boy Kitten and Girl Kitten cowered behind her.

Crouched in front of her was the male cat, even larger than I remembered. His claws were extended and his mouth opened to show wicked fangs. Big Kitten slashed once, then again, cutting only air, while the male, just out of reach, hissed with dark malevolence. He was not backing away. He was hungry and determined to have his prey. He darted out his own paw in a murderous swipe so near Big Kitten's face I thought she had been struck.

My instinct was to run forward and leap on the attacker, but his claws were impossibly long and sharp. As they sliced through the air again, frighteningly close to Big Kitten, she jerked her head back. A swat from the big male would end the struggle with one blow.

If I attacked straight-on like a dog, I would be killed. But I was not going to let Big Kitten face the hunter alone. I remembered the lumbering, stinky predator who came after the kittens when I was with Dutch. Dutch knew that if he circled around the back and assaulted from the rear, the enemy would give up the fight. It was how dogs did things—if your attacker was larger and more ferocious and you had a pack, you surrounded it.

The cat caught sight of me sneaking forward, and his eyes widened. Now there were two enemies for him to face.

Big Kitten slashed at the male as I darted around behind him, and I bared my teeth and lunged, snarling, aiming for the base of his tail. The cat whipped around and I knew he had me, but even as he raised his paw Big Kitten pounced and swiped at him with her own claws, raking his shoulder. The big male bellowed and turned to face her and I darted forward again, my teeth tearing at his rear leg until I dodged away.

I saw out of the corner of my eye that Girl Kitten had impulsively joined the fray. Her face was fierce as she came out from behind her mother to get at the big male.

No! She'd be killed!

Big Kitten and I charged at the same time, both of us directly at the male, and it was too much for the huge cat. Though he was in a perfect position to strike me, he instead turned and scampered away.

I wanted to pursue, but Big Kitten didn't move, so I stopped. It was more important to stay with the cubs than it was to chase a threat farther away.

Boy Kitten and Girl Kitten seemed overjoyed to see that I had returned from the town of panicky people. I sensed their relief as I endured their jubilant greeting. They had been hunted and survived the attack, and now I was back with them.

Big Kitten was not as elated. She stared at me, and I wondered if she was disappointed that I hadn't jumped on the big cat's back. But then she lowered her head and pushed it against me, and I knew that she still loved me.

I could smell the male cat out there, even with the rain tamping down his scent, but the distance continued to grow—he was still on the move away from us. I remained vigilant, standing in the rain and staring off in the direction he had fled until I caught no trace of him in the mist.

With the danger truly gone, I decided to return to town. I still felt like a bad dog. If Mack wanted to take me for a car ride, now, I would go.

I sniffed the kittens, who obviously had no sense that this was goodbye. Mack's car ride was about to take me back to Lucas, so I would not be returning to them again. But they were safe—the predator had been chased off by dog and cat. They had their real mother to protect them.

Big Kitten was impassive as ever, staring at me unwinkingly as I went to her, wagging. All this time with a dog, and she still didn't know how to behave around one.

I would miss my cat family so much. But I had said goodbye to Dutch and Gavin and Taylor, and would say goodbye to anyone, even Big Kitten, if it meant doing Go Home to my boy.

With one last glance at the frolicking kittens and my good friend, I trotted away.

Big Kitten made no effort to follow me.

I journeyed back to the ridge of rock from which I could see everything below. Something remarkable had happened in the few moments I had been engaged with the predator. Down below me, the outside lights of the small houses and buildings were beginning to glow with more force as the sun left the sky. It was still raining but the sounds of cars in water had ceased. From where I stood, and from what my nose told me, there were no cars left in town at all. Everyone had decided to take their dogs and go for a car ride. Even Mack's truck had left. The whole town was completely devoid of people, movement, and any life at all. No dogs barked. The only sound was the steady drone of rain showers landing on roofs and roads.

Was the fire coming back? Was that why everyone left? Clearly the black mountain across from me, looming up to my side, had been stripped of plant life by flames, which I had come to believe meant the flames would not be coming back—they never seemed to return to a place that had been denuded by fire. But with all the pointing and frantic movements and shouting, it was obvious the people were afraid of something up there.

I wondered what had happened and what I should do now. The option to get on the truck with Mack and take my own car ride no longer seemed to exist. I decided I should climb back down into town and see if there were bins with food that I could knock over and perhaps bring a meal back for Big Kitten and her family. Certainly, there was no danger of being struck by a passing vehicle.

I began picking my way down the slope again when I felt a sudden transformation, as if the air itself had snapped in two. I saw and smelled nothing, but I had the sense that everything was changing. I halted, bewildered by the strange sensation. And then I saw something I could not understand.

Over on the hulking black mountain, the skinny trees that were sticking so forlornly up toward the sky all at once began falling forward. As they did, the ground in which they were rooted began sliding downhill as if the mountain's surface was turning into a river. Beneath my feet, the soil was shaking and heaving, though in contrast to the steeper slopes across the way, nothing was moving. I instinctively turned around and scrambled frantically back up to the ridge, my whole body seized by a thunderous vibration, louder than anything I had ever experienced. When I reached the ridgeline, I whirled around and watched in utter amazement as the entire face of the mountain gathered itself and with ferocious speed slammed into the town. Houses flattened and the lights all went out and I saw rooftops separate from homes and splinter under a wall of mud and trees and rock. Everything was smashed with such vicious force that when a wooden fence snapped into the air like the tail of a cat, it landed far from where it had started. Poles fell, a boat split in pieces—nothing was spared, everything was scattered as the overwhelming punch took buildings and trees and forcefully laid waste to them all.

I was shocked. I had seen something much the same before, but with snow, not liquified soil. The day I met Dutch, a whole mountain had collapsed, burying a man who I'd helped Dutch try to dig out. Gavin and Taylor arrived to assist and then Dutch and I went to live with the two men.

I lifted my nose. Gavin and Taylor were not here now, and neither was Dutch, despite the similarities.

The sight of the black mountain taking aim at the town and destroying everything in its path was so dreadful and inexplicable I wanted to turn away, even though the destruction had ceased. I left the ridge and ran to the lair, but Big Kitten had fled the shaking and roar. She and the kittens were gone.

Big Kitten was faster than I was, though her cubs slowed her down. I focused on finding her, tracking her scent, and after a time caught up to where she and the cubs were cowering in the rain.

I went to them and tried, by wagging, to let them know that

while I had no comprehension of what I had just witnessed, I did not feel like we were in any danger. Eventually, the tension left them, and Girl Kitten invited me to wrestle.

The night was dark and wet with the steady rain. We found a hollow in the rocks and Big Kitten did not hunt, though she was awake, staring out at nothing, until near dawn. Was she worried the male cat would return? I could detect no sign of him in the misty air. I curled up with the cubs.

In the morning, most of the storm had dissipated, leaving the sound of drips and the gurgle of small streams to replace the ceaseless patter.

I wanted to see in daylight what I had witnessed unfold during the night. I returned to the ridge and looked down at where there had once been a town, but now I saw almost nothing but mud, rocks, debris. Along one street, houses still stood, untouched, but the rest of the dwellings were sagging relics of the structures they had once been, or were gone completely, swept away by the anger of the black mountain.

I decided to make my way down there because I still felt guilty about disobeying Mack. I could not smell him, but I thought I could find the place where I had last seen him.

I hoped that he and his friends in the truck had not waited for me. Mack loved me and would want to take me back to Lucas, but the devastation by the black mountain would not have spared his truck.

In the valley, I did not find Mack, nor could I locate the place where I had seen him. Everything was buried in a huge layer of mud. Around the fringes lay fragmented remains of what had once been buildings full of people.

I found no life, no dogs or humans, but I found no death, either. Everyone and everything was gone. I circled the edge of the enormous pile of rubble, aimlessly exploring, distressed by the magnitude of the devastation.

My searching led me to a mostly intact structure that had

been broken cleanly in half. From inside it, a delicious scent came to me.

I cautiously approached. I could smell plants, I could smell milk, I could smell meat. I could smell cheese. No animals, no people, but food.

I gingerly climbed inside the ruined building, conscious of dripping noises and tantalizing odors. Soon I arrived at a huge, refrigerator-like box that had been toppled. Inside, I saw solid pieces of cold meat.

I pulled one out. It was big enough to share—I could barely lift it—so I wasted no time in making the slow, steep climb back to Big Kitten and her cubs.

The felines were grateful for the meal, but when I turned to retrace my steps for more hunting, Big Kitten did not want to go. She stared expressionlessly when I gazed back over my shoulder in a clear beckoning—a gesture I had learned from her. I was frustrated, but, recalling the broken building with the delicious meats, I decided to revisit the place on my own.

And then something unexpected happened. I glanced back behind me and Big Kitten was sitting and not moving, but the cubs made a decision. First Girl Kitten, and then Boy Kitten, bounded after me.

This was not good. We were no longer a cat family separated from Big Kitten. We were reunited with their real mother. The cubs should remain with her.

But they had made their choice.

Thirty-one

Boy Kitten and Girl Kitten were clearly confused. Since Big Kitten had first disappeared, I had served as their mother cat. They'd followed me in the day, slept with me at night. A dog always leads a pack, but this was more than that: their survival had depended on them doing what I did. So when I headed back for town, they felt compelled to stick with me.

I, too, was confused. When forced to choose between people and the cubs, I had picked my cat family. I still missed Lucas, but I had deliberately decided to remain a lost dog when I could have run to Mack and gone for a car ride back to my boy.

I glanced over my shoulder as I reached the point where the hill met the jumble of debris and mud that had been the town. The kittens were still scampering after me, trusting me.

The sight of them warmed me the way a t-i-i-iny piece of cheese warmed me, made me feel loved.

My nose told me before I turned and looked that Big Kitten was now reluctantly tracking us, following her cubs, who were following me. I picked a now-familiar path around the wreckage, licking my lips at the thought of what awaited us.

Big Kitten paused several steps from the ruined building, not trusting anything made by human hands even as I climbed confidently into the half-collapsed space. Her cubs had no such compunction and bounded after me. They were as delighted as I had been to find the cabinet full of cool, delicious meat. Soon we were all feeding greedily.

Drawn by eating noises, Big Kitten crept forward until she stood just outside, where the wall had been torn from the rest of the building. For me, it was an open doorway to a meal; to her it smelled of people and therefore danger. I could tell that she wanted to come in out of the light rain, but she didn't think it was worth the risk.

When it became obvious that she couldn't be tempted to join us, I decided I wasn't doing a good job of taking care of my friend. She was a member of my pack and was watching us with hungry eyes. I clamped my jaws down on a large piece of meat with a bone in it. I dragged it across the floor to her, and she accepted my gift, lifting it easily with her immense strength. Her kittens, meanwhile, had found fish and were delightedly feasting on it. I like fish but it's not my preference when fresh meat is available. The felines who lived across the street with the cat lady always had fish on their breath, so I knew it was a cat favorite.

After eating, I was tired and joined Big Kitten. I lazily watched her sniffing suspiciously at the twisted metal and broken glass outside the building. I wasn't very interested when she found a hard, white ball and began clawing at it. The thing was much too large for me to get my mouth around. The smell of turkey reached me, and I sniffed the air curiously. Big Kitten began batting impatiently at the thing, and it went skittering out across the mud. She pounced on it, gnawing at it and hitting it again.

The cubs, having eaten their fill, pursued. And then I realized that Big Kitten wasn't hunting, she was playing. She was knocking the frozen turkey around so that the cubs could chase it and pounce. I sat and watched them enjoy themselves like cats will with a new toy.

We spent the evening right there, gorging on meats and fish. When night fell, Big Kitten, her belly visibly distended, led us a short distance away and we curled up into a pile near a sheltering rock, out of the rain.

As always, having a food source meant we ceased migrating in favor of staying put. Big Kitten made no move to bury the meat, perhaps because there was so much of it.

When the sun illuminated the morning, we were still being pelted by light showers. Big Kitten and her cubs curled up for a daytime nap, while I sniffed around the town. The black mountain's assault had unearthed unusual smells—animals and food and people odors mixing with mud and burned trees.

When the rain let up for a time that night, Big Kitten left, presumably to hunt. The cubs, I noted drowsily, remained with me.

She returned as the light changed from night to a rainy dawn. I could smell that she had not found prey. I made room for her in the den, sighing myself back to sleep, but I raised my head sharply when I sensed something.

Machines were coming. Machines . . . which meant people.

Big Kitten stared at me, clearly understanding that I was reacting to something. She climbed to her feet when she, too, picked up on the approaching sounds. Her cubs felt her alarm and bolted awake, staring at us for guidance.

Big Kitten padded out into the rain, moving fast. She was headed for the ridge; she wanted no part of the humans and their rumbling machines. The two kittens immediately pursued, but I hesitated, considering. . . . The machines might mean Mack was coming back for me. This could be my opportunity.

I was distressed when Girl Kitten suddenly halted, turning to gaze back at me in confusion. She took a few halting steps in my direction. Then Boy Kitten stopped and stared at me as well.

Big Kitten made a low, moaning growl, clearly admonishing the cubs, but they were obviously reluctant to abandon me. I felt like a bad dog, taking them away from their mother cat. So once again, given a choice between rejoining humans and remaining with my cat family, I chose cats. I lowered my head and climbed up the hill, the cubs accompanying me joyously.

At the crest, I took my post overlooking the town. I could see that at the far edge of the mound of debris, large machines were snorting and moving slowly, and people were talking and pointing. None of them was Lucas, none was Mack. I wagged a little, as if their human hands were petting me and their voices were calling me a good dog.

I was surprised when Big Kitten bypassed the den we'd used and kept us moving briskly, as if she had a Lucas of her own to whom she was doing Go Home. This had happened before, the dynamics of the cat pack changing, no longer led by the dog, but by the cat who did not know which way to go. The cubs were glad we were all together, but I wanted to find Lucas.

The sun stayed behind the rainclouds all day, but I sensed it leaving the sky as night approached, and still we were on the move.

All at once, Boy Kitten darted away, moving with such speed I was startled.

A black squirrel of some kind was rooting alongside a fallen tree, and Boy Kitten had spotted it. He was hunting. Girl Kitten joined him while Big Kitten stopped and watched impassively.

I could teach the cubs how to hunt squirrels, but it was dusk already, and if the squirrel hadn't had a white stripe, I would not have been able to see it at all. I approached where the kittens lay on their bellies, preparing to give chase. I could smell the squirrel now, and it carried a different odor than the ones who climbed the trees in our neighborhood.

Most squirrels wisely flee the moment they see a dog, but this one was busy digging around and seemed oblivious to the presence of an entire pack stalking it. Boy Kitten was crawling forward, and Girl Kitten turned her head to see if I was going to help. Her brother might be leading, but I expected Girl Kitten would pounce first.

As if sensing my thoughts and wanting to deny his sister the triumph, Boy Kitten suddenly rose and lunged for the squirrel.

I knew how this would end—the thing would dart away, find a tree, and then chatter at us from a branch. So, I was astounded when, just as Boy Kitten was right on top of the creature, he suddenly backpedaled, his face contorted in a wince. I watched, bewildered, as he fled right past me, trailing an odor so strong my eyes watered.

Whatever it was that laid such a heavy stink upon the air, Girl Kitten obviously smelled it as well, her ears going back on her head. It was so alien and offensive that the black squirrel with the white stripe was forgotten. Girl Kitten sought comfort from her mother cat, who turned and led us in the direction Boy Kitten had taken. I brought up the rear. The rain made the stench even more powerful than it would have been on dry air, something I could taste on my tongue. My nose wrinkled in revulsion.

When we reached him, Boy Kitten attempted to climb on his mother, but Big Kitten shoved him away. He was the source of the hideous odor, which made him unbearable. Spurned by his mother, he tried to rub against me, but I dodged his affections. If a piece of bacon had been on the ground in front of me, I couldn't have enjoyed it, so overpowering were the fumes. (I'd have eaten it, but I wouldn't have enjoyed it.)

When we stopped moving and found a suitable den, Boy Kitten lay by himself, miserable in the falling rain, rejected by the rest of us. Whatever he had done to bring on such a horrible stink, we were not welcoming him to curl up by our sides.

The odor of Boy Kitten filled my nostrils and kept me sleeping fitfully, the normal smells of the mountain and rain utterly extinguished.

When the day came, the storm had lessened, but not Boy Kitten's stench.

I moved away from my cat family so I could breathe. We had left behind the town that was buried under black mountain, though I couldn't tell how far we had gone because my nose was so filled with Boy Kitten.

I stood in the drizzle unhappily. Big Kitten was leading me away from Lucas, or at least not *to* him, which was much the same thing. The big meals from the broken building had given her renewed strength but also new determination. I could sense the change in her. There was a place she wanted to go and she expected me to accompany her.

But I was a dog who belonged to a boy named Lucas. I lived in a house with him and Olivia and slept with a Lucas blanket on their bed and nearly every evening had a t-i-i-iny piece of cheese, fed by his loving hand. I was not meant to be a dog following a giant wild cat, helping to protect one female kitten and one stinky kitten.

I was, I realized, forming a decision. With Big Kitten leading us, we were no longer doing Go Home. She was forcing me to make a final choice between Lucas and our cat family.

Had it not been for the imminent threat of the male cat, I would have gone with Mack. The thought, had I done so, that I might already be reunited with my boy, made me physically hurt. Yet more and more, it seemed I was destined to be a dog lost, a dog who lived with cats regardless of what I wanted.

The all-pervasive stink of Boy Kitten was simply unbearable, interrupting my thoughts. The falling rain had yet to scrub the stench from his fur. Disgusted, I decided to get away and find some clean air.

I followed a rutted path worn into the rocky ground by the hooves of some animals I had never met. Every step into the wind took me farther from the sickening odor of Boy Kitten. I wondered how he had become so smelly and if he would ever go back to being a normal cat. I supposed I would still love him either way, but it was much easier to love him when he didn't stink.

Boy Kitten's foul malodor refused to stop pursuing me, blocking the usual smells—the wet rocks, the smoke, the animals who had created the trail down which I was walking. Obviously, Boy Kitten was tracking me, which meant his sister was back there, too. Boy Kitten did not have the courage to go anywhere without his sister. But I couldn't find her when I turned my nose back down the trail—her scent was obliterated by his.

Ahead of me, a body of water, possibly a river, beckoned with the promise of a drink. I followed the trail until it veered away, and then I was setting my own course through the mist.

Lucas was on my mind so heavily that I didn't trust my ears when I heard a human voice shout, *"Bella!"*

It was Lucas, and I was headed straight toward him!

He was close.

Thirty-two

There was no mistaking that voice.

No dog heading to dinner has ever run with my eagerness as I galloped as fast as I could between wet, dripping rocks and over blackened, felled trees. My feet pounded the mud as I kicked up clods. With each bounding leap, I sought my boy's scent, knowing that it would swiftly grow stronger and more clear.

And behind me, faithfully following in pursuit, were Boy Kitten and Girl Kitten. My obvious determination was attracting them as powerfully as anything could.

Behind the two cubs, Big Kitten trailed more slowly. I believed that she was unhappy with this turn of events, much as she was unhappy to be out in the open in the day. And she certainly couldn't be glad she was being rained on.

Lucas had not shouted again, but it didn't matter—my nose had him now, advising me that he was straight ahead even as my ears filled with the sound of moving water.

I stopped short when I came to the high bank of a stream, heart pounding. I was on a rock bluff a considerable distance above cold, rushing rapids.

There he was. My boy, Lucas, on the other side of the river. He wore a wide-brimmed hat, from which water dripped steadily. He was standing and watching the rapids with his hands on his hips. On his side of the stream, the banks were flat, sloping only gradually toward the moving currents, whereas I stood on a cliff.

He raised his hands to his mouth, half turned so that he was facing downstream, and bellowed at the sky. "Bel-la!"

He was calling my name, but he wasn't calling *me*, exactly. There was a forlorn, hopeless quality to his voice.

Lucas was searching for me in the mountains. My heart filled with love for my boy.

He did not see me because I was so high above him. I wagged, knowing that in moments we would be together. When I barked, Lucas jerked his head up sharply and registered me standing above him. I saw the shock on his face.

"Bella!" he cried delightedly.

I danced in a circle, my joy uncontainable. I could not wait to feel his hands on my fur. I wondered if he had remembered to bring my t-i-i-iny piece of cheese.

I looked down, hesitating. It would be a long plunge from this height. I wanted to go to him, but I was being held back by a different sort of invisible leash—the pull of an instinct deep and undeniable that feared undertaking such a dangerous leap.

And what of the kittens? Would they follow me, jumping into space and plunging far, far down into the violent, soot-filled current? I remembered swimming with the kittens' napes clutched in my teeth. Even if I made it across with Girl Kitten, how could I return for her brother?

I whimpered, unsure. Once in the river, there would be no scaling the rocks back up; they posed a sheer wall with no path for a dog. I put my paws on the ledge, lowered my head, then pulled it up sharply, barking my frustration.

Lucas ran to the edge of the blackened water. "No!"

I cringed from the word, thrown out with such ferocity it was obvious Lucas was angry at me. What had I done? I wanted nothing more in that moment than to have him pet me and call me a good dog. I peered again at the surface of the stream, calculating. The kittens hadn't followed into the last stream, but this time could be different. . . .

"No! Don't jump! Stay! You can't survive the fall!"

Was he upset that I was here and he was there? I regarded the rushing water. Though full of debris, mostly small bits of burned wood, it was flowing fast, an angry boil made black and hostile with all the ash and charcoal. I could not tell if it was deep or shallow. I lowered my head, bunching my shoulders for the jump, lifting first one paw, then the other. I whined again.

No. . . . A leap from this height seemed impossible. I paced, panting, searching for a different way. I looked to a large tree on Lucas's side of the stream that had clearly suffered the effects of the big fire. It was denuded of branches, and had sagged across the river, some of its roots visible where its hold on the opposite riverbank had given up. Rainwater dripped steadily from its trunk, falling silently into the river far below. It was tipping in my direction, its top hanging just over my head. It was far higher than any bed I'd ever jumped up on. This was not the same as the tree that had smashed Gavin and Taylor's wooden fence. For me to try to leap up and land on the tree and then climb down to him . . . it seemed an impossible task for a dog. Big Kitten could get up there easily, and I had seen her navigate far more treacherous paths than this tree trunk spanning the river. If she carried the kittens one at a time, she could take them to my boy. But then what? Would she come back for me? I had trouble picturing her teeth on my nape, lifting me and holding me above the rushing water.

If she did that, I decided, if she carried the cubs down to Lucas, I wouldn't make her come back for me. I would take the plunge into the river and swim to him, even from this great height.

"Bella! Don't jump!" Lucas cried again.

I knew he was desperate to tell me something, but I didn't understand. He seemed less angry, but he was still upset.

The wind was blowing from directly behind Lucas's back, and I could smell rather than see Olivia and knew that she was approaching from somewhere in the blackened forest behind him. I wagged at the thought of seeing her again. I stepped to the edge of the cliff-like bank, looking down. It was so, so far.

A motion caught my eye and I glanced over. Some distance away, Big Kitten had maneuvered in front of Boy Kitten and Girl Kitten and was preventing them from advancing any closer to me. She had pushed them away from the river as far as she could. They were huddled against the rock wall behind them, and the kittens seemed to understand the message: this was a dangerous place for any animal, and they were not to approach the edge of the cliff. I glanced up at the tilted tree over my head. Would Big Kitten understand what she needed to do?

I saw my boy react and realized he saw Big Kitten, too. He put his hands to his face and shouted at me, "Stay there! Bella! *Stay!* I'm coming!"

I saw Olivia emerge from the woods as Lucas ran to the leaning tree. He tested it, shaking the trunk, and then climbed up and straddled it. Even from this distance I could see the burnt bark blackening his palms. Above me, the tip of the tree trembled.

"Lucas!" Olivia screamed at him. "What are you *doing!*"

He turned to look at her even as he continued to climb, making his way gingerly up the tree by pulling with his hands and then moving his legs astride the trunk.

"There's a cougar! Bella doesn't see the cougar! I've got to get to her."

Lucas was coming to me! Humans always know what to do.

"Stop!" Olivia yelled. Now she was dashing toward him across the opposite bank.

Lucas looked directly at me. "Stay there! I'm coming!"

I knew the word "Stay." It meant I should do Sit and wait and eventually I would get a treat for doing nothing more than remaining still. But it made no sense in this context: How would doing Stay be the right thing here?

I looked again at the water, which to my eye was visibly starting to rise. Why would that be happening?

Olivia was running hard in the rain, stumbling and tripping across the blackened rocks, and when she reached Lucas, she didn't hesitate. She launched herself onto him, tackling him and dragged him off the tree.

I did not understand and whimpered in confusion.

Lucas pushed Olivia away. I could tell he was angry. "She'll be killed! She doesn't see the mountain lion!"

"You can't climb up there! It's not safe!" Olivia shot back.

"She doesn't know she's being hunted!"

"Stop, Lucas. Just stop. You can't help her."

Lucas turned back to the tree and as he reached for it, Olivia seized him by the shoulders. "Lucas, you can't!" She turned him to her and screamed in his face. "I'm going to have a baby!"

Lucas stared at her while I watched in concern. Something had just happened to him, and now he was holding himself very still.

"You can't risk it," Olivia pleaded. "I need you. You can't risk leaving me and our child. Not even for Bella."

I wagged my tail a little because I could see Lucas's posture softening. Olivia was nodding at him. They momentarily hugged each other, then Lucas turned and shouted at me. "Run! Run, Bella!"

I did not know what he was saying, and I looked again at the water far, far below. Was he telling me to jump?

I had been so focused on my boy and Olivia, I had not noticed that there was a roar building, a roar like the fire, but without the attendant smell of smoke. It was thundering at us from upstream. I turned and stared but saw nothing, only the black stream twisting and vanishing behind the high cliffs. The farther upstream, the sharper and higher the rocks rose on either side.

Something was coming, but what?

I could tell by the way Olivia and Lucas were reacting that they'd heard the roar, too.

"Bella! Run!" Lucas shouted again.

I wagged uncertainly as they both turned and fled upward

toward the woods from which Olivia had emerged only moments before.

The ground beneath my feet began to tremble in a way that was frighteningly familiar. I stared as the sound grew larger and more powerful. Still nothing visible, though Big Kitten's ears had flattened against her head and she, too, was focused on the river upstream.

When it came, it came fast, a moving wall of water propelling black tree branches and rocky debris. It smashed hard around the tight bend through the high banks, and I cringed at its violence. It reminded me of what I saw when the town was buried by the mountain. But this wasn't mud, this was black water and limbs and boughs, and it was louder than even Mack's truck. I turned and watched in dismay as Lucas and Olivia reached the woods and kept going, climbing steadily into the ruined forest. And then the water was upon us, smashing the tree Lucas had been straddling and swallowing it in its path. In an instant the river rose high and wide and boiled with incredible force, so loud there was no hearing anything else.

Somehow the rapids had gone from a stream to a savage flood, propelling black limbs and tree trunks with incredible force. It was as if the waters could hold back their rage no longer.

It did not seem that the surface would rise as high as I was standing, but Big Kitten did not know this. She fled, terrified, and her cubs followed.

I needed to be with Lucas. I wanted to chase him and Olivia into the woods. But what had started as an impossible leap would now be a crossing of a treacherous deluge that contained more than just water. I stared, watching whole trees twisting in the brutal currents, thrusting up and banging into one another as they fought their way downstream.

After a moment, I turned to search for Big Kitten and her cubs.

Lucas was close, and he had come to find me. Soon he and I and Olivia and Big Kitten and the cubs would all be together.

Thirty-three

The cats kept running away from the thundering flood, which made sense—the destructive waters were smashing trees into splinters and tossing boulders like dog toys in the park. But before long, we traveled far enough to be safe, and I felt we could stop and reflect on what we had just learned, which was that Lucas and Olivia were nearby. We had seen my boy. He had *called* to me.

But although Big Kitten slowed, she did not stop, keeping a rather brisk pace. It was as if, once at the head of the pack, she didn't dare stop, lest her cubs decide to start following me again.

No matter how I tried, I couldn't manage to get Big Kitten's attention. She traveled swiftly and without relent, as if pulled by an invisible leash of her own. This was not like her—when Big Kitten traveled, she preferred to dart to camouflaging trees and rocks and pause there to consider her next move. This was more of a straight-line attack, meant to cover distance, sacrificing stealth and safety. She still found shadows and protective cover, but only briefly; if she came to a field of rocks or grass, she plowed straight through it instead of searching for a way around.

Her cubs followed uneasily, not liking that we were spending so much time out in the open. I brought up the rear, as much to protect the kittens as to try to slow Big Kitten's pace by lagging behind. Why the urgency?

I always knew where the cubs were, even if they vanished in

the undergrowth, because Boy Kitten still carried that inexplicable stench on his fur. The rain helped—I could track that stink dribbling off him and into the dirt.

It sure was taking a long time to fade.

When the rain ended, dark clouds pulled away and a stark moon lit up the path ahead. I wanted to stop and sleep, but Big Kitten didn't even glance at me when I slowed and then halted. Her cubs anxiously pooled at my feet, stressed by how far away from us their mother was getting. Finally, I resigned myself to renewing my pursuit.

With dawn, Big Kitten finally found what she considered a safe place next to some felled trees, and we all tumbled together in an exhausted pile. At sunset, though, she nudged me with her snout and stared at me. This was not her normal going-hunting behavior. I felt I understood the message and reluctantly climbed to my feet. I fell in line behind the two kittens, and we went back to traveling.

It made no sense to me that we were trying to cover so much ground, especially given that we were hungry again. It only made it worse that we were traveling farther and farther away from Lucas and Olivia.

Water was plentiful; it was pooled and running in tiny streams. We crossed burned areas that seemed alien and lifeless, and then we would find a field or a forest that had been spared the effects of the flames. If it were dawn or dusk, small squirrels and other rodents darted away from us as we approached, and I was too tired to give chase, even for fun. The kittens both came alive and alert when they saw a squirrel leaping across the ground and up into a tree, but they seemed to understand that to expend energy on squirrel pursuits would mean falling farther behind their mother. At times, Big Kitten drew so far ahead that it was up to me to lead the kittens because only I could smell where she had gone.

If Big Kitten were a dog, like Dutch, I might have comprehended what we were doing. Big Kitten was driven, that was obvious, so much so that she ignored me and her own cubs. And every step conflicted directly with what drove *me*: the need to do Go Home to Lucas.

As a dog, I trotted openly and reliably, while the kittens, seemingly adopting the behavior on their own, had taken up the curious habit of slinking from tree to rock to bushes, moving in a jagged, interrupted gait. Cats might be faster in bursts, but in the end, I'd rather walk a trail with a dog.

The kittens displayed no sign that they comprehended what we were doing any better than I did. Did they sense the tension between their animal parents? Were they concerned over Big Kitten's odd compulsion to march as far as possible every night in one dedicated direction, not even pausing to hunt?

Seeing her so far ahead of us filled me with despair. Whenever I had roamed with Big Kitten in the past, I had always felt that we were cooperating toward the common goal of doing Go Home to Lucas. When we reached the point where the next logical step was to descend from the mountains down to the city where Lucas lived at the time, Big Kitten was too timid to proceed, but she had accompanied me loyally up to that moment. Back then, I was her mother cat, but since having cubs of her own, the dynamic between the two of us had changed.

I finally reached the decision that I could not go on like this. We were climbing down into a deep, unscorched valley, the sun just beginning to light up the morning sky, and I sat down as firmly and purposefully as if Lucas had just opened the refrigerator for a t-i-i-iny piece of cheese.

At that point, neither the cubs nor I could see Big Kitten, though I could track her scent easily enough. She was not too far ahead.

Boy Kitten and Girl Kitten seemed relieved that we were taking a pause in our dogged trek. They trotted up to me, too weary to play or do anything but lie at my feet.

I waited. The sunlight grew stronger, until it was bright enough that I knew Big Kitten would want to stop for the day.

I recognized precisely the moment when she doubled back, because her scent strengthened. I waited until Big Kitten slid out from behind a rock and strode grimly toward me, her face, as always, expressionless.

Her cubs greeted her with tired enthusiasm. Big Kitten came straight to me and, for a moment, I contemplated the power in her limbs and the fatal points on her claws. She had become *that* unknown to me in these days of flight from so many threats.

For the first time in my life, I was afraid of Big Kitten.

I held perfectly still as the huge cat stood so close that I could smell the heat of her breath. Her kittens sat, observing the adult animals attentively.

After staring at me, Big Kitten suddenly dropped her head and rubbed it on my shoulder, her body thrumming. My apprehensions were misplaced—she would never harm her own mother cat. When she turned, took a few steps, and looked back expectantly, I felt I had no choice but to follow.

We were a pack.

We descended into the lush valley, pleasantly alive with birds joyously telling each other that another day had dawned. Big Kitten pressed on with the same determination, even out in the sunshine.

And then, suddenly, after leaping nimbly across a small brook, Big Kitten relaxed. The change was startling. She turned to play with her cubs, she greeted me with a purr and another friendly rub of her head, and she led us to a place high in the craggy rocks where a natural overhang made for a den that was redolent with her smells.

This was, I realized, Big Kitten's version of Go Home. Whatever this place was, she had been here before, and the tension that had been driving her had left her body the way we all wished Boy Kitten's stench would leave his.

After so many days spent migrating, it was wonderful to curl up with the cubs and know we were staying put.

Now it was all about hunger. Big Kitten ventured out hunting that night and returned with nothing. She nosed her cubs, who climbed on her, trying to communicate their need for food.

I was famished, too.

I stayed close to the den during much of the second day, hoping that Lucas was out there at the other end of my invisible leash, but not finding him.

What I did detect, however, was another human. A person produces a variety of odors when they live in a house. I can always find tangy food smells, and other odors peculiar to humans residing nearby.

We needed to eat. The sun was still up, though it was starting its descent toward the horizon, when, with a glance behind me at my cat family, I went off to find the person whose presence was drifting on the air.

The kittens followed. They still thought of me as another, probably better, mother cat, and a roaming adventure was always more exciting than resting in the den. I knew Big Kitten would soon be stealthily tracking us, uneasy that I was leading her offspring away.

I followed my nose and soon picked up smoke, garbage, and other odors emitting from a small cabin in a stretch of woods that had been untouched by the fires. I circled the house, inhaling something so tantalizing I had to lick my lips to keep from drooling. In that house was fresh meat. And a person. I found my way to a door and saw that there was a dog door built into it. I advanced carefully, but could find no signs of a canine. Nothing barked at me, and there were no marks on trees or stains of female dog urine in the plentiful grasses. If a dog had lived here once, it had not done so for a long time.

When I tentatively shoved my nose through the dog door, I was greeted with an astounding meat bouquet. It yanked me into the warm home like a leash.

A man was standing at a big thick table in the middle of the room. He wore an apron. He had no hair on his face or his head. He was bent over, with several big chunks of red meat arrayed before him. His head stayed down as he vigorously sliced away at one of these. Then he caught sight of me and glanced up, startled.

"Whoa!" He staggered back a little, his eyes wide. "Where did you come from?"

I wagged.

"Who are you?"

I heard the question and decided that the situation called for a good Sit. I put my rump on the floor and stared at him imploringly. He had meat. I was a good dog. Surely, he would make the connection.

He blinked at me several times and some of the tension eased out of his shoulders. "You found your way in through Cody's dog door, didn't you?" He gestured with the knife. "He's been gone for some time now. Never occurred to me some other dog might use it." He frowned. "You sure are skinny. I'm cutting up meat for my beef jerky. I make it for the farmers' market down in Denver. I'm gonna cure it and take it down on Sundays. Should last me until around Halloween."

He was talking to me, and I knew he thought I was a good dog because he wasn't shouting or acting at all angry at my trespass. But he wasn't feeding me, either. I wondered what other inducements I could offer. I decided to do Lie Down. My Lie Down has been admired by many humans over the course of my life. There . . . I was lying down. Now would he give me something to eat?

"I think maybe you're trying to ask me for a handout, here," he observed with a chuckle. He picked up a thin, long slice of red meat and tossed it to me. I snagged it out of the air, which is one of my great talents, and choked it down. He stared at me while I did so. "Been a while since you had a meal, hasn't it?"

I went back to doing Lie Down, since it worked so well before.

"Well," he decided after a moment, "here's a bigger piece." He

carved at the large chunk of meat under his hand and then tossed
me something so marvelous I nearly swooned: a thick slab of delicious beef. I leapt to my feet to eat it. It was almost big enough
to take to Big Kitten, but I was too hungry and could not restrain
myself.

I could smell that the cubs were close now; their odor was
drifting in through the thick curtain that was the dog door. They
must have seen me push through it to come in, and they surely
were able to smell the meat—at least I thought so.

I finished the big portion of meat and did Sit, watching the
man expectantly.

He chuckled again. "I wouldn't be much of a businessman if I
gave away all my product for free," he lectured.

He bent his head and started cutting again. "You seem like
you're a lost dog. I don't need a dog, exactly, but if you don't belong
to anybody, I suppose you could live here with me."

He wasn't saying any words that I recognized except "dog," but
he was still cutting meat, so he held my attention. That is, until
Girl Kitten forced her face through the flap of the dog door.

Thirty-four

Girl Kitten peered about suspiciously, then focused on me. I had the sense that she had thrust her head forward to see for herself what had happened to her favorite dog. It warmed me to consider she might have entered such a foreign environment out of concern for my fate.

The man was concentrating on what he was doing with the meat and did not glance up until Girl Kitten burst all the way into the room and then he staggered again, this time with a hand over his chest. "Oh my God! Oh my God!" Some dishes clattered as he fell back against the counter. He stared at Girl Kitten, who trotted up to me, sniffing accusatorily at my mouth.

"Okay, okay," he babbled. "You're a baby, right? You're just a baby, you're not going to hurt me. A baby mountain lion. Oh my God, I have to get my phone. No one will *believe* this."

The man opened a drawer and started rummaging around in it, setting things on a counter. Then Boy Kitten made an appearance, tentatively squeezing through the dog door and freezing once inside, his head ducked down in a way I had come to believe meant he was intimidated. He had learned to follow Girl Kitten, who had learned to follow me, and now he was in a people house. He looked unhappy, but the smell of fresh meat was undeniable; it permeated the room, igniting twitches in the noses of both kittens.

The man stared. "I've never . . . I don't know what's going on. I don't understand."

Retreating, eyes on the cubs, he fumbled his way back to the table where he'd been working. "So . . . so you're with the dog? You're being raised by a dog?" He shook his head. "That can't be right." He sliced with his knife and I watched intently. Girl Kitten took two steps into the room, while Boy Kitten remained flattened against the door, his head bobbing frantically, ready to flee but seemingly unable to figure out how to pass through the dog door from this side. The man hefted a piece of meat between two fingers and flipped it at Girl Kitten. It landed right in front of her and she flinched but then lunged forward and snapped it up. After a moment of hesitation Boy Kitten went after it as well. She turned her face away to deny him even a bite. Boy Kitten gave me what I interpreted as a wounded stare.

I noticed that neither cat was doing Sit or in any way indicating that they would like more treats. It was as if the kittens had no idea how to act around humans. I wasn't even sure they understood where the scrap of beef had come from—it was just suddenly there on the floor in front of them.

I hoped I would be on the receiving end of another throw—catching a piece of meat out of the air was probably the most satisfying trick a dog can perform, and I was eager to demonstrate.

The man kept busy with his knife. "Here, here." He tossed a few more chunks in their direction and I watched approvingly as the two of them gobbled up the treats. Already they were more comfortable in the house, and Girl Kitten, at least, seemed suddenly to draw the connection between the man's hand and the beef falling from the air, because she kept staring up at him.

"Okay, now, I can't wait to post this." He held up a phone in front of his face. "I am feeding two mountain lion cubs in my own home," he intoned. "They came in through the dog door, following this big dog. I was just cutting some meat to make jerky. Waltzed right in. Watch."

He picked up some more thin strips of meat and tossed them at the kittens. They pounced on them, though one came close enough to me that I took that for myself. Boy Kitten shot me a surly look, which I ignored. My actions seemed justified: I had, after all, found the dog door and the man.

The house, the person, the food: all reminded me that our goal had not changed. Would this man know to give us a car ride to Lucas?

"They must have smelled the meat, and the dog came in, and then the cubs followed. It's like they're a family or something. Or maybe they're tame. Somebody raising cougars illegally and has a dog? I dunno. It's just the most amazing thing I've ever seen." The man put his phone down. "Okay, I'll give you each a bigger piece, now, like I did the dog," he told the kittens. He worked his knife and tossed two much larger chunks of beef onto the floor.

The kittens ate ravenously.

"You two are as hungry as the dog, huh? Did you run away from home, somewhere? You're not going to bite me, are you? I guess I need to call the game warden. Man, this is a trip." He crinkled his nose. "One of you tangled with a skunk."

While the man babbled, I picked up something happening outside. Big Kitten was close by, her unmistakable scent coming to me through the folds of the dog door, and I could sense that she was uneasy. Her cubs had willingly entered the dwelling of a human. This could not make her happy.

When the kittens were finished, we all looked up at our benefactor expectantly.

"More?" He carved off large pieces for each of us. Mine hit the floor first and I snatched it and then turned abruptly from Boy Kitten, who seemed to feel he should share it with me. He was fed next while Girl Kitten gazed up at the man, and she received a nice helping as well.

Big Kitten was now directly outside. Her shadow passed over the thick material of the dog door as she sniffed at it.

The man shook his head in wonder. "I can't believe you three are still hungry."

The man was standing, watching us eat with a satisfied smile, when Big Kitten shoved her huge face through the dog door. She instantly took it all in—her kittens and me actively chewing, a human standing over us. Her eyes met his and her lips drew back in a snarl.

The man screamed and turned and ran to a big glass door and slid it open with a bang and stumbled out into the night. I padded over to the doorway and watched him wildly flee down a hill and into the woods, taking any chance of a car ride with him. He never looked back at me.

Big Kitten did not come through the dog door. I don't think she would have fit. But she did make her way around to the back of the house. Her kittens joined her outside, through that big open door, but Big Kitten still did not come in. Instead, I stood up on my back legs and managed to drag the enormous hunk of meat off the counter and onto the floor. With great effort, I managed to haul it outside and lay it at the feet of Big Kitten. I made two more trips into the home, each time returning with one of those big, heavy sides of beef. We fed right there, and it felt so good to have my stomach stretched by such a hearty meal. When we couldn't eat any more, we still had one small piece of meat and a big hunk that was virtually untouched.

Big Kitten picked up the enormous piece in her jaws, and Girl Kitten lifted the smaller one. Moving together, the cat pack returned to the den area where we'd spent the night. Big Kitten scuffed dirt and twigs over the large chunk of meat, her cubs watching approvingly. Then, Girl Kitten buried her smaller piece.

It was just what cats did.

With full bellies and a nice food source, the cat family slept well, and Big Kitten did not hunt that night. When I awoke, I decided to get a drink and trotted down to the small babbling stream nearby. Not for the first time, I admired Big Kitten's choice of den.

Standing there by the water, a placid wind in the trees, I felt a new peace come over me, and realized, after a time, the source of this gentle contentment: Big Kitten and the cubs were safe in their lair. I had come with them all this way and protected the kittens, but now I was free to pursue my own goals on my own time.

I roamed somewhat aimlessly that day, searching for but not finding the scent of my boy. That night, Big Kitten again didn't hunt, though the kittens were awake and active. I trotted off in a different direction the next morning, and this time I noticed that the cubs were tracking me, so I did not venture as far. No matter—I still could not locate Lucas on the air or find the insistent tug of the invisible leash. He was not close.

Big Kitten hunted successfully that night, and the family fed at dawn. I watched them, thinking that my travels were hampered by the kittens. So I waited patiently with them in the den, watching Big Kitten's eyes blink shut, and when the cubs curled up with their mother, preparing to sleep the day away, I crept away, secure in the knowledge that they were all unconscious.

I struck out in a new direction, heading uphill toward thinning trees, and hadn't gone far when a stirring sensation revealed something wonderful.

Lucas was near. Somehow, he had managed to come close enough that I could feel him as strongly as I could sense when he was returning home from work.

I knew then that, even while I was doing Go Home to Lucas, he had been doing his own version of the same thing: searching for me. My boy loved me, and he was trying to find me, guided by the opposite end of the invisible leash.

I went to find him.

The sun had slipped past its high point in the sky when my nose told me I was very close to my boy. It was an area of craggy, slippery rocks, and I picked my way carefully through them.

And there he was.

Lucas was lying with his face to the sky, his head on his back-pack, his eyes closed. I could not help the joyous bark that escaped my lips as I ran clattering over the hard, rocky jumble to reach him.

His eyes snapped open and he sat up. "Bella?"

My boy! My Lucas!

"It's you! It's really you!"

And then I was all over Lucas, jumping on him and licking him and whining with relief. All this time, all this searching, and I had finally found my boy.

He hugged me, his face dampening with tears as he kissed me on the nose and ears and scratched my chest with one finger.

"I *knew* it. I knew we'd find you, Bella. Even with all the sightings, everyone told me you couldn't possibly still be alive, but I knew that you were the dog who took two years to come all the way across the Rocky Mountains. I knew you were headed home, and I knew I'd find you. I knew you were close. I could *feel* it!"

It felt so good to be with my boy.

"Oh, Bella, Olivia's going to be so happy." Then his voice changed tone and lowered. "She went to get help, Bella." He smiled at me ruefully. "I fell like an idiot and the rocks slid and my foot got trapped. No way to get free without help. And no signal up here, so Olivia left this morning. She should be back soon." He regarded me thoughtfully. "How did you survive, Bella? What did you do for food?"

I loved hearing my name being spoken by my boy.

When Lucas stiffened, I looked in the direction he was staring and there she was: Big Kitten. She was standing in front of Girl Kitten and Boy Kitten. The cubs must have tracked me and, of course, she had felt compelled to follow them.

I wondered if Lucas would put them in the Jeep so we could all go back to the house together. That's what I wanted.

After a long moment, Lucas reached for his pack and carefully pulled out his phone. He was not looking at me now; he was staring at Big Kitten. Then he turned his head slightly, glancing at his phone while he touched it with his thumbs. He cleared his throat. "Olivia . . ."

His voice choked off and I sniffed him in concern. Waves of emotion were pouring off him, fear and sadness like I'd never felt from Lucas. How, I wondered, with a good dog back in his arms, could he possibly be unhappy?

"Honey. I have so much to tell you, and I don't know what sort of time I have. First, look." Lucas tilted the phone and I glanced at it, but it was just a phone. "Bella found me. It's . . . crazy. I don't understand any of it. And I want you to know, our family, you and me and Bella, has given me so much happiness."

Lucas wiped at his eyes and I whined quietly. "Just, when you find this . . . just know you're the best thing in my life, Olivia. From the moment I met you, I knew I would never love another woman. I'm so proud to be your husband. And I want to say, no matter what happens, I know you'll be the best mother in the world to our baby."

He took a deep, shuddering breath. "I'm looking at a full-grown mountain lion. She's about twenty yards away. She's stalking me and Bella. It might be the same one from before, at the river. I'll try to fight her off if she comes down here. But if I don't make it . . . I love you, Olivia. God, I love you. I maybe didn't tell you that every day but I thought it every minute I was awake."

Lucas wiped his eyes. "I'm going to stop recording, now. I wouldn't want you to . . . to watch. My last thoughts will be how much you mean to me."

Lucas set the phone down. He looked at me, gazing into my eyes. "Something very bad is going to happen now, Bella," he murmured.

Thirty-five

Lucas stretched out an arm, visibly straining, gritting his teeth until his hand reached a rock shaped like a big toy ball. He clutched it in his fist and pulled it close. "She has young with her . . . that makes her more dangerous than anything," he told me quietly.

I sniffed curiously at the rock. Lucas still hadn't stood up, and now he was going to throw the rock for me? If he did, I would go get it because I am a good dog, but it did not look like it would be much fun to pick up with my mouth. I looked from his phone to the rock to my boy's face.

We remained frozen there for some time. I could feel Lucas's heart beating in his chest. His jaw flexed tightly as he breathed fast and hard. I realized then that he wasn't just afraid, he was terrified, even though I could see nothing to alarm him. Was the fire coming back? I sniffed the air. No, and if it were, I was confident Lucas would start digging energetically with a shovel.

This was something else.

Girl Kitten separated herself from her mother, dodged around her brother, and edged forward curiously. Her approach looked unusually cautious, so I wagged to let her know everything was all right.

She bounded a few more steps forward and stopped. Lucas tightened his one-armed hug, rock still clutched in his other fist. All of Girl Kitten's attention was focused on my boy. I wondered if she was remembering how, just a few nights before, a man had thrown her scraps of meat in his house. I had been friendly with that man, and obviously I was friendly with Lucas. Was she thinking that Lucas would feed her as well? I figured there was a strong possibility that was precisely what was about to happen. I pictured how Girl Kitten would react to a t-i-i-iny piece of cheese. She probably had never tasted anything so wonderful before!

Girl Kitten kept staring. Maybe she didn't understand that Lucas had his arms around me to love me, not to trap me.

Lucas was still sitting perfectly still. A seated animal, even a human, doesn't pose much of a threat. This was my boy letting Girl Kitten know there was no reason to be afraid.

"Bella," he said with sudden urgency.

I wagged.

His arm dropped from around me. The sensation of losing his hug, when I had been craving it so much, was like a sudden gust of cold air.

"Run," he whispered. He gave me a small shove. "Get away. Okay? Go!" His voice rose on this last word.

I shook my body and stood. I thought I understood what he was saying, so I skipped gaily up to Girl Kitten, who impassively watched my playful approach. She was more like her mother every day, her face less and less expressive.

"No! No, Bella!" Lucas called in anguish.

I was not doing anything for which "no" seemed appropriate. He wasn't saying "Come" or "Heel," either. Did Lucas, a boy who loved cats, think I was going to hurt Girl Kitten? To demonstrate that nothing could be further from my intentions, I closed the distance and play-bowed and wrestled with Girl Kitten, though she wasn't fully engaged and clearly wanted only to stare at Lucas.

I heard him breathe, "No way. . . ."

Now, I hoped, Lucas would understand that this was my cat pack, that Girl Kitten and the still-reticent Boy Kitten and Big Kitten were my family. I would never hurt them. With that settled, I turned away from playing and picked my way back through the loose rocks to Lucas. This time, Girl Kitten decided it would be all right to follow me. Together, we approached my boy. His eyes went large in his head and he sat without moving while Girl Kitten sniffed his outstretched hand.

"No *way*!" he whispered again.

Humans say things all the time to dogs, but we rarely know what they mean.

Boy Kitten was watching and when he saw Girl Kitten so close to Lucas, he took this as a sign that everything was safe and left his mother and scampered down to us, perhaps worried that his sister would be fed fresh meat and he wouldn't. He was much more cautious than his sister had been, but he joined us, and Lucas reached out and touched Boy Kitten on the back, stroking him, a look of wonder on his face. Then he lifted his palm to his nose.

"Skunk," he said.

I could see that my boy was no longer afraid. He was happy, I thought, because he understood that I had been a good dog, taking care of the kittens.

Big Kitten was taking this all in without any visible reaction. I decided I needed to do something to let her know that my boy would not hurt her. While the cubs continued sniffing curiously at my boy, probably wondering when the raw meat would make its appearance, I trotted up to their mother, play-bowed, and then moved close, touching her with my nose. Big Kitten examined me carefully, smelling the human scent on my fur.

The kittens had already become bored with Lucas and were wrestling with each other right in front of him. He let go of the rock he had been clutching in his fist, perhaps understanding that a cat would care even less about fetching a stone than a dog would.

I took a few steps back to Lucas, then looked expectantly at Big Kitten, who glanced down at my boy, and then at me. She decided to move. I led her as she flowed languidly down through the broken rocks.

Lucas's eyes grew large again as she approached him. He caught his breath, gulping.

Big Kitten stopped just out of reach of Lucas. She sat, staring at him for a long, long moment. Lucas stared back. I got impatient with both of them. Why didn't Lucas call her? Why was Big Kitten holding back? I demonstrated how much I loved my boy by licking him on the cheek.

Finally, Big Kitten's curiosity seemed to get the better of her. She closed the remaining gap between herself and my boy. He was breathing shallowly, and did not move as she sniffed him up and down. When he raised his hand, she did not react. I saw he was trembling as he touched the top of her head.

"Oh my God," he whispered.

Big Kitten was as unimpressed with Lucas as her cubs had been. She turned and strolled casually away, glancing over her shoulder in a way that I knew meant that she expected her family to accompany her.

Lucas shook his head in wonder as the kittens scampered after their mother.

I looked to Lucas, knowing how much he loved cats. And there were no better or more special cats than Big Kitten, Girl Kitten, and Boy Kitten. He should call them back. If necessary, he could even take Big Kitten in a tight hug so she'd understand she needed to remain here with us, because I certainly wasn't about to abandon my boy.

When Big Kitten reached the top of the jumble of rocks, she paused and twisted around to peer at me, and I knew what she wanted. She expected me to follow the family. I studied my boy and saw no sign he was willing to do anything but let my cat pack go.

I left his side and clawed my way up through the uneven terrain until I reached Big Kitten. She drove the top of her head into my shoulder, knocking me back a little. Then I lowered my nose to Girl Kitten and Boy Kitten, who were playing and oblivious to what was happening.

But I knew.

This is goodbye, Big Kitten. You are a good mother cat. Your cubs need to be with you. But I am a dog. Dogs need to be with people.

The cats moved off, and I watched them go. I recalled saying goodbye to Big Kitten a long time ago, when she sat on a rock and watched me return to Lucas. Now it was I who sat on the rock, watching them, and every time Big Kitten turned back to look, I wagged my tail a little.

At one point, Girl Kitten stopped and stared at me, confused. Why wasn't I with them? What was I doing?

I had been the other-mother cat for a long while, but the kittens were already starting to watch their real mother more carefully, to move like she did, and to bury their perfectly good dinners in dirt. They had followed me to meet two humans, but Lucas hadn't offered any meat, and ultimately sat pointlessly in the rocks.

Girl Kitten was a good kitten and would remain with her mother, now.

And that is exactly what happened. Big Kitten and Boy Kitten continued to walk away, and Girl Kitten, after taking a few hesitant steps in my direction, made the right decision. She turned and scampered after her mother.

At the top of the trail, where the path twisted and vanished behind big boulders, Big Kitten paused and glanced back for one last look. Both cubs sat at her feet and regarded me solemnly. We all shared a long, lingering moment until they turned and disappeared from sight.

Wagging, I trotted back to my boy. I could smell sweat on his skin, and he was shaking his head at me.

"Is that how you survived?" Lucas put his hand out to touch me and I smelled Big Kitten and stinky Boy Kitten on his palm. "You lived with a family of mountain lions? How is that even possible?"

After a while, Lucas relaxed. I did not understand why he didn't stand up, why we didn't go for a walk or do something more interesting than sit there, but he seemed to want to remain right where he had been the whole time, so I lay down and put my head in his lap.

Suddenly, he stirred. "I know what you want."

I sat up and watched alertly as he rummaged around inside his backpack. There was a delightful crinkling sound and then he brought out a morsel so pungent and wonderful I immediately began to drool.

"Bella? Do you want a t-i-i-iny piece of cheese?" He extended his fingers and I delicately pulled the delicious cheese from between his fingers.

T-i-i-iny piece of cheese meant that Lucas loved me.

The treats didn't stop there. He pulled out another packet and opened it. "I've been carrying around dog food for just this moment." He unfolded a bowl and poured the contents into it. I ate greedily; it had been so long since I'd had real dog food.

I was happy.

Lucas and I had both fallen asleep when the air was suddenly split with a heavy thumping. Lucas looked up into the sky, the source of the noise, while I nudged him and tried to crawl into his lap for reassurance. I had felt percussions like this before, and associated them with a very bad time under wet blankets.

"There's the helicopter. Here they come."

A short time later I saw someone come around a bend in a trail and heard the most wonderful sound: "Bella!"

Olivia.

I ran to her, at first carefully, because I was still in the jumble of rocks, and then, on stable ground, I galloped toward her as she dashed to me. I leapt up to give her kisses on her face and she sank to her knees and kissed me back. "My God, this is impossible! You are so amazing! How did you find him, Bella? You are the best dog in the world!"

There were two men and a woman with Olivia. They seemed nice, and I wagged at them. They were carrying big boxes. When they reached Lucas, they all touched hands with him, and then set about working with chains and long metal bars.

I did not know what we were doing.

"I'm not dreaming, right? This really is Bella, isn't it?" Olivia asked Lucas.

Lucas nodded. "Oh yes. I was sleeping here and she just showed up out of nowhere."

Olivia smiled down at me. "Absolutely amazing."

The other people were straining with chains, and I saw the rock near Lucas budge a little and he winced. Then he looked at Olivia. "Oh, that's not the amazing part. You're not going to *believe* what I'm about to tell you."

I sat with Lucas and Olivia and their new friends, who loved playing with rocks. Then I lifted my nose because the air brought me a scent I recognized as well as I would my own. Big Kitten, Girl Kitten, and Boy Kitten were not far, though I could tell from the way their scent was receding that they were still headed away.

I loved them. They were my cat family. Just as Olivia and Lucas were my people family. But a good dog belongs with a people family. I would never forget Big Kitten and her cubs, but I was happiest when I was a good dog.

Epilogue

Things soon changed in the human world in ways even a dog could observe.

Immediately upon returning to our home, Lucas began wearing a thick, heavy boot on one of his feet but not the other. I sniffed it, but it wasn't any more interesting than any of his other shoes. He abandoned it after some time.

The biggest, most immediate difference is what happened to the Room of Things. This was a place with two windows and a nice summertime breeze and chairs and pillows and boxes. Whenever friends came over for dinner in the past, Lucas and Olivia would run around our home, grabbing items and throwing them in this room, and usually that's where those things remained. But now Lucas and Olivia, in the space of a few days, moved everything out of the Room of Things, and Lucas applied a foul-smelling liquid to the walls, and Olivia frowned and said, "Now that it's up, I don't like the color," and so he did it again, and she said, "Much better."

The main new object in the Room of Things was a small wooden bed. It had high sides to prevent a dog from jumping up to nap there, but otherwise, when I stood up on my back legs to examine it, I found it about as interesting at Lucas's boot. It smelled like a bed that no one had ever slept in, and that was it.

Winter came and applied blankets of snow and then the weather warmed up and Olivia stopped leaving for work in the morning. She had decided it would be better to remain with their dog. It was, in my opinion, the right decision.

I expected Lucas to go back to the lake and retrieve the Jeep, but he didn't. Instead he wheeled into the driveway one day in a big, boxy car. I learned a new word: *minivan*.

"Not much longer," Lucas told me one afternoon. I wagged, hoping he was telling me something about bacon. He turned to look into the living room. "Honey, I'm going to take a shower."

"Okay!" Olivia called back.

I loyally tracked Lucas into the small Room of Intriguing Odors and did a Sit while he stood behind a rubber curtain and the smell of damp boy filled the air. I wagged when Olivia came in, one arm cradling her stomach, which was how she chose to walk now. She pulled aside the curtain. "Hey, can I use your phone to call mine? I can't find it."

"Knock yourself out," he told her.

I padded out after her and sat on the couch when Olivia eased herself down. She held a phone in her hand. Soon a small sound trilled from their bedroom. "Well, it's in the bedroom, but now I don't feel like standing back up," she advised me. I wagged and curled up on a pillow. "You look so cute. Hang on, let me take a picture."

My eyes started to ease shut as Olivia held the phone in front of her face. Then she continued to sit, examining the phone as if it were a piece of chicken. Suddenly she sucked in a breath. I snapped my eyes open, alarmed. She was weeping silently, tears flowing down her cheeks.

I joined her as she struggled to her feet and, making tight, choking sounds, returned to Lucas.

He was standing in the same room, toweling himself, and glanced up in concern when we entered. "What's wrong?"

"Oh my God. I never knew you took a *video. You thought you were going to die.*"

Olivia dropped the phone and pulled Lucas in tightly, her sobs barely audible.

Soon after that they kissed and I shoved my nose forward, participating in the love. Then they took a very active nap. I did not participate in that.

The woman Lucas lived with when I first met him, named "Mom," came over to visit every so often. I was always glad to see her, especially when she showed up one day with a mostly white, mottled little dog named Charlie. I loved it when people brought over dog friends.

It was far easier to teach Charlie proper dog games than it had been with Boy Kitten or Girl Kitten. My favorite was when I had a squeaky toy and Charlie tried to get it from me.

Sometimes Charlie had the squeaky toy, which I knew could not be as much fun for him.

Then things *really* changed. Mom and Charlie spent two nights with me, and Lucas and Olivia were gone the whole time. Charlie wanted to wrestle constantly, but I was worried my boy wouldn't be coming home and kept breaking away to sit expectantly at the front door. One day, I sensed that Lucas was finally returning, felt him drawing closer and closer, and he walked in the door with Olivia and a baby human named Emma.

Emma slept in the high-sided bed and wasn't much fun, though Olivia and Lucas spent a lot of time passing her back and forth, trying to get her to play. I demonstrated to the baby what could be done with a squeaky toy—you can toss it, pounce on it, shake it, and, above all, squeak it—but Emma couldn't catch on the way Charlie had. When she watched me, she had the strangest expression on her face, as if she really weren't paying attention (which was ridiculous—*no one* can ignore a squeaky toy).

"You're a good dog, Bella," Lucas told me.

That and *t-i-i-iny piece of cheese* were my two favorite things to hear from my boy.

Snows had come and gone again, and the air was clear and dry when a woman a little older than Olivia arrived to stay with us. I smelled more than one cat on her clothes and skin. She slept on the couch and I slept at her feet to be polite. For houseguests, sleeping with a dog is always better than without one.

"Bella, this is my sister Alexis," Olivia told me when the woman arrived. I didn't understand any of it except "Bella," but with enough repetition I figured out that the woman's name was Alexis. She was nice to me and would give me a treat if Lucas handed it to her first. I didn't question the process but didn't understand why the handoff was necessary.

Alexis was mostly interested in holding Emma, but Emma at that point was mostly interested in crawling around on the floor and putting things in her mouth so that Lucas would pick her up. Sometimes Emma would seize a piece of furniture, haul herself upright, and wobble, beaming at Olivia and Lucas.

Emma, I had come to understand, was Olivia and my boy's baby human. Sometimes her pants smelled very interesting.

"Look at the big girl!" Lucas would say in exactly the same tone of voice he used when he praised me. He'd be looking at Emma, though. I noted that when he talked to me like that, I got a treat, but he didn't give her one.

Having Emma live with us, crawling over to me and seizing my fur in her little fists, somehow made being away from Boy Kitten and Girl Kitten less sad for me. It was complicated, but I felt a little like Emma's mother cat.

The second night Alexis stayed with us, Lucas and Olivia ran around picking up baby toys and dog toys and stuffing them into the closet, which I had come to regard as a smaller version of the Room of Things. All three of the adult humans showered, though not together, and Alexis changed clothes several times.

"You look fine," Olivia assured her. "Your hair is amazing."

"I think these jeans make my butt look fat. Don't you think I look fat?"

"Come on."

There was a tension in the room, and I yawned, feeling my unease rise. Alexis was the most anxious and Lucas was the calmest—except maybe for Emma, who was mostly absorbed in trying to eat her own fingers.

I went to the door when I heard a car in the driveway, and wagged when my senses told me there was a dog in my yard. I assumed it was Charlie. "That's them," Lucas announced.

The moment he opened the door, I recognized the odor. It wasn't Charlie—it was Dutch!

I burst out and crashed into my old friend and we immediately started to wrestle. Gavin and Taylor were with Dutch, laughing.

"Bella!" Gavin called. He knelt and opened his arms and Dutch barreled into him, licking his face. "Okay, Dutch! Okay!" He reached past the big dog and gathered me in a hug, and I gave him a kiss, wagging. I loved Gavin.

It made me very happy that Gavin and Taylor and Dutch had figured out how to do Go Home, but that couch was going to get awfully crowded.

Taylor carried what looked like a suitcase, but there was a baby in it, staring at me with solemn brown eyes.

The humans all clustered in the living room while Dutch and I climbed on each other. He was as big as I remembered.

"This is Noah," Taylor said, pulling his baby out of the suitcase. The child clung to him. It was a boy, almost exactly the same size as Emma.

Taylor passed Noah to Olivia and Lucas handed Emma to Gavin and the adults all spoke to the babies with happy faces and sing-songy voices.

I thought I understood why Alexis had been tense—somehow, she had known Dutch was coming—but my friend's arrival did nothing to calm her down. I went to Taylor and he bent down to speak to me.

"It's so good to see you, Bella," he murmured.

I loved Taylor.

"Noah took his first steps yesterday," Gavin announced proudly.

Taylor looked up from where he was petting me. "Actually, it was more like you stood him up and dragged him across the carpet."

Everyone laughed, so Dutch and I wagged.

"Emma's got standing up figured out, but I think she's going to stick with just that for a while. I keep saying, 'Come to Daddy,' and she gives me a look like, 'No thanks, I'm good,'" Lucas told them.

Everyone laughed again. There's just something about having two dogs in a room that makes people happy.

Gavin held his hand out to me and I sniffed optimistically, but there were no treats. Yet. I hoped he remembered how to do *t-i-i-iny piece of cheese*.

"I can't believe you lived with lions!" Gavin told me, then grinned at Lucas. "When I opened that link and saw the footage I almost fell out of my chair. But you're right, that was our Bella with the cougar cubs."

"Oh, there's more to the story, I promise," Lucas replied.

Then I heard someone else outside the door. The bell rang and Dutch barked, but I did No Barks because I am a good dog.

"Dutch! Stop barking!" Gavin commanded loudly. The words weren't clear but I thought I understood their meaning anyway. When Dutch looked to me, I wagged in sympathy.

Lucas opened the door and it was Mack! Everyone stood up and the sudden tension flashing off Alexis startled both Dutch and me as we glanced at her. I went wagging to Mack, who for some reason clutched a bunch of plants in his fist. Lucas took them from him. "Great to see you, Mack, thanks. I'll put these in a vase."

Everyone wanted to grab hands, but no treats were exchanged. Then Olivia stepped up to Mack, hugged him, and turned to Alexis. "Mack, this is my sister Alexis. Alexis, this is Mack."

"Nice to meet you," Alexis told him.

"Happy," Mack replied. Then he and Alexis laughed. "I mean I'm *happy to finally meet you in person*. Oh my God."

Eventually Mack reached for me and hugged me. His hands no longer smelled like smoke. It felt so good to be held by him.

I loved Mack.

I could tell that Dutch did not know who all the people were, and that he understood that I *did* know, but it didn't bother him. Dutch never really seemed bothered by anything, except the big stinky bear creature with the enormous claws. He and I did wonderful Sits by the table during dinner, but despite our efforts, no one threw any food to us.

After dinner, the humans sat there, laughing. The two babies were put on a soft spot on the floor and they stared at each other.

Dutch was tired, and so was I. When the children lay down and slept, Dutch and I sprawled next to them.

Lying there, with a huge dog pressed close and two tiny humans nearby, it reminded me very much of sleeping in a den with Big Kitten, Girl Kitten, and Boy Kitten.

I did not know when I would see my cat family again. I only hoped that, wherever they were, they were as happy as I was.

Acknowledgments

It has now been a year since I lost my number one salesperson. My mom, Monsie Cameron, would attempt to force everyone she ever met to buy a book or, failing that, she would just *give* the person a copy. She set up a table in her church and accosted people on their way in and out of services—people sat in pews with my books stacked up like hymnals. When the priest took her aside and suggested that perhaps running a bookstore in the church was not really what it said to do in the bible, she listened respectfully and then was back the next week at the same table. My mom weighed around 80 pounds and was hardly a threat, but he gave up in defeat. Her favorite way of greeting strangers was to ask, "do you like dogs?" If they said yes, she gave them one of my books. If they said no, they didn't like dogs, she gave them one of my books to convince them they *should*.

My mother was in the middle of a conversation with a nurse when she passed away suddenly at age 89. I've not spoken to that nurse, but I can only assume my mom had asked if the nurse liked dogs.

This novel, *A Dog's Courage*, grew out of my desire to advance the story of Bella, Lucas, and Olivia, whom we first met in *A Dog's Way Home*. When I began writing it, huge fires were on my mind, because I've lived in both California and Colorado, where such conflagrations are common. I had no idea, though, that after turning in my final draft, a historic fire disaster was slated to hit the western states. I promise you, I was utterly shocked at how seemingly predictive *A Dog's Courage* is. That the devastation in Colorado came from the Cameron fire is a further odd coincidence.

My agent, Scott Miller at Trident Media, didn't know about my mom's sales abilities or surely he would have bragged about her in the cover letter for the first submission, *A Dog's Purpose*. Thanks Scott, for getting the job done on that, and every novel since.

My publisher for every novel my mother hand-sold, meaning, force-fed, to people has been Tor/Forge. Thanks very much to the team there—Linda, Tom, Susan, Sarah, Lucille, Kristin, Eileen. There are probably others and I apologize for not calling you out by name. What a great group of people, dedicated to the hugely difficult task of bringing books to market. There are a lot of steps! Probably you have other authors but I never feel like it when I call.

Thanks Ed for being my editor—you're great at it, and assume that's why your parents gave you that name.

I'm typing these words right now, but much of my writing is no longer poked out on plastic keys, but is dictated, using an Apogee electronics microphone. The microphone sends my words to an FBI surveillance team, where every word is transcribed. Thank you everyone at Apogee, especially Betty Bennett and Marlene Passaro, for the donation of the microphone.

I put every novel through a couple of drafts and then hand it to my wife. Her notes, thoughts, and comments are always key ingredients in every success. Thank you, Cathryn, for your hard work on everything except that time you hit me in the face with a pie. I am still not sure how that sells books, and our dog Tucker was equally perplexed. (There's a video of this whole sordid scene that's gotten more than two million views. I can't believe that many people have nothing better to do with their time than to watch an author get a pie in his face.)

And thank you Sheri Kelton, manager, for everything you do for my career. You ask me what I want and then try to get it for me.

I am convinced that if I wanted to play basketball you'd get me a tryout with the Lakers.

If, as we'd expect, I wow the Lakers coaching staff with my ability to throw the ball several or at least two feet into the air, attorney Steve Younger would be the person to negotiate with the team for what color seats I want in my private jet. Thanks for that in advance, Steve, I like the cream-colored accents, and also thanks for navigating the treacherous waters associated with turning my novels into filmed entertainment.

Gavin Polone has produced the movies based on my books, but what I really want is for him to direct. Thanks for always supporting me and for caring about the dogs, Gavin.

Whenever someone tells me I have a right to remain silent, I call Hayes Michael, my personal attorney who has thus far convinced people I am not guilty by reason of insanity. I appreciate having you in my corner, Hayes.

Thank you Olivia Pratt for organizing our operations and running them single-handedly. We couldn't do it without you. Heck, without you we can't even find time to *eat*.

Thank you Diane Driscoll for matching us up with Olivia.

Thank you Jill Enders for helping run our social media, especially since I don't really understand what it is.

What I do understand is that there's a Facebook "Secret Group." The Secretary disavows any knowledge of their actions. If you are a member of this group, you sometimes receive free gifts, you always receive news and updates before anyone else, and once a year we have a fabulous convention except for the years when we don't. Thank you for being a member! (If you are not, but belonging to a special gathering of extraordinary people with superpowers sounds like fun, track down Susan Andrews on Facebook and send her a message asking her to introduce you to the group.)

Having lost my mom, I must turn now to my two sisters to individually sell all of my books. Amy Cameron has made it her mission to support educators by creating CORE compliant study guides available free on my web site—much easier to download than my original idea, which was peanut butter sandwiches. Julie Cameron is a doctor who diagnoses all of her patients as having W. Bruce Cameron Novel Deficiency Disorder. There's a cure: she dispenses my books in her waiting room, which works better than an injection for treating this serious medical condition. Dear sisters, Mom would be proud of you.

If you are an alert reader, you may have spotted some of my family names cropping up here and there in various works of fiction. Thank you Georgia, Chelsea, Chase, Gage, Eloise, Garrett, Ewan, Gordon, Sadie, and James for your support. And thank you Evie Michon, Ted Michon, Maria Hjelm, and Jacob, Maya, and Ethan Michon for being family and also for supporting my work and lending a name or two to my novels. I love you all.

I also have two goddaughters. They used to be cool kids and now they are cool adults. Carolina and Annie, you're the best. Making me the godfather was an offer I couldn't refuse.

I mentioned the study guides earlier. For my younger reader novels, Judy Robbens writes the study guides. You can find all of them, free for download, at adogspurpose.com. No peanut butter sandwiches, which my web team says would be "too impossible." You just can't get good help these days.

One of the coolest and most talented authors I know is Samantha Dunn. I'm just bragging that I know her.

As I write this, we're working on a project so Secret that even the Secret Group doesn't know about it yet. Thank you Mick, Will, Connor, Rob, and Elliott. I'd pit you guys against SEAL Team Six any time. I mean, I'd bet on the SEAL Team, but I'd pit you against them.

Sometimes you have friends who are just there for you. They're the type of people you can call for bail money at 3 AM and have them hang up on you. So thanks to Aaron Mendelsohn, Gary

Goldstein, Ken Pisani, Mike Conley, Diane Driscoll, Susan Walter, Margaret Howell, Felicia Meyer and Mike Walker for being such good friends, and for forming the Committee To Make Fun of Ken Pisani.

Thank you Dennis Quaid for publicly declaring you want to be in all of my movies. It's a deal.

Thank you Larissa Wohl for picking my novel, *A Dog's Perfect Christmas*, as the very first novel in your world-wide book club. What an honor!

Thank you Tucker for keeping the pillows pinned to the couch.

Over the years I have worked with and donated to over 300 animal rescue charities. Two of the best are Best Friends Animal Society and Life is Better Rescue. Let's Save Them All.

As I write this, 2020 draws near to an end, and the world is still in the grips of a great contagion. Many people are suffering from disease or the damage wrought by disease. Book stores struggle to survive, some schools are closed—hopefully, by the time you are reading this, we've emerged from the worst of the crisis, and our species is recovering in every sense of the word. My prayers are with all who have been affected.

When I was young, fourth grade, in fact, so I was probably sixteen years old, I declared that my life's ambition was to be a novelist. As these acknowledgments imply, getting there was a journey that required many assisting hands. I'm thinking specifically of some of the authors who I admire who helped—Nelson DeMille, Andrew Gross, Lee Child, T. Jefferson Parker—but then my mind goes to friends from my whole life who have shown up for movie premieres and book signings and the rest, even though I have never gone up to their work to cheer them on, not even once. Pretty much if I know you, you've been a big help to me. My acknowledgments might not call you out by name, because if I did that this section would be as long as a phone book (they were these big printed books of names and phone numbers . . .

oh, never mind) and I don't think my publisher would let me do that. But know I feel blessed by all you've done for me. Next time we meet, I will buy you a PDF of a peanut butter sandwich.

And Mom, I know you're reading this right now. You can rest. We'll take it from here.

W. Bruce Cameron
Los Angeles, CA
Monday, November 23, 2020